Love is
a time of enchantment:
in it all days are fair and all fields
green. Youth is blest by it,
old age made benign:
the eyes of love see
roses blooming in December,
and sunshine through rain. Verily
is the time of true-love
a time of enchantment — and
Oh! how eager is woman
to be bewitched!

DOM

**Library at Home Service**
Community Services
Hounslow Library, CentreSpace
24 Treaty Centre, High Street
Hounslow TW3 1ES

YOUR COMMUNITY
YOUR SERVICES

| 0 | 1 | 2 | 3 | 4 | 5 | 6 | 7 | 8 | 9 |
|---|---|---|---|---|---|---|---|---|---|
| 410 | 7751 | 3321 8963 | 7704 | 715 | 3/6 | | 818 | 639 | |
| | 0321 | | 344 | 533706 | | | 588 | 32 | |
| | 7781 | 942 | 613 668X | | 30786 | | 338X | 09 | |
| 3150 | 3491 3321 | 0862 | | 904 8855 | 33 46 | 9977 | | 0 519 | |
| | | | | 7745 6306 | | | | | |
| | | | 3074 3235 | | | | | | |
| | | | 995 | | | | | | |
| | | | | | | | | | |
| | | | | | | | | | |
| | | | | | | | | | |
| | | | | | | | | | |
| | | | | | | | | | |

P10-L-2061

# SMOKE ON THE RIVER

Wealthy Llewellyn Saucier found his daughter Charmian his only consolation when his wife died. Charmian met Pierre Gregoire, a French peasant boy, and her father's over-protectiveness was to intertwine their destinies forever. This was St. Louis of the 1840's, the golden era of the city's development, a time of contrasts, when anything could happen.

## Books by Anne Tedlock Brooks
### in the Ulverscroft Large Print Series:

ONE ENCHANTED SUMMER
FIRE IN THE WIND
ISLAND NEIGHBOR

ANNE TEDLOCK BROOKS

# SMOKE ON THE RIVER

*Complete and Unabridged*

# ULVERSCROFT
*Leicester*

First published in the
United States of America


First Large Print Edition
published June 1992

British Library CIP Data

Brooks, Anne Tedlock
 Smoke on the river.—Large print ed.—
 Ulverscroft large print series: romance
 I. Title
 813.54 [F]


 ISBN 0–7089–2655–X

Published by
F. A. Thorpe (Publishing) Ltd.
Anstey, Leicestershire

Set by Words & Graphics Ltd.
Anstey, Leicestershire
Printed and bound in Great Britain by
T. J. Press (Padstow) Ltd., Padstow, Cornwall

# Foreword

All resemblance to authentic places of historical St. Louis is fully intended. It is no coincidence that Clabber Alley, Battle Row, Happy Hollow, and Shepherd's Graveyard are mentioned in this story, for no story of St. Louis in its heyday of steamboating could ring true if these were left out. Chouteau's Pond, where seven tenanted coffins were found floating one day during the cholera epidemic, was the idyllic rendezvous of many a romantic swain and his lady of the Ripple Boat Club. Montesano Place, Planters' House and the Southern Hotel were famous gathering places. Compton Hill and Lucas Place were becoming the elite section. Saloons were scenes of lusty brawls, and steamboat pilots were known to carry around thousands of dollars which could be lost at the turn of a card.

St. Louis, in its golden era of development, was originally a French village which burst its bounds to become a great city with growing pains upon the advent of the steamboat. The wharves bustled from morning until night with the activities of as many as forty great river steamers which often lay docked in a single day. Steamboat landings and departures were exciting occasions when the crews threw pitch pine in the furnaces and the funnels belched black smoke on the river. Many of the steamboats referred to in this story were actually floating palaces — here today and gone tomorrow.

The main characters are fictitious, although it is not unlikely that certain prototypes may be studied for recognition by romantic-minded descendants of early St. Louisans.

ANNE TEDLOCK BROOKS
St. Louis, Missouri.

# 1

THE Mississippi lay sparkling in the morning sun. The wharf road bustled with activity. Drays, wagons, carts filled with produce inched along the thoroughfare. An elegant carriage pulled heavily over deep ruts and fell into line with other carriages going down to the docks. The coachman sat stiffly in his seat, holding the reins firmly and occasionally swishing the tasseled end of the whip across the bays' sleek backs.

Inside the carriage, Llewellyn Saucier was so deep in thought that he barely saw the street, was unaware that his little daughter's eyes were wide under their long black lashes as she moved closer to her nurse's side. It was hard for a nine-year-old to keep still on a ride like this, for there was so much to see. But when her father wore that deep line between his brows, she must be as quiet as a mouse, for he was concentrating on some problem concerned with his shipping line and must not be disturbed.

A shining carriage similar to the Sauciers' passed them, and a wave of a cane from the white-haired man within indicated that Mr. Cyrus Manley was also on his way to the docks. The two coachmen did not even exchange glances. They would remain formal to the last turn of the carriage wheels.

Saucier's newest boat, the *Euphrasia*, lay at anchor. It was a floating palace — sharp contrast to that first steamboat which had plied its way into the Port of St. Louis twenty years before. The boat was getting up steam and the tall stacks belched a heavy stream of black smoke, ribboning it out on the rain-washed morning air.

Charmian Saucier leaned out of the carriage and watched the sweating Negroes below as they rolled barrels of molasses from the Sugar House down the gangway of the *Arcadia Belle*. A pile of cotton bales, a great heap of cordwood, a little band of slaves, stood waiting in hetergeneous collection. Pascal drove slowly now. His master liked to see what was going on every morning.

"Humph!" exclaimed Saucier. "The *Arcadia Belle* has turned into a dirty freighter!"

"What's that, sir?" asked Pascal over his shoulder.

"Look! The *Arcadia Belle*! Nothing but a freighter! Manley ought to be ashamed of it. The way his new boat's run down is a sin to crocket!"

"Yes, sir!"

"I'll not load my boats with that kind of slop!" He was talking about molasses. Even Charmian knew what he meant; she had heard about 'dirty freight' before.

"I say that when you start taking on that kind of freight you might as well say good-bye to your first-class passengers. And I'm not hauling any filthy slaves down to New Orleans on any of the Saucier boats."

"No, sir!"

"No, sir, we won't, will we, Papa?"

Charmian was accustomed to her father's silences and thought nothing of his failure to answer. She looked at him only a moment, her little oval face serious in the reflection of his own expression. She scowled, and the tiny line which

3

appeared between her brows was a faint replica of the deep furrows between his black ones.

"Good-bye, little daughter. Mind, you be a good girl today."

"Yes, Papa."

"Take good care of her, Brigette. And you, Pascal, look sharp as you go back through Clabber Alley."

"Yes, sir!" Pascal, red of face, was pushing the reins into the hands of a black boy and struggling with the door clasp in embarrassment, because Saucier was impatiently opening the door himself. Charmian saw that Mr. Manley's coachman was holding the door of the Manley carriage open with a great show of possession, and knew that Pascal was writhing inside. Saucier turned to her once more.

"A kiss this morning, my rosebud?"

"Yes, Papa. And Papa, you almost forgot your flower!" Laughing dark eyes, a shake of the little head which set the black curls to dancing on her shoulders, and a quick shaping of her lips for her father's kiss brought a smile to Saucier's face.

"You're like your mother, my daughter." Saucier kissed her tenderly, took the rose from her hand and, stepping back, was gone in another moment.

"An' if your poor mother had lived," sniffed Brigette, "ye'd not be allowed to come nigh the wharf."

Charmian had heard this plaint so many times before that she gave it no heed this morning. She continued to watch the scene at the levee.

"No dallying in the Alley, Pascal. Now let us go!" Brigette called out sharply.

"You'd think you were the mistress instead of just the child's nurse." Pascal touched the backs of the bays with the tassel of the whip, and they were off for home. They drove down Front Street with the horses' hoofs making a clopping racket over the cobbled street.

"Stop at the stalls while I pick out the fowls. And mind you, you can pick out the fish and the vegetables. Fresh and green. Remember, Pascal."

The coachman obediently slowed down to a walk as they neared the big open market stalls. This part of the morning drive was almost as exciting to Charmian

5

as the dock itself. Brigette bustled out of the carriage and helped her little charge down from the step, lifting her carefully, smoothing the gray cape down over the pretty morning dress which reached Charmian's ankles.

"It's beautiful you are," Brigette said proudly, pushing back Charmian's curls and wiping her damp brow with a fine linen handkerchief.

Charmian scowled a little. Brigette was always fussing over her, smoothing her dress, picking at her curls, brushing off imaginary flecks of dust. Charmian was anxious to go on to the stalls.

She shivered a little at the stiff white forms of the geese and ducks hanging head downward, and watched with awe while Brigette went over and selected two of the plumpest birds. She wrangled with the man every morning. They began, Brigette's voice calm and low at first, then working up to an unpleasant pitch until she attained the price she had set.

"Come on, little one. I've fetched the vegetables. Give the man his money and let's be off." Pascal's voice had laughter in it, and he cupped Brigette's arm with his big brown hand, only to have it shaken off.

"Keep your hands to yourself, Pascal."

"And wise to do so," added the man she had just bluffed. "I'd not want the likes of that tinderbox. Flares up — *pf-ff-t!* Like that!" He snapped his fingers and tossed his dark head.

"*Pf-ff-t!*" mimicked Brigette. "Yes, yes, I flare up. Asking two prices for your ducks! Why, we wouldn't give away such stringy-fleshed birds as these in our market in Dublin."

"Give me back those ducks. You needn't buy, my little tinderbox!" The fat man looked as though he would burst, and Charmian trembled with anxious excitement. Would Brigette give them back? Sometimes she did.

But Pascal was taking them from the nurse. He led her toward the carriage and helped her and Charmian into it.

Charmian turned back and waved a hand to the blustering man at the stall, and when Brigette was no longer looking as the carriage rolled away, she blew a kiss to him. He shouted and threw one back and waved at her with both arms. Charmian giggled and Brigette said, "There you go again."

"But, Brigette, he likes it. He always lets you set your own price."

"I know. He just loves to haggle."

The row of stalls was fast filling with produce for the housewives and cooks who were gathering on Front Street. You could see them coming, some in elegant carriages, some in smart traps with wide fringed parasols above the seats, but most of them on foot. St. Louis was bursting with its gain in population, and fat German women brushed skirts with French women, both staying clear of the Irish sisters, who were quick with their tempers. How the voices sharpened! The clatter of foreign tongues was as confusing as the noise of the livestock tethered to posts in front of the stalls.

Brigette looked on all this with disdain, and with a queenly mien said, "Drive home, Pascal."

"Very good, my little tinderbox."

Brigette's face grew red and, picking up Charmian's ruffled parasol, she poked the coachman between the shoulders with the point.

"Leave off now. I take it back!" Pascal, convulsed with laughter, hunched his wide shoulders and leaned against the seat.

Charmian squealed with excitement. The game was progressing. After her father left them in the morning, there was a continuous round of excitement until Pascal got Brigette under the shelter of the side porch. There he always succeeded in kissing her. Brigette would pretend that she didn't like it, and Pascal would give her a little slap and send her scuttling for the kitchen. 'Where you really belong,' he often called after her.

They were turning into Clabber Alley now. Pascal touched the whip tassel to the backs of the bays and the carriage lumbered over the crooked road where clabbered milk and other refuse glutted the muddy wagon tracks. Children were playing in littered yards before the dilapidated wooden houses that crowded against each other on either side of the waterfront alley. Charmian sat very still and looked out anxiously.

A little knot of boys stood just beyond the road bend. They were silently poised

— waiting. As if by signal, they suddenly broke apart, spreading out on both sides of the wagon tracks.

Pascal shouted at the bays, urging them on. A flying stone almost lifted his tall black hat; clods of the hardened clay flew thickly about the windows; the carriage lurched in the ruts. Brigette pulled Charmian close to shield her.

"It's the last morning, so 'tis! There'll be no more of this!" Brigette said sharply between thin, straight lips.

The horses reared, the boys hooted, and Pascal shouted again. The din brought a few housewives running to their doors, others lolled indifferently; this uproar was not uncommon in Clabber Alley.

"Look, Brigette! There he is again! That boy who tried to stop them yesterday," cried Charmian, pointing to a thin lad who stood apart from the rest, his hand upraised, pleading with them.

"Down with you!" cried Brigette. "Mind you keep your head hidden. The nasty little varmints! This is your last ride through here. Your last morning, so 'tis! Slow down, now, Pascal."

10

"Stop, Pascal!" cried Charmian, looking back. "Stop! He's down! Stop!" She escaped Brigette's clutching hands, and as Pascal drew the bays to a standstill, Charmian jumped.

Brigette's mouth stood open. "Better come down, Pascal," she said, and went scurrying after Charmian.

Charmian's appearance in the Alley, her flying curls, her pretty dress, silenced the wild hooting of the urchins. She was leaning over the fallen boy, who had struggled to a sitting position.

"Here, let me help you up." She put out her lace-gloved hand and the little boy stood up, staring at her.

"Come back to the carriage!" Brigette's long fingers clutched Charmian's shoulders. "Come back to the carriage."

Charmian ignored her. "What's your name? Do you live in the Alley?" She took a white linen handkerchief and pressed it to a trickle of red which ran down the side of the boy's white face. "What's your name?" she demanded.

"Pierre. Pierre Gregoire."

"Here's the provost. Now we'll see!" exclaimed Brigette. "Why don't you do something? Those horrid little rats overrun the place like varmints!"

"I'm sorry, miss," panted the fat Irish provost. "Sure an' I turn me back one minute an' the little rapscallions are loaded with stones an' ready to fire. G'long with ye now." He tapped Pierrre's shoulder. "An' if I catch ye throwin' stones again, me lad, it's into the hoosegow."

"He wasn't throwing stones. He stopped the others. Haven't you any sense?" demanded Charmian.

"So you did, me lad? Well, be off with you. Don't be botherin' the Saucier carriage or the folks inside. it." He smiled at Brigette, the smile dying as he saw Pascals's scowl.

"Come, Charmian." Pascal picked her up and carried her back to the carriage, Brigette following. Charmian strained backward to call, "Thank you, Pierre, thank you."

"Into the carriage with you, little lady, and not a word of this to anyone, hear me?"

"Yes, Pascal."

"Nasty varmints," said Brigette again.

"This is your last ride through here."

"Brigette," wailed Charmian, "I want to come to the levee. I will come to the levee!" She began to cry, her breath coming in great sobs, paying no heed to the splotch of blood on the handkerchief from the little French boy's cheek.

"Hush, Charmian. Hush! If Pascal will have the officers rid the street, then we will see."

Without warning, a sudden clod, as though in final salute, clipped the tall hat from Pascal's head. Reaching down, he grabbed it off the dash. He wiped the sweat from his face with his stock and clapped the hat back on his head.

There was no sound in the carriage for a while but the soothing endearments slipping from Brigette's lips as she patted and pulled at Charmian's cape, brushed and smoothed her curls; and then with exasperation she gave bent to a torrent of scolding directed at the calm back of the coachman.

Pascal drove on silently until he turned into their own street and up the tree-shaded lane to Ginger Blue. A flock of guineas went clacking across the road and a bevy of quail, barely out of their shells, fluttered into the tall green grasses. A Negro boy stood waiting at the side porch to take care of the horses.

Charmian cried, "There's Whistlejackets! Oh, wait, Pascal! There's Whistlejackets!" A little brown pony came whinnying to the pasture gate and thrust his head over it and stood watching them. Pascal obediently paused, but Brigette would not let Charmian get down out of the carriage.

They drove on to the porte-cochere. The Saucier house was one of the finest in St. Louis. The tall three-storied structure had been fashioned according to the plans brought by Llewellyn Saucier from Virginia, where his own father had built an imposing mansion on the land grant given to his father before him. The red brick had been made on the place; the long white galleries were reminiscent of the big houses on the flourishing estates the owner had known in his boyhood. The wood was Weymouth white pine and was put together with wooden pegs instead of nails.

"Blue, hitch the horses and help carry

in the produce," said the coachman to the Negro. "Here, lambie, let me lift you down."

"Oh, I can jump, Pascal," Charmian said, poised on the step.

"No, no, Charmian. Remember you are a little lady."

"Oh dear! Sometimes I think it must be nice to not be a little lady!" Charmian pouted her pretty lips and tossed her head, and Blue hid a quick, wide grin from his superiors, bending down to pick up the long-necked fowls.

"Take the ducks to the smokehouse and hang them high till Sabetha can pluck them. Mind you, save the feathers."

"Yas'm, Miz Brigette."

"Come, Charmian."

They entered by the side door. The dim interior of high ceilings, rich hangings, and heavy furniture seemed cool after the bright white heat of the late June sun. Charmian's hair was curling damply under her bonnet with its sheer white ruffled edging. She pulled impatiently at the white satin bows.

"You must go straight up to your room and change into something cooler — your pink sprigged lawn — and then it's time for your lesson on the pianoforte," said Brigette.

"But, Brigette, then it will be time for lunch, then I shall have to sleep, and then it will be time for dinner, and when, I pray, shall I ever have time to ride Whistlejackets?"

"I won't have you ripping and tearing over the hills like a common — like a common — " Brigette stopped, at a loss what to call the daughter of a man as wealthy as Llewellyn Saucier.

"A common little good-for-nothing?" supplied Charmian.

"Charmian!" sharply. "You've been listening to Pascal."

"*You* don't have to listen, Brigette. He calls you that many times."

Brigette's ears were red and her face looked as though it might burst into flame. She fluttered her hands nervously. She almost wished it were time for Charmian to enter the Academy of the Sacred Heart.

Brigette took the little girl by the hand and led her towards the great circular stairway. She looked at it and felt a

16

little dizzy. Would she ever get used to looking up at that beautiful, winding stair of which Llewellyn Saucier was so proud?

Brigette shuddered as she recalled her master's words. 'It keeps me from taking too much wine. If I didn't remain steady enough to negotiate the stairs, look how far I'd pitch down to the floor below.'

On the wide landing at the second flight Brigette leaned against the mahogany balustrade and looked down. She could see the big double parlors, where fingers of light touched the polished floors, the satinwood and rosewood furniture, the tall gilt-edged mirrors.

It was a good vantage point. She could check on Florry's dusting, could call down orders, because from here there was an echo that lengthened and distended her voice and made it more commanding.

"Florry! You good-for-nothing black trash behind the portieres! Come out of there! Come out, or I'll march right back and pull you out and give you a hiding!"

The portieres moved slightly, then ballooned widely, and a slender young

17

mulatto came out, pushing aside the heavy claret-colored material. There was a hint of voluptuousness in her figure, unlike the other Negro women of the household. She stood there sullenly, not looking up.

"Florry, get your turkey-wing brush and clean up every fireplace in the house."

"Yas'm."

"And the featherbeds — did you spread them out in the sun?"

"Yas'm. Yas'm — I mean, no'm!"

"Florry!" Brigette's voice was like thick brittle ice which formed in the wooden pails on a winter night. "Florry, don't try to lie to me. Get to work and don't let me catch you lolling about the parlor again." Brigette moved on up the last steps, holding her backbone stiffly — 'like it almost rubbed her stomach,' Florry had described it to Sabetha.

Charmian stood watching and saw that Florry looked back sullenly, hate stamped upon her yellow face. Florry had promised Charmian that she would some day take her down to old Granny Popo's cabin, behind the slave quarters in the little patch of woods beyond the last field. Old Granny was an ancient yellow Negress who claimed to know all about voodooism. Just thinking about her made Charmian shiver and remember Florry's description of the bayou country, where long moss hung from giant trees, and alligators poked their hungry heads out of black water to snap down their prey.

Florry had asked Granny Popo to make a charm against Brigette. Only Charmian and Florry in the Big House knew it. That was their secret. Somehow Charmian knew that it had something to do with Pascal.

Charmian shivered again and then she ran up the stairs ahead of Brigette, whose lips were set tighter than ever.

# 2

PIERRE GREGOIRE was always dazzled by the appearance of the Saucier carriage in Clabber Alley. The bays were sleek and well fed, the carriage itself was sleek, the coachman's tall hat well brushed and shining.

Pierre rubbed his eyes and stared after the rare elegance, which was gone in a moment. Someone bumped him fiercely from behind. Then they were upon him, the ragged little urchins who had made life miserable for him ever since he had come to live in the Alley.

He turned upon them fiercely and struck out rapidly. His defiance surprised them and in another moment two of the smaller boys had fled with howls and bloody noses.

"So you'll fight today, me lad?" cried the tallest boy. "Come awn, Mike, poke him! Poke him!"

An elbow in the pit of his stomach, a fist in his right eye, Pierre grunted. Blood gushed from his nose, but before he was blinded by it, he struck the oldest boy.

A streak of white face and tumbled black hair sailed into the mellee, and Pierre, cheered by reinforcement, hit harder and faster. Grunts, blows, screeches — and then he was sitting on top of the big boy, pummeling, pummeling, pummeling.

"'Tis enough, lad!" shouted the provost, running up to them. "Up! Get up! be off with you now! Get along, or I'll take you all to the calaboose. Go along with you, Mike, and you, Tim. Wait here, you two." The big man stopped Pierre with a touch on his sleeve. "What's your name, lad?"

"Pierre. Pierre Gregoire. And this is my brother Sydney."

"No more fightin'. Understand? Though they deserved what they got. Mind you, no more fightin'." The provost looked at them severely and, turning them loose, trudged on down the Alley. Rough little whelps, they were, those little rapscallions. These two new ones would take care of themselves, no doubt. But 'twas time to clean up the Alley. Cyrus Manley and Llewellyn Saucier were raising cain over the pack of hoodlums who threw stones at their carriages.

Pierre brushed off his worn little jacket, His twin brother suddenly gave over to deep sobbing. Rubbing his dirty fists into his eyes, he said, "I hate this place. I hate St. Louis. I want to go back home."

Pierre said gravely, "We can't go back, Sydney. We have to stay here, and you must not hate it."

"I'm afraid."

Pierre had been afraid, too. He longed desperately for the coolness of the little thatched cottage and the funny crooked streets of the French village, but all that was past. They did not like this new world, but they would stay here, and some day perhaps they would learn to love it. The only good thing he had seen since he had been here, and the only beauty in all this dirty placed called Clabber Alley, was that shining carriage which passed through every morning at the same time.

How he admired the splendor of the coachman's uniform, and how he stared at the little girl sitting so close to her handsome father.

"I dare you, Syd, to steal a ride on the back of the next wagon and go down to the wharf," he said to his brother. That would take Syd's mind off his troubles, and Pierre wanted more than a glimpse of that wharf again. All the way, as he had traveled with his family up the great Mississippi from New Orleans, he had thrilled to the steamboats and life along the wharves.

Sydney stopped rubbing his eyes in sheer surprise. Pierre was always hanging back from adventure, and here he was, suggesting it.

"Here we go," whispered Pierre. He darted to one side, grabbing the shoulder of Sydney's heavy blue blouse, and they stood silently waiting for a wagon to pass them.

The driver was singing lustily, his hat pulled down over his eyes. He saw only two thin little boys politely standing aside out of his road.

"Now," whispered Pierre.

They were so much alike that you had to look twice to make sure you weren't seeing double. Sydney's face was dirtier than Pierre's — that was the only real difference. The same wide-spaced, deeply set dark eyes, fringed with long upsweeping lashes. A dark lock of hair, worn in a ruche above high foreheads, and thin, eager little faces, pointed at chin and pinched looking from a kind of hunger which was caused not so much by the lack of food, but the sameness of it.

"When we get to Front, slide down or somebody will tell him. That's a long whip," Pierre could almost feel the sting across his shoulder blades. He had seen one of the other boys catch it just yesterday, doing this same thing, stealing a ride on a load of cotton.

*Roll the cotton down, boys, roll the cotton down,*
*Johnny's gone to N'Orleans, so roll that cotton down.*

*The deck's all wet, the sail's all set,*
*So roll the cotton down,*
*Oh, roll the cotton down, boys, roll the cotton —*

"Why, blast it, ye little devils, git away from there!" Pierre looked at Sydney, but they knew the driver couldn't see them. He was shouting at some other boys trying to hook on.

"They'll tell! Slide down, Syd, slide!"

But the other boys were darting away and, strangely, they hadn't pointed out the two on the wagon.

This was a new kind of code. This mere gesture made Pierre feel a loosening up in his chest; and he sat on the back of the wagon, swinging his bare legs and thinking. Sydney, thankful for the respite, was pulling cotton from the bales, looking at it curiously, sniffing it, and chewing it a little as if to analyze this white stuff of which they had seen great heaps on docks all the way up from New Orleans.

The wagon was turning the last corner into Front. Pierre touched his brother's arms and they slid down simultaneously to duck out of sight behind a water barrel.

They stood waiting while the wagon passed on down the street, then Sydney bent his head toward the barrel. Pierre caught him just in time.

"I'm thirsty."

"You'll be sick. Horses drink there."

Sydney paled, and Pierre, swallowing the saliva which rose in his mouth, gagged a little. They were remembering the stench of the horses and cattle in the hold of the ship in which they had come over to America.

They followed the wagon discreetly, down to the very wharf, avoiding the Negroes and the raw Irish immigrants and, of course, keeping out of the way of the roustabouts. There were other boys of their own age hanging around watching the deck hands carrying impossible loads under straining backs, with muscles standing out like knotted cords in their forearms and backs.

Pierre whispered to Sydney and they went along the wharf's edge reading the names of the steamboats in flourishing gold letters on the paddle boxes. They watched the captain of the *Lady Genevieve* as he walked swiftly up the gangpank to board it. You could swagger slightly when you walked, in that splendid uniform, with your buttons shining in the bright sun so that they hurt your eyes to look at them, Pierre thought.

The pilot of the *Genevieve* pulled down upon the whistle cord. The air trembled about Pierre's ears and deafened him. Then the pilot released the cord and the echoes came booming back from the shore buildings. This brought a sudden clatter from the lower decks, a great screeching of wheels, the crash of heavy boxes, the clang of metal.

Roustabouts began to move at a trot up and down, up and down, with the passengers moving and dodging among them, carrying bundles and carpet bags, valises and boxes.

"All aboooard! Clear the way, clear the way, folks, Watch it on the labbord side — Watch it, you ape! Easy there — easy does the job," shouted the mate.

Household goods from St. Louis factories, cases of dry goods from wholesalers, and pig iron and castings from the foundries in Pittsburgh which had been brought down this far to be transferred to the Mississippi boats still lay on the wharf. Two roustabouts were lugging a heavy casting on board, and Pierre and Sydney crept unseen up the gangpank behind them.

The *Lady Genevieve* vibrated and creaked as her burden grew. From the main cabin on the boiler deck, which strangely did not carry the boilers, came the sound of cutlery and the clash of dishes as the long tables were being set for dinner.

In spite of the noise, Pierre was aware of the steam surging in the boat's boilers and of the engines churning gently to keep the pressure regulated.

The captain was standing on the open hurricane deck, forward on the texas, watching the loading of his boat. After a while Pierre saw him reaching out to tug a rope attached to the clapper of a big bell suspended at the forward edge of the hurricane deck. Three taps sounded and the confusion increased at this last warning.

"We'd better go now, Syd," whispered Pierre.

But the deck they were on was suddenly almost deserted and he knew they would be seen. They hugged the side of the cabin and waited for another chance to reach the gangway unobserved. Finding it, they ran safely behind a fat man who had come to see his daughter and her shabby brood off to New Orleans.

The boys stood on the bank and breathlessly watched the *Lady Genevieve* cast off. The levee near her had been swept clean of drays and carts and teamsters who were on their way with a backward look now and then.

"Slow ahead!" called the captain from his position at the guard rail.

"Aye, aye, Captain," answered the pilot's ringing voice as he reached down and twitched a lever on the bell board.

A jangling of bells sounded below on the main deck. The boat seemed to take a deep breath, the frame trembled, and the *Genevieve* nudged forward, slacking the headlines. Far up the levee, the deck hands slipped them off the anchor rings and came in at a lope.

"Slow astern!" called the captain.

The boat lay between the *Swiftsure* and the *Tamerlane*, making it difficult to back out into the river, but she began to move along slowly with a great fuss of stopping and starting the huge paddle wheels. The engines of the side-wheeler were opposed or operated singly to work her out without scraping against the other two.

"Good work!" shouted the mate of the *Tamerlane* as the *Lady Genevieve* swung free and was finally out in the main channel.

Pierre's body was trembling with the excitement of the departure and he crept closer and closer to the edge of the river. He stood there a long time, even after the last wisp of smoke had uncurled itself and disappeared behind the bend in the river, and the last of the backwash had eddied into the smooth, glassy surface of the muddy water on the far banks.

Some day I'll own a boat like the *Lady Genevieve*. Some day *my* boat will be that grand and I'll be standing on the deck waving my handkerchief to someone on the wharf . . .

Somebody was tugging at his sleeve. He turned with a start. Sydney was grumbling, "We'd best go. It's getting late."

Pierre's lagging steps faltered over the cobbled street. The river had cast its spell upon him and he was never to escape it.

# 3

EVERY window of the mansion glowed with candlelight. Outdoors the night breeze, as soft as thistledown, moved the leaves gently on the great trees. The carriages were still rolling up on the block by the broad white-pillared piazza. The porch lights disclosed the elegance of beautiful clothes, and the blazing candelabra inside increased the dazzling effect.

Within the reception hall where Llewellyn Saucier and his small daughter stood shaking hands with the guests, there was a rustle of silks and satins.

Charmian saw hazily the white head-dresses of feathers which some of the ladies wore, drifting past the statuettes on the stairway. Softly lined capes, high silk hats, glittering, shimmering lights flashing from jeweled bosoms, dazed the little girl, and she moved restlessly.

"Tired, my litle rosebud?" her father smiled at her.

Charmian nodded. "Yes, Papa. When may I go and play with Dennard?"

"Soon."

Dennard was the son of Mr. Cyrus Manley, who had already arrived. Mr. Manley was in the the dining room near the punch bowl, carefully filling glasses for two sparkling young ladies.

One was Gabriella Darby. Saucier had not really expected her tonight, although she had stopped her carriage to tell him this morning that she would be here, even if she had to slip away from her aunt, in whose care she had been left when her parents died. Gabriella, as though feeling Saucier's eyes upon her, turned her head coquettishly and smiled at him, pulling her fan halfway to her lips. She excused herself and came quickly across the polished floor, all eyes following her.

"It's nice that you could come, Miss Gabriella," said Saucier. He saw the excitement in her eyes and knew that although it was quite early, she had already had more than one serving from the punch bowl.

"It's a wonderful party, Llewellyn,

simply divinely wonderful." The name of her host slipped out daringly. Her green eyes fell on his small daughter. "Hello, Charmian. Having a good time?"

"No." said Charmian.

Gabriella laughed, the sound ringing clear in the great hall, her head thrown back, her white teeth flashing.

Llewellyn scowled for an instant, then, catching the infection of Gabriella's laughter, followed suit. Charmian pouted her lips and thrust her hand into her father's. Gabriella frowned at the little girl.

Charmian looked up at her father. He was still smiling, watching Gabriella as she started walking slowly up the stairs, as though she were aware of the picture she made, the light catching the radiance of her auburn hair.

Saucier watched Gabriella to the landing, where she turned to smile down upon him. Her white dress stood airily out from her body as she poised on high heels, and the staircase waved a moment in Saucier's eyes.

"Let me go now, Papa?" Charmian begged, pulling at his hand.

"Ho! So that's the way the wind blows?" he tweaked her arm gently. "Doesn't like to help Papa receive the guests? Wants to go play like the hoyden she is!"

A surge of love went through Charmian. Papa was so handsome standing there. He was still youthful; his black hair had only a few white strands in it, his dark eyes were full of fire. "Run up and let Brigette tie your ribbon again."

Charmian, glad to be free, started up the stairs, but almost tripped on her long dress. She crept up carefully, holding her skirt as Gabriella had done a moment ago.

As she neared the top she heard her name.

"He needs someone to mother that dear little Charmian, but Llewellyn Saucier will never wed again." That was Mrs. Shaffner's voice, thought Charmian.

"He'd be a catch for any woman. So rich, so handsome — so everything a woman would want in a husband. And think of Ginger Blue! Well, little Miss Gabriella Darby will have to look elsewhere for a man, although anyone can see she has her cap set for him!"

"Llewellyn Saucier will never allow any woman to take Charmian's position in his affections!" said Mrs. Shaffner.

"Don't be so sure!" cried a flippant young voice. Charmian paused as though Gabriella's voice had cut her. "Don't be so sure. Oh, I'll put Charmian in her place when I'm Mrs. Llewellyn Saucier!"

Charmian rounded the curve above and came upon the two plump matrons looking in shocked amazement after Gabriella, who was disappearing into the cloakroom.

"Well! I never!" said Mrs. Lamont.

"What did she mean?" asked Charmian, perplexity written on her face. The two women turned, aghast at her appearance on the stairs.

"Don't bother your pretty little head, Charmian. My! What a beautiful party dress, my dear," said Mrs. Shaffner.

"But what did she mean? Put me in my place?" demanded Charmian.

"How pretty you look tonight, Charmian. This is a lovely ball," said Mrs. Lamont.

Charmian stared silently at the door of the cloakroom, then her hands fell slowly to her sides and she turned and went downstairs. She walked up to Dennard Manley and said, "Let's go away from here, Denny."

She looked about for her father, but he was talking with Mr. Shaffner and Denny's father. She felt closed in, as though the flowers blooming all over the great house and the overbearing fragrance of perfume and colognes were contriving to suffocate her.

She had almost liked Gabriella, whose gaiety made her seem so young. But Gabriella had ruined the evening for her. Charmian saw her coming downstairs again and the overwhelming desire to get away came to her once more.

"Don't you want to join in the Grand March?" Dennard asked.

Charmian watched her father smile at Gabriella as she joined him.

"No," she said, "I'd rather go into the garden and play with Timkins and Peebee."

"*Phoebe*, Charmian," said Dennard a little crossly. "Not Peebee. And I don't want to go into the garden; the dust will spoil my pretty slippers."

"You sound like a girl. Don't you want to have fun?"

"It's according to what you call fun. If you think playing with a couple of niggers is fun — "

"Don't you dare call Peebee and Timkins *niggers!*" Charmian's eyes flashed and her red lips clamped together as she stood with her hands on her hips. "Don't you dare!" She glared at him and hated the way his whitish-colored hair curled up in a mass of ringlets high over the side of his head. His eyebrows and lashes were very light, and his eyes, though dark, lacked fire. She didn't like him, but she tolerated him because of her loneliness. Brigette would hardly ever let her play with Peebee and Timkins. Only sometimes Brigette was too busy to notice what Charmian was doing.

Denard tried to avert her anger by asking, "Aren't you afraid you'll spoil that beau-ti-ful gown?"

She glanced down at it. It was of sheer white *mousseline de chaine*, with five rows of ruffles mounting from the hem which barely showed her matching pantalettes. Each ruffle was hand-embroidered with a running design of blushing roses; her sleeves were a waterfall of ruffles, and around her narrow shoulders was a fichu with more of the roses, fastened by a deep rose brooch. Her curls, lustrous and dark, were held in place with a small lace cap at the back of her head, and a single red rosebud peeped out of the cluster at the side. Her dainty feet were encased in heelless slippers of white satin, tied with black velvet ribbon.

Dennard caught her glance and looked down at his own costume. His knee breeches were of bright blue corded material; the cream-colored satin blouse had ridiculously long bishop sleeves, and a cascade of ruffles down the chest, topped off with a black satin bow tie just like the one his father was wearing.

"You're not going to play in the garden in that!" he insisted, pointing to her dress.

"Oh, I won't hurt it any. I'll not run, I guess. We could sit in the moonlight and tell ghost stores." Charmian took his reluctant hand and half pushed him toward the side door. No one was looking and it would be a simple matter to slip outside.

She hesitated only a moment to locate Brigette, and, catching a glimpse of her in the dining room, she stepped out into the white moonlight. Dropping Dennard's hand, she skimmed quickly over the grass, calling back to him, "Hurry! Denny! Hurry, ol' slowpoke."

The orchestra was playing 'Salut à la France,' a song new to many of Saucier's guests. No one noticed the children leaving.

Charmian paused at the white gate which led into the rose garden. She puckered her pretty lips as Pascal had taught her and whistled a high-trebled three-noted signal. A kinky head was thrust out of the nearest clump of shrubbery.

"That you, Miss Ch'meen?"

"Come out, Timkins. Where's Peebee?"

"Heah." Timkins came out quickly, pulling a shabby little yellow girl with him. "Mammy say we gotta go to bed, but Peebee done slept some a'ready."

Phoebe hung behind her brother, clutching at the strap on his worn breeches, staring out at Charmian with big round eyes.

Charmian turned a searching glance back over the grounds for Denny but he semed to have been lost. He'll probably go back and tell Papa where I've gone, she thought bitterly.

"You promise' today that we could peek inside at de folkses," reminded Phoebe, moving near Charmian's elbow and looking up solemnly into her face.

"Oh, if you must, go ahead." Charmian was impatient to escape the brightly colored silks and satins, the perfumes and the heavy atmosphere of the warm June night. She thought it would be the very time to slip down to old Popo's cabin while everybody in the house was busy. Phoebe could guide her to the cabin.

They crept up through the garden again and were now hugging the broad piazza. Phoebe's and Timkin's eyes flashed white in the candlelight which fell and flickered with the changing pattern of leaves in the giant trees. Laughter and music and excited female voices, with the constant undertone of masculine talk, floated out of the open windows.

The two Negro children were staring their eyes out at all the gorgeousness within the Big House.

"Dat's Blue, a-wavin' de switch acrost de tables of victuals," whispered Timkins. "And Florry! Mah Godlemighty! Don' she shine in dat riggin'?"

Charmian reached across Pheoebe's back and pinched Timkins' arm. He whooped with pain and ran from her.

Charmian followed him. "Hush! Oh, hush, Timkins. Don't ever say Godlemighty like that again." She was panting and furiously afraid that he would run away; she knew that she and Phoebe wouldn't dare go to the old crone's cabin without him.

Timkins sank down in a heap of misery, but his sobs stopped and he wiped his eyes and nose with a long sweeping gesture, keeping his hand up in front of his face for a moment and peering out to see if 'Little Miss' was angry.

"Go back and get Peebee," she commanded. "We're going to Popo's."

"No. No, suh, you cain' do dat, Miss Ch'meen. Miss Brigette said on no 'count to evah tak you."

"I'm going. I'm going tonight. Peebee'll take me. But you got to go, too, or you'll probably die and go to hell-fire for takin' the Good Lord's name in vain. If you take me, I'll pray for you tonight when I say my prayers."

Timkins got slowly to his knees. He was badly shaken.

He was afraid to take Charmian to Granny Popo's, and afraid of the hell-fire with which he had been threatened. The new overseer said Godlemighty all day long, shouting it out at the blacks in the fields, and nothing ever happened to him.

"Go get Peebee," Charmian said again.

"Yas'm. But de field'll ruin de slippers."

Charmian stood on one foot and removed the shoe from the other, then, reversing position, she said triumphantly, "I'll carry them."

"But de weeds'll snag yo' dress."

"Oh, hush, Timkins! Hush! Peebee! Peebee!" I'll get her myself, Charmian thought as she turned and sped back toward the house.

Phoebe was still standing in the

shadows, fascinated by the vision beyond the windows. Someone had joined her and the two of them stood silently drinking in the picture of the ball.

"Peebee!" Charmian said.

The other two children whirled quickly and Charmian saw that the boy was white, not one of the slaves' children. He looked vaguely familiar. He started to walk away, but Charmian stopped him.

"Who are you?" she asked. "I've seen you somewhere."

"I," he answered in his broken English, "I am Pierre Gregoire. I brought some pastries from the *confiseur*. My mother bakes for him." He moved again toward the edge of the piazza.

"Oh, I know now! I remember. You tried to stop the boys in Clabber Alley from stoning our carriage!" Charmian was excited and peered at him. Coming up beside him, she nodded her head. "You *are* the same boy, aren't you?"

"Yes." He moved again and she touched his arm.

"Don't go away. Please don't go away. Do you like ghost stories?" He did not answer and she went on, "You can go with us. You ought to see old Granny Popo. Did you ever see a voodoo 'ooman, Pierre?" she asked, pronouncing the word as the Negroes did.

He shook his head. "I don't know what you mean. I came over the ocean on a big ship to New Orleans. Then we came up the river to St. Louis. I don't know voodoo 'ooman." He backed away, clutching his basket.

"My father owns ships. Did you come on one of my father's boats from New Orleans?"

He did not answer. It seemed difficult for him to speak.

He turned back to the windows again, as though fascinated by the house and the colorful dresses of the women moving about in the brilliant light of the candelabra. He had never seen anything so entrancing. It made him feel hollow inside and he shivered although the night was quite warm.

"I think you're brave," said Charmian, remembering the incident in Clabber Alley. "You're braver than Denny Manley. Denny wouldn't try to stop anyone from stoning our carriage. He wouldn't go with me to Granny Popo's. He's a coward. But you'll go, won't you, Pierre?"

"I must go home."

"Oh, come on, Pierre. You're brave. You're as brave as my papa." She turned to Phoebe and put one hand around her thin little arm, digging into it a little with her thumb.

"Peebee, come now and take us to Granny Popo's."

"No." Phoebe's eyes were big in the moonlight. She could already feel the keen-edged whip over her shoulders. "No." She began to sniff a little. "No. No."

Charmian stamped her foot. "Don't stand there saying no!" She caught up Pierre's hand. He stood five inches taller than she and she looked up into his face. "Come on, Pierre. I know the way. Florry told me."

Pierre followed the touch of her hand. He was impelled to go, although he knew he should return home after delivering the cakes. They crossed the broad terraces and crawled over a rail fence. Charmian paused briefly once to point to the outlined shape of Whistlejackets. "That's

45

my pony. I ride him every day."

Pierre's hand was hot and he pulled it from her roughly. She was the daughter of wealth and he the son of poverty, and he felt it as keenly as though they were man and woman grown. He had no pony to ride every day, he had no fine house to live in, no shining carriage with a coachman to drive it, no boats on the river. But give him time and some day he, too, would own all these. He threw back his shoulders and smiled in the darkness, proud of his secret. No one knew it but himself, not even his twin brother, Sydney.

He continued to follow the little girl. Charmian stopped abruptly once and turned back to see if Timkins and Phoebe were following. Satisfied, she laughed a little and said, "They'll come. They always mind me."

The row of stone cabins where the Negroes lived stood beyond the first field. A soft, mournful tune from a mouth organ sounded through the night air, and they could hear the humming undertone of mellow voices. Charmian had heard the tune many times in the evening when the night breezes wafted it to the piazza. She knew some of the words:

*Oh, Lawd, oh, Lawd oh, Lawd!*
*Come an' tak me Home.*
*Home to Heab'n an' de Pea'ly Gates*
*Oh, come and tak me Home.*

"It's just the slaves. They're singing." Charmian said.

"It scares me a little." Pierre's eyes felt the sting of tears although he knew not why. There was a loneliness surging through him and a feeling of sadness for his old home that he would never see again. The dim shapes lounging around the cabin doors loomed big and frightening and he was glad when his new little friend skirted the cabins and they crept unseen through the edge of the woods.

"Where are we going?"

"To Granny Popo's, the voodooo 'ooman. She's yellow, like Peebee, and she came from the swamp country. She ran away from her master and they caught her and took her back, but he wouldn't have her any more and sold her to my father."

"Sold her? Sold a woman to your father? You mean like flour?"

Charmian stared at him. "Don't be silly, Pierre. *Of course!*"

As if that were enough explanation, she ran on ahead of him on the narrow path hedged in by underbrush. The moonlight was white above them, and he could see a small shanty in another clearing. But the windows were dark and there was nothing but silence around them.

"Old Popo's asleep, I guess," whispered the little girl. She stood there, half afraid to go farther, and Pierre could feel her fright.

He jumped as Timkins whispered behind them, "We'd bettah go back, Miss Ch'meen. Ol' Popo don' lak to be waked up outa sleep."

An owl hooted and Charmian clutched at Pierre's hand.

"Let's run," whispered Pierre.

But Charmian, now that her first fear was gone, stood still, knowing that she might not get back for a long, long time. She peered beyond the bright patch of

48

moonlight toward the shadows of the cabin. Something moved and a blurred shape crept out of the shadows to stand in front of the door.

The children stared as the old crone emerged. They could see the wrinkles set hard upon her face like furrows in a field, the skin so tightly drawn on her yellow forehead that the shape of the skull showed through it.

Charmian shivered and drew against Pierre and put her hand into his. A weird sound caught at their ears as the old hag began to chant. Charmian pulled at Pierre's arm and they edged closer and closer to the shack, her heart drumming.

The old woman knelt in the dust and, swaying to and fro, her eyes closed, she chanted in rhythm. A long, loose gown of grayish sack covered her bony figure, tattered fringes partly hid her skeleton-like arms. She reached into a fold of her skirt and withdrew a glowing object. Suddenly, in horror, Charmian saw a snake about old Popo's neck.

A feeling of nausea engulfed Charmian but, fascinated, she could not move. Her feet had turned to stone and she could not will them. The huge snake uncoiled itself. The old woman placed on the ground the strange object she had taken from her skirt, and the winding reptile looped itself and suddenly swallowed the thing whole.

Charmian screamed. Her wild, piercing shriek rang out again and again. Pierre grabbed her hand and began to run, pulling, half dragging her with him. Through the field, across the stubble, they sped into the dark woods. Charmian caught her foot in a vine and pitched headlong and Pierre stopped to pick her up. They came to the second clearing, Pierre half carrying her.

"Charmian! Charmian!"

Her father's voice dissolved Charmian's terror into tears.

"Papa! Papa!" she sobbed.

Lanterns bobbed about the garden and Charmian realized that the whole place was in an uproar. Her father broke through the shrubbery and stopped short at the sight of Pierre half carrying his daughter.

"Charmian! Charmian! Are you hurt,

Charmian?" he lunged toward them and took her in his arms and turned furiously upon Pierre. "Get out. Get out before I kill you! Leading my daughter away into the woods. I'll whip you within an inch of your life!" He cuffed Pierre sharply, his hand ringing on the boy's cheek.

"But I led *him*, Papa," wailed Charmian, burrowing deeply into the hard, warm cloth of her father's coat.

"White trash! No better than the Negroes," Llewellyn Saucier shouted. "Get out!" He turned and strode toward the brightness of the house.

Pierre's face burned. Saucier's tone lashed him and he stood abjectly watching the man go, humiliation weighting his feet like lead. He brushed tears of rage and anguish from his eyes.

"I'll show M'sieu Saucier. I'll be rich some day. I'll show M'sieu!

Saucier, carrying Charmian, disappeared into the hall. He marched grimly up and up the stairway. From the crook in his elbow, Charmian's wide eyes saw all the faces upturned below them and she squirmed in shame. Gabriella was smiling. Brigette, panting, came up the stairs behind them, her face taut.

They came to Charmian's room where the candles sputtered in their brackets. Saucier set his daughter upon the floor.

"I thought you were lost." His lips were white. He brushed aside her hand. She shivered and put it out again timidly but he ignored it.

"I have always hoped, Charmian, my daughter, that you would be a little lady. I have despaired sometimes, but it is true that I have wanted more than anything in my life for you to grow up like your mother." He turned furiously upon Brigette. "Brigette!" he roared.

"Yes. Yes, sir?"

"You were given a charge two years ago. You have never neglected that trust until tonight. Mind you, watch yourself, Brigette."

Charmian felt the hot tears pressing tight against her eyelids, which she had closed to shut out the awful sight of her father in anger. He had always been so gentle, always so soft-spoken. She peeped out between her fingers to look at him again and he reached across and pulled her hands down from her face.

"Look at your gown. The beautiful gown that came all the way from Paris especially for this party. Don't you have any shame?"

"Very little, I'm afraid, Papa."

"Brigette, strip her and wash her before you put her to bed. Good night, Charmian, I shall see you tomorrow."

She watched him striding from the room, then threw herself sobbing upon Brigette. She could not bear for Papa to be angry with her. She could not bear it!

But somewhere within her a voice was saying. *He didn't ask you where you had gone. He didn't ask you.* Relief flooded over her until she remembered those dread words. 'I shall see you tomorrow.' She cried louder. She had known in the beginning there would be an accounting.

# 4

THE youth stood on the deck of the *Eagle*, entranced as always with the leave-taking. He was more excited than usual, because the *Eagle* was going to race the *Friar Point* to Natchez.

Many things had happened to Pierre Gregoire since he first arrived in St. Louis. The years had dealt hard blows to his parents, and harder ones to the brood they left when they died two days apart. Pierre and Sydney, the twins, had stayed on in the little cabin in Clabber Alley for a while, but their sisters, Marie and Emilie, had gone into the home of the owner of the confectionery shop where their mother had worked.

Pierre, at the age of thirteen, had run away from the leather shop where he was apprenticed and become a cabin boy on a steamboat. Sydney was taken in by the good doctor who had signed his parents' death certificates. Sydney wanted to be a doctor himself, and at the age of nineteen still lived with Dr. Whitten, studying every evening and making calls with him.

Pierre had advanced rapidly from cabin boy to deck hand and he had just become a cub pilot. With hard work he had developed great vigor and he now stood a few inches taller than most of the crew of the *Eagle*.

He was stealing a few moments to look over the scene at the levee. He loved the confusion and noise of the departure. The big paddle wheels turned slowly, beating the muddy water with their first sluggish, swishing strokes. Steam hissed from the open cylinder cock and ribboned away over the brown river. Pierre's eyes fastened on the pair of gilded antlers on the pilot house, which the *Eagle* had won from the *Itasca* last month.

The mate looked up and called, "All ready, sir!"

Captain Porter rang the bell. The mellow note was echoed by the bells of other boats ready to start. Loudest of all by the *Friar Point*, which was working her way into the channel.

Most of the passengers, stirred by excitement, were on deck. Back on the levee, people were still making bets: sportsmen, shippers, friends of the passengers, officers of other boats, hackmen, porters, stevedores, newsboys, pickpockets, and the usual run of gamblers.

The wheels stopped and Pierre leaned over the edge to watch the black roustabouts take the mooring lines aboard. The bells jangled in the engine room, then the reversed wheels beat the water, exhaust steam hissed up through the coroneted escape pipes, and the *Eagle* backed into the current, belching a great cloud of black smoke from her two tall chimneys. Pierre heard the chant of the darkies, and the people on shore and passengers on the decks picking it up:

> *"Juba in and Juba out*
> *Juba, juba, all about;*
> *Dinah, stir de possum fat;*
> *Can't you hear de juba pat?*
> *Juba!"*

The first line was softly sung, the second louder, the third became a stirring shout, and the final *Juba*! was a roar that vibrated against the very banks of the river. Pierre loved it all with a deep and satisfying love. He could close his eyes and see the wharves of New Orleans all along from Canal to Julia Street, piled high and deep with white bales of cotton, and from there but a short distance to the Girod Street landing where the packets that steamed from New Orleans to Memphis, St. Louis, Louisville, and Cincinnati lay three abreast in the water.

After he had once been cast alone upon that crescent-shaped levee at New Orleans, with its mile-long bank of boats from the Ohio, the Tennessee, the Arkansas, the Missouri, and the Mississippi, Pierre had known that he would never be anything but a river man.

Now the surging excitement of the crews, the high thrill of departure, stirred him, and he joined in the plaintive lines:

"*Farewell, brothers if you's gwine fo'
   to go,
We'll weep fo' to see you' face once
   mo'.*"

Some of the women passengers joined in the refrain:

*"On de levee by de river side,*
*I've left my gal in New Orleans,*
*Fo' she is young, jes' in her teens.*
*On de levee, by de river side."*

Swinging Jake, a huge brown roustabout, broke in with a rollicking tune:

*"Ducks play cards and chickens*
*    drink wine*
*An' de monkey grow on de grapevine.*
*Cornstarch puddin' and tapioca pie,*
*Oh! de gray cat pick out de black*
*    cat's eye!"*

A great shout of laughter went up. Swinging Jake's voice was deep and mellow and the crew loved to hear him sing.

"Sing Miss Loo, Jake, sing Miss Loo!" shouted someone.

Jake walked over to the deck and leaned his arms agains the rail.

*"Walk that, Loo, O Miss Loo,*

*Ah! Ah! Here we go!*
*For we're gwine fo' to leave you,*
*Good-bye, good-bye;*
*Fo' we're gwine fo' to leave you.*
*Good-bye, good-bye."*

The *Eagle* was out in midstream now, the people on the levee almost out of sight, and the crew must begin the serious business of the race.

No more sooty smoke was pouring out of their chimneys. Pierre knew that was only a showy trick anyway, accomplished by throwing powdery coal over the fire. The fires were clean now, and white hot, and the pilot rang for full speed ahead. The *Friar Point* was considered one of the fastest boats on the river, a racer without any fol-de-rols; and both crews, from scullery boys to captains, were racers above everything else.

They were off to the first landing. The smaller packets in the stream dropped behind as the *Eagle* and the *Friar Point*, intent on the race, forged swiftly ahead. Running side by side, they led all the rest between the low-lying banks.

Pierre was one of the first to spring

down the gangplank at the Donaldson Levee when the rush of loading and unloading began. He grinned at the cursing of the mate standing on the capstan, urging the crew on to more speed. It was a few minutes before nine and they were already ahead of schedule, but the *Friar Point* was panting at their heels.

The bells clanged and the boats rounded into the stream once more, the *Eagle* still a few minutes ahead of the *Friar Point* at the second landing.

The light from the open furnaces shone weirdly on the glistening bodies of the firemen. High above the cabin lights, above the darkened pilot house, showers of sparks flew; gleamed, and died into darkness. The people at the last levee, having shouted themselves hoarse, were nothing but a faint call in the inky black of the night.

Baton Rouge. Unloading and loading again. The water was patterned with lights at the wharf and the persistent fishy smell was thick in his nostrils as Pierre, still so near the life of a deck hand, helped the crew. He was too excited to sleep after they got started again, and stood by the rail watching the moon, which had not come up until after midnight. Most of the passengers had retired, but there was still a throbbing of excitement all over the boat.

A few men lounged about the bar, among them two of the most noted gamblers on the Mississippi. They had bet heavily upon the race, but wouldn't let it interfere with their regular business. Pierre looked in upon them, but returned to the rail until time to go to bed.

Pierre's favorite run was from St. Louis to New Orleans, and he told himself that when he owned his boat that was where he would travel. In his mind was the map of the river, its shape and appearance in high water and low, the depth of the channel at every point, at all stages. He knew the name of every point and bend, island, snag, and wreck. There were countless wrecks whose lurking dangers made it imperative that the pilot sense their presence to enable him to make the journey safely.

The Mississippi was full of tricks and inconsistencies. Where a sandbar lay on the downstream trip, it might shift in the treacherous current on the upstream. The bed was as changeable and rapacious as the muddy water which flowed above it. In his six years on the river, Pierre had learned intimately its subtle whims, its vagaries, its covetousness.

Restless, he wandered back to the furnace door to watch the firemen. They were having trouble with the wood they had picked up at the last docks. "Too green! Takes too much time to get started. By God! We're barely crawling!"

They threw pitch in with it and the smoke rolled black, but the firemen continued to curse, for they knew they couldn't hope to keep up enough steam to run ahead of the *Friar Point*.

Pierre slept fitfully in his bunk when he finally went to bed. With the morning light he went on deck to see how they were faring. The *Friar Point* was not in sight.

"Are we behind?" he asked.

"The *Point* slipped past us in the night. That green fuel cost us the race. Our mate's fit to tie!"

"We've got a chance yet," said

Pierre, grinning.

He went to the galley for coffee, and Cooky Jensen poured it into a heavy white mug. "Set down, Pete. Might's well have yer ham and eggs. Set right down, sir."

Pierre smiled. It was still a little strange to be treated like a gentleman after all these years of rough life. Cooky was rattling on.

"The paint's blistered on our chimneys. But this ain't no race." He shrugged his fat shoulders and wiped the sweat from his forehead with the back of his hand. His squint eyes peered into Pierre's face as he set the platter down in front of him. Cooky hitched up his dirty apron and poured himself a cup of coffee.

"It was nip and tuck till arter midnight and that green wood put the kibosh on the *Eagle*.

"Don't be so downhearted, Cooky. Maybe we'll win yet."

"No, sir, not a chance, Pete. Cap'n Porter's got the resin barrels handy, but not a goldarn chance to beat the *Point*."

Pierre finished his eggs and held out

his cup for more coffee. It was good and black, not any of that half chicory stuff they gave the passengers on the first boat he had worked on. He had been spoiled on New Orleans coffee, strong and as thick as syrup. Pierre stretched for a moment, his arms going up over his head, pulling fatigue from his muscles and showing his great length from lean waist to shoulders and the length of his legs in their leather boots and whipcord breeches. Cooky went back to the galley stove to finish getting the captain's breakfast and Pierre went to the wheelhouse.

It was a beautiful morning, but he could tell it would be a hot day. The sun was ready to burst forth, and the reflection of it was shimmering down the river ahead in the bright blaze Pierre had grown to love. Mist was rising from the banks and he could feel the steam of the day's heat.

The pilot was glad to be relieved as Pierre took over, anxious to feel the wheel beneath his hands.

Pierre had learned to tell a reef mark from a wind mark on the water, and he knew that a dimple in its surface meant a rock, that a streak resembling a wake was a snag waiting to stab at the boat. He avoided a spot ahead which looked like a boiling caldron. Oh, every line and every peculiar mark had a meaning of its own and he had learned to read them like a chart upon a wall.

The sun was getting higher and passengers came out upon the decks. The *Eagle* neared another landing where they would take on wood. Pierre grinned to himself.

As they rounded the next bend, he blew the whistle and it rang out and echoed hollowly, resounding from the cliffs rising sharply from the water. Pierre saw the first barge piled high with cordwood waiting at the point in the stream previously designed. He heard the passengers call to one another in excitement as they saw what the *Eagle* intended to do.

Pierre nosed the boat up to the barge and one of the crew caught the line as the grinning bargeman tossed it to him. They refueled the *Eagle* without stopping, cutting the barge loose down the river after the Negroes had taken all the wood on board, tossing the huge pieces to one another midst the excitement of the passengers.

Presently Pierre felt the response of the *Eagle* to the new, dry wood, heard the quickening of the engines, the higher note of the threshing paddles, the louder hiss of the exhaust, and the cursing of the firemen.

The wheelhouse door opened and Captain Porter put in his head. "Here's someone wants to meet you, Gregoire. Colonel Reaves and Miss Reaves." He stepped aside and excused himself to go back to his cabin.

Surprised, Pierre looked into a pair of the bluest eyes he had ever seen, gay, laughing eyes fringed with long black lashes. The girl was very pretty standing there with a friendly look, her blond curls peeping out from a lace-frilled bonnet.

"That was a right smart trick, Mr. Gregoire," the large man with her was saying. "Captain Porter says you're responsible for it! I've got a bet placed on the *Eagle*, son, and something tells me we've got another chance now."

"The *Friar Point* can't be too far ahead

of us. After their next stop we'll have a better chance, sir," said Pierre, keeping his eyes on the river after that one swift look and his embarrassed nod at their introduction.

"That was some pretty good piloting, taking on those barges without scraping the boat."

"Thank you, Colonel."

"I'm so excited!" said Miss Reaves. "I wouldn't have missed the race for anything, would you, Papa?"

"I should say not, puss. Well, we'd better run along now. We'll see you later, Mr. Gregoire."

Pierre nodded and smiled at them, his eyes leaving the water long enough to see that the girl was as pretty as he had thought in the first place.

"Good-bye, Mr. Gregoire, until later," she said from the doorway, her arm linked through her father's.

Soon after they took on another load of wood from barges waiting in the stream, they passed the *Friar Point* standing at the levee, its mate cursing while the roustabouts refueled. The *Eagle* came around the bend, passing the docks, smoke streaming out of her chimneys, horn blowing, the passengers shouting from the decks.

With a clanging of bells and blowing of horns, the *Friar Point* backed out into the channel once more.

Now's the real test of speed, thought Pierre. He could hear the orders from the officers aboard the *Eagle*. The roustabouts worked like beavers tossing the wood from the pile to the furnace doors, down the lines. Flames burst furiously every time the doors were opened. The firemen's curses never slackened, and the whiskey barrel sank to a lower level. The proof of the *Eagle*'s lines and engines and boilers, of her officers' skill, of the crew's endurance, were all at stake; and they worked, keeping up their vigilance, heat-pitch high. The passengers shouted until they were hoarse, for the *Friar Point* was lunging like an angry monster close in their wake.

Sweat poured down Pierre's forehead and dripped in rivulets from his chin. His shirt was wet and his arms and legs cramped as he clung to the wheel, now plowing down the channel, now nosing out a bit to avoid a floating log, now straightening her up a little, and so on and on and on. Presently the long low buildings on the levees of Natchez came into sight, and the passengers on the *Eagle* gave a vast, rousing cheer that lifted the heavens.

The shouting died away, and big brown Jake, standing on the forecastle, sang lustily:

*"Juba in and juba out,*
*Juba, juba, all about"*

Natchez!

The golden antlers stayed on the pilot house of the *Eagle*.

As Pierre swung his carpet bag out to get his clean clothes, Captain Porter came to his cabin door and said, "Colonel Reaves would like to see you, Gregoire. Wants to congratulate you, I guess."

"I'll clean up a bit first, sir." Pierre hurried because the passengers were already beginning to leave the *Eagle*, and a few minutes later he tapped at the colonel's stateroom door.

"Come on in, Gregoire," said the colonel, withdrawing the pipe from his mouth and motioning to a chair. "You're a fine pilot, son, and I wanted to tell you so!"

"Thank you," said Pierre in embarrassment, turning his cap about in his long fingers, his eyes sweeping Miss Reaves, who sat holding her parasol and long gloves.

"I've some business at the cotton mart, and then my daughter and I would like for you to have dinner with us at Natchez House."

Although Pierre was astonished, he managed to say, "Why, thank you, Colonel Reaves, but I'm not dressed for the Natchez House, sir." It was an elegant place, one of which he had often heard, but had not hoped to enter.

"Come, now, no objections! Pshaw! We'll have it in our rooms. Then my daughter will retire and we'll see a few sights."

"Papa! Indeed I shall not retire. Pray, why do you think I came along? Let us all dine together in the dining parlour

— not in our rooms."

"Very well. Come along, Mr. Gregoire. We've counted on you."

They made a striking picture going down the gangplank: the handsome colonel with his white flowing hair and black stock, dressed in white linen; Pierre, the tall, comely youth in shabby but clean work clothes; Antoinette Reaves, who tripped along gaily, her blue eyes sparkling, her lips curved upward; and the Reaves' big black servant, Jamaica.

"It seems to me the life of a pilot could be almighty appealing," said Colonel Reaves when they were settled in the carriage. "Do you hope to own your own boat some day?"

"I do, indeed, sir. Some day I shall."

Pierre's embarrassment grew with the moments he sat facing the colonel and his daughter. Her peach-bloom skin, the gold of her curls, and the beribboned hat, fascinated him almost as much as the music in her soft voice.

"I hope you get your boat, Mr. Gregoire," she said, smiling at him to make his discomfiture complete.

"Pull up!" Colonel Reaves called to

the driver, and Pierre saw that they were approaching the cotton mart. "Please stay here with my daughter, Mr. Gregoire, Jamaica will come inside with me."

An hour passed in which Miss Reaves talked on subjects of purely feminine interest; Pierre was unable to say anything but an occasional murmured, "Yes, ma'am," and "No, ma'am." But he learned something about social life on the big Reaves plantation near Vicksburg before the colonel and Jamaica reappeared.

"I can tell that you were successful, Papa," said Miss Reaves as her father seated himself in the carriage.

"Yes, my dear, your father knows how to trade."

Pierre sat back in a red plush seat in the lobby of the Natchez House, waiting for the Reaves to come downstairs. He was impressed with the extravagance of the decorations. The carpeting underfoot was thick and beautiful, the cut-glass chandeliers sparkled in the last rays of the evening sun which came in at the western windows. The elegance of the upholstering on the love seats and the ornate carving of the backs of the heavy mahogany chairs entranced Pierre.

He sat up as he saw two of the gamblers who had been aboard the *Eagle*, Cappy Rals and Big Dick Benders, go up to the clerk and ask him a question. The clerk nodded toward Pierre, and he felt the two men's hard, sharp scrutiny.

A few minutes later, Pierre heard the voice of Antoinette Reaves on the stairway and saw her descending arm in arm with her father. If he had thought her pretty this afternoon, he knew now that she was beautiful. Her blond head, with a fantastic jeweled headdress, was held proudly; her white dress, cascading rows of lace-edged ruffles, was the most exquisite gown Pierre had ever seen.

The colonel studied the younger man's face. He knew the expression of a man who was seeing something untouchable. He had seen back in their rooms that his daughter was breathtakingly lovely tonight and had said, "You ought to be ashamed, Toinette, dressing like that. You know he has never seen a girl half so beautiful!"

"Then it's time he was seeing one,

Papa. But you flatter me; I know that some of the girls in St. Louis are very beautiful. I remember your talking about them!"

"Yes, but this river rat has never seen them."

"He may have been a deck hand once, but he's no river rat, Papa. You heard him say, too, that he hoped to own his boat some day." She whirled about for her father's benefit.

"Mind you, no coquetting tonight. Remember, there's your young man in Vicksburg."

"Oh, yes, Papa, I'll remember." She rolled her blue eyes up at him. "I'll remember — that he *is* in Vicksburg!"

"Fie! Fie on you! Every day you're more like your father!"

Pierre's fingers were hot and awkward on the rim of his cap and he glanced down in dismay at his whipcord breeches. Toinette, seeing his glance, rippled into conversation designed to set the shy young man at ease as they entered the dining hall.

The waiters brought strange new dishes: baked lobster with a piquant sauce, creamed chicken on tiny biscuits, light, tender gingerbread which melted in Pierre's mouth, and fragrant, tantalizing drinks that he could only swallow and wish for more of; brown roast pork, braised ribs, stuffed young guinea, tiny garden peas, a dessert made from the roots of an exotic fruit which grew in the swamps of the Everglades that left him mystified. It felt cold on his tongue, yet warm the next instant and pleasantly satisfying. Pierre's eyes caught a glimpse of himself in the shining coffee urn. He thought, My brother Sydney would be at home here, no doubt.

"You're eating nothing, Gregoire. Fill your wineglass!" said the colonel.

"Thank you, sir, no more tonight."

"Good evening, Colonel and Miss Reaves," said a voice, deep and pleasant.

"Good evening, gentlemen," said the colonel.

Toinette inclined her head slightly.

Pierre knew without turning that the two gamblers stood behind his chair. He sat silently, waiting for them to pass on.

"Enjoying your meal?"

"The very finest I've ever had in Natchez," said the colonel extravagantly. "Come join us, gentlemen, and we'll drink a toast."

Benders drew out a chair near Pierre and the other man sat down facing him. "Your friend?"

"Young Pierre Gregoire, cub pilot on the *Eagle*."

Benders raised a black brow and nodded. "I haven't seen you around, I guess." His eyes drifted over Pierre's long frame.

"No," said Pierre briefly.

After a round of toasts, Toinette coughed to get her father's attention. He responded by rising. "Well, gentlemen, I have some papers to go over."

"Shall we see you later in the evening, Colonel?" asked Benders after bowing courteously to Miss Reaves.

"Not tonight, I'm afraid."

Pierre, falling back of him and Toinette, saw the two gamblers exchange glances. "How about you, Gregoire? How about a little game?"

Pierre bowed politely. "Thank you, I do not play cards." He eyed them coolly, knowing they were not interested in his wages. The colonel's cotton money was their concern.

They parted in the lobby and the colonel and his daughter retired to their rooms, Pierre bidding the girl goodnight. He looked at her gravely when she changed his 'good-bye' to "*au revoir*," and stumblingly repeated, "Ah, yes, until we meet."

But I shall never see you again, he thought, although some day, perhaps, when I own a freighter, I may carry the colonel's cotton to market.

He stopped short suddenly on his way out of the hotel. A carriage was drawn up outside and the gamblers waiting, probably for a prearranged rendezvous with Colonel Reaves. The colonel's little subterfuge about having to go over papers — that, thought Pierre, was for his daughter's benefit.

It was getting late, but Pierre, loath to go back aboard the *Eagle*, started walking toward Natchez-Under-the-Hill. It was dark all along the street of the gambling district, except for the lights behind shabby lace curtains — beacons which were contemptuously whispered about by stiffly corseted dowagers in respectable drawing rooms.

Pierre stopped outside a saloon. He seldom joined the other members of the crew ashore, but he knew that this was where they usually spent their nights in Natchez. He opened the door and strode in. Several of his fellow crew members were drinking at the bar and greeted him with friendly cheers.

"By God! It's Pete! The fines' damn' cub pilot that ever walked the deck of a side-wheeler!"

Pierre felt their friendliness closing in, urging him to the bar and lifitng his spirits. They pushed a glass to him and he grinned companionably.

The outcome of the race and his clever trick in refueling the *Eagle* without stopping her had been told and retold this evening and Pierre had rapidly gone up the scale in the crew's estimation.

He was facing the door when it opened and Colonel Reaves and the two gamblers entered. They went to a table in the corner of the big room and began dealing cards. The small flame in an oil lamp fretted against the smoked chimney, casting a flickering yellow light on the men's faces.

Pierre watched while the cards were dealt again and occasionally glanced at the table where the men played. The colonel seemed to be enjoying the game, the smile never leaving his face. His servant, Jamaica, sauntered past the open door, and Pierre saw him look in a moment at Reaves. The colonel's smile grew as time went on, and although Pierre was tired, he remained at the bar, talking, yet watching the men at the table.

The game went on and on. The colonel won, then Big Dick won, then the colonel won again. It seemed endless, but the colonel kept ahead. Men began edging up to the table, watching and murmuring with excitement. The room was quiet then except for the colonel's occasioral chuckle and the voices in betting. Finally Colonel Reaves looked at his watch.

"Well, boys, I've had enough. Have to get some sleep."

Rals objected politely, but Benders shrugged a heavy shoulder.

Pierre, sleepy now and feeling the length of the day upon him, slipped out of the side door to the street. He saw Jamaica waiting in the hired carriage, holding the reins. Colonel Reaves climbed into the carriage and Pierre watched a moment from the shadows while they drove off.

He heard a clock striking midnight as he walked along the shadowed street. Two blocks further, he halted in astonishment. Dimly he saw the colonel's carriage had been stopped and drawn to the side of the road.

He saw an unfamiliar dark figure holding the horses, and then in the fitful moonlight saw another man standing on the step of the carriage. He realized that Colonel Reaves was being held up. Pierre shouted and began to run toward the carriage.

The man on the step jumped down, there was the sound of a gunshot, and the horses, loosed by the other man, reared high. Pierre saw the two men dash for the shadows of a nearby building, and then the sound of running feet over the cobbled ground came to his ears.

Panting, he came up to the carriage.

"Are you all right, Colonel?" he cried.

"Yes," answered Reaves. "Jamaica's shot though!" he leaned over the slumped figure of his servant in the driver's seat. "Humph!" he said as Jamaica moaned and sat up. "Needs more'n a bullet to take care of this big black rascal of mine. Feel all right, Jamaica?"

"Yassuh."

"Nothing but a light scratch, I guess. Well, it looks like those footpads got away, lad."

"I don't think they'll bother you again, but I'll drive with you to the hotel if you wish."

"We'll make out all right," said the colonel. "That was a close shave — too close to be comfortable. You got here in the nick of time." He nodded toward Jamaica. "We'd better go along now. The next time, Gregoire, that you're in Vicksburg, I'd like for you to come and see me."

"Thank you, I will," said Pierre.

# 5

STEAMBOAT trade was at its height six years later when Charmian Saucier returned from the Academy of the Sacred Heart to Ginger Blue. Her father's shipping line had flourished during the interim and now, in 1848, he was one of the wealthiest men in St. Louis. The Saucier boats carried passengers and freight: cotton, hemp, tobacco, sugar, and meats; steel goods from the east, and imported goods and raw materials from Europe. They made the run from St. Louis to New Orleans on the Mississippi; from St. Louis to Westport Landing on the Missouri; another line also had three fast steamers which plied the Ohio.

Her school days behind her, Charmian found that the social whirl which her father enjoyed seemed strange to her after the quiet life she had led. Llewellyn Saucier had not changed greatly in the past ten years, although there was a little more white in his dark hair. He came and went to his offices daily and sometimes wore a harassed expression to the supper table. He dined often with Gabriella Danforth, whom Charmian saw frequently at social gatherings.

Charmian soon grew restless and spoke to her father about doing charity work among poor families on the waterfront.

"You can't imagine the squalor and the filth, daughter. Battle Row is dirtier and less reputable than Clabber Alley and Happy Hollow. The Guards are always being called to clear out drunken brawls."

"But I'll be careful, Papa. Pascal can drive me and Brigette can go along."

"Let's not discuss it," he said.

But she brought up the subject again a week later.

"You have duties as my hostess, my rosebud," her father said. "We entertain often at Ginger Blue. There's many a young lady who'd like the chance to help me."

Gabriella Danforth would, of course, thought Charmian a little bitterly. In all fairness to her father, though, she must remember that he had been lonely while she was away, and Gabriella was very attractive. Even Brigette had linked her father's name with Gabriella's on the first day Charmian was at home. It was really partly because of his interest in Mrs. Danforth that Charmian wanted to do social work. She felt a greater distance between her father and herself now than when she had first returned.

With a tinge of bitternes in her tone, she said, "yes, I'm sure that Gabriella would like that, Papa."

"Yes," he answered, "Mrs. Danforth loves Ginger Blue. And," he added, not noticing the bitterness in his daughter's voice, "she agreed with me entirely about your idea. We don't want you going into those vermin-infested, disease-ridden houses!"

*We!*

Charmian trembled. Saucier and Gabriella were inevitably linked in that one word, *we.*

Gabriella was a widow now. Everyone had thought she would make a fine marriage, but she had married poor, indecisive Lewis Danforth, who hadn't been any more successful in his printing business than anyone had predicted. Danforth had died two years earlier, leaving his wife a small income and the modest house he had built for her.

"Gabriella has no right to decide what I shall do!"

"Only the right of a very dear friend of your father's. I simply don't want you in those districts."

Charmian's voice was thin as she said, "We've been all through this before, Papa. Ever since that first summer I went with you to the levee, I've been sorry for those people."

"I forbid you to go into those places!" Saucier shouted.

"Then I shall go without your permission."

"I'll lock you in your room!" he stared at her, his eyes dark and deep-set in his white face. Then he turned and went out of the house, shouting for Pascal to drive him to his office.

Charmian would always remember her first trip down to the waterfront again. Pascal, his stiff sideburns bristling with gray, his eyes still dark and merry, drove the carriage for her, and Brigette, who had been his wife for seven years, sat stiffly beside Charmian as though the girl were still in her charge and as naughty as ever. Charmian laughed over that excursion many times during the first month at home, but there were weeks later when she rarely laughed.

One late winter's day she picked her way carefully from her carriage to a cabin in Battle Row. She was going to call upon Emilie Vigo, whose newest son had just come into life in the shabbiness of the tiny house. A light mantle of snow which had fallen the night before had begun to melt, and spring was forecast in the dirty rivulets in the wagon tracks.

Charmian uttered an exclamation as she crossed the yard and saw a yellow-green shoot upthrust through the soil. It was the first concrete evidence of the new season and a glow of exhilaration went through her slender body. She tapped gently at the door of her cabin and pressed it open at Emilie Vigo's weak call from within. The shadowed room was untidy and cold, but a newly built fire shot sparks on the hearth.

"My brother came and built the fire. I sent the boys with their father this morning," said the woman on the bed.

Charmian crossed the room and stopped beside the fire. Her cheeks were flushed with the cold morning air, her dark eyes shining. The snapping logs gave up a brightness, touching her black curls and sending out a new radiance. Charmian stood there, tall and slender in a dark red woolen redingote trimmed with fur down the front and on the hem of her skirt. She wore a matching fur toque on her head and her hands were still tucked in her muff for warmth, but she drew them out and unfastened her coat.

"My brother went for soup meat and vegetables," Emilie Vigo continued. "He will be back in a little while. He is good to me and would help more if Alexis would let him, but my husband is too proud. He says that my brother always did look down on the rest of us. He has given me money, but I dare not let Alexis know."

Charmian laid aside her hat and coat and began tidying the cabin, picking up the boys' clothing, hanging it on nails behind the door, making up their tumbled little bed and putting fresh sheets in the small cradle.

"The baby's so tiny to put in there all alone," said Emilie, eyeing the cradle and smoothing her son's fuzzy head.

"Oh, not a fine big lad like that! He'll tire you too much if you keep him with you all the time," said Charmian cheerfully. "You must rest so that you can feed him. I'll make the soup when your brother comes, and it will be good and nourishing."

"You've been so kind. I don't know what I'd have done without your help this week." Emilie's eyes were sunken and there were hollows in her white cheeks.

Charmian waved aside her words. "What does your brother do?" she asked. She wondered why she had not seen him or heard Emilie Vigo mention him before.

"He owns a passenger steamboat and two small freighters. He just came in from New Orleans last night. He — " She broke off at a tap sounding at the cabin door. "There — there he is now."

Charmian saw him in the bright sunlight of the doorway, tall and well built, with broad shoulders tapering to a lean, hard waist. He was not actually handsome, but he had an arresting look. He was wearing a fashionably cut suit, and she saw that the cravat fastened at his throat was of soft blue silk. He bent his head a little to enter the low door and then hesitated as he saw Charmian.

"Won't you come in?" she asked. "I'm Charmian Saucier."

"How do you do, Miss Saucier," he said. "I appreciate your coming and helping my sister. She was speaking of you a while. ago. I am Pierre Gregoire."

'Pierre Gregoire. Gregoire.' The name stirred her memory and she added quickly. "Oh, I remember you!" Suddenly she knew that she had never forgotten the white-faced boy who had stood out from among the little urchins in that dirty street called Clabber Alley.

He was certain that she would have forgotten him, and her remembering so quickly embarrassed him. She was beautiful, unbelievably beautiful, here in this shabby little house of his sister's, and the contrast between the pinched look of Emilie's face and the soft, rounded contours of Charmian's struck him forcefully.

He slowly removed his hat and then held out a brown package. "I brought some things for soup."

He was looking about the room curiously, almost disbelievingly. In the short time the girl had been there, a change had come over it. The untidiness had given way to neatness; the boys' garments were off the floor and hot water was steaming from the black pot on the stove. A contented sucking noise came from the blanket on his sister's arm.

He went over and stood by the bed and turned down a corner of the coverlet to gaze upon his new nephew for a moment. He looked a little awkward standing there, but an expression of tenderness was on his face, lighting it up from within and softening the whole of it. It was a strong face, Charmian saw, with a firm, jutting jaw and a showing of bony structure underneath the tan skin on his cheeks with their fresh, scrubbed look.

Charmian moved forward, asking, "What became of you? I remember that you tried to stop the boys from stoning our carriage in Clabber Alley. Then I recall a ball that my father gave, and you looked in the window. And we ran through the dark woods. Do you remember?"

"I remember." He straightened up and came to meet her, forgetting his sister on the bed. She had wealth, family, position. What did she want here in his sister's poor little cabin?

"You asked what became of me. I was an apprentice in a leather shop, but I ran away and became a cabin boy, and have been on the river ever since." He paused, remembering the heat on the burning summer decks, the ice in the winter when he was a stevedore. "I have three boats now; one is a passenger, the others small freighters." He paused again, then asked. "And you, Miss Saucier? I have seen your father many times and I recognize the coachman in your carriage — but you?" His voice had faint mockery in it for this girl who was playing Good

91

Samaritan to the poor.

"I was sent to the Academy of the Sacred Heart. I was furious because my nurse, Brigette, talked my father out of the trips to the levee after that one summer. She was so afraid it was not ladylike for me to drive along the riverside."

He smiled a little and she knew that he was remembering her running barefoot through a dark patch of woods. That hadn't been very ladylike, either. A flush spread over her face.

She turned swiftly back to her patient on the bed. "Can I get you a drink, Mrs. Vigo?" she asked.

Pierre stayed on only a few minutes longer. Then, picking up his cap, he said, "I'll be going now. I want to thank you again. Good-bye, Emilie. Take care of that new son." he was whistling after he left the house and Charmian recognised the tune, 'The St. Louis Polka.'

The cabin seemed cold and cheerless without him, after the door closed. Charmian put the meat on to cook, hanging the pot from the crane above the fire. She assumed a cheerfulness that she could not feel, and forced herself to finish the tasks she had set before she could leave. She finally put the vegetable and meat stew on the back of the built-in oven, and dipped up a bowl of it for Emilie. She opened the basket she had brought from home, taking out fresh bread and a roll of butter from the Saucier springhouse. Then she went to the window and peered out to see if Pascal had returned for her.

He was waiting, and she could see from his stiff posture that his indignation was thriving on his impatience.

"I've arranged for Mrs. Lane to come in to stay with you this afternoon. She promised that she would come early," she said, turning to Emilie.

"I'll be all right," Emilie said. "I mustn't keep you any longer."

Charmian had two more calls to make. Pascal slowed the horses before the door of the first house, farther down the street.

"Brigette said to tell you that she had the batch of bread made up just to please you this one more time, Miss Charmian. My old woman is getting harder and harder to live with every blessed day that passes."

"Shame on you, Pascal! Maybe you're getting harder and harder to please. So Brigette is rebelling again!" She reached up and adjusted her hat, partly closed one eye and murmured, "We'll have to keep on the good side of Brigette."

She reached across and opened the big basket on the seat, sniffing hungrily at the buttered brown crust and, unable to resist, pinched off a bit of it between her fingers and ate it.

In a house overflowing with richness, where servants fell over themselves getting out of work, it would be strange if she could not have a few small chores performed for her that would do so much good. She had no patience with Brigette, and much less with Florry, who avoided physical labor as she would the plague. Brigette was bitterly resentful of the mulatto girl and would never get over it as long as they worked in the big house together.

After Brigette's duties as nurse were over, she had firmly picked up the reins as housekeeper, and had never relinquished them in the slightest, despite Pascal's continuous warning, "You must learn the driving hand, my little tinderbox. Hold the reins lightly, yet firmly. The black devils are like horses; they can tell by the feel whether they've got the lead or if you have it. You drive 'em too hard and they don't like it any more than the bays when I checkrein them too tight."

"Oh, go on with your silly talk, Pascal. Blacks are animals all right, but they've not the sense the bays have."

Charmian heard such comments daily. Sometimes she saw humor in their sallies, other times she grew weary of their everlasting hacking at each other, like a poor woodsman cutting down a staunch, contrary pine.

# 6

AS Charmian got back into the carriage from her last call she was glad the day was over. It was a short day, she admitted to herself, but one that had taken toll of her energy. The chief bright spot in it was seeing Pierre Gregoire this afternoon. She wondered if he would be at his sister's house tomorrow when she went back.

"Home now, Pascal. Drive by Chouteau's Pond, please."

Pascal touched the brim of his hat. The young mistress looked tired. Some of the bloom was gone from her pretty rounded cheeks, and her dark eyes had a look of fatigue. He drove fast, thinking the wind whipping through the carriage would revive her. As they neared Chouteau's Pond, the three stone towers of the flour mill rose ahead of them. Disconsolate boys with ice skates in their hands stood by idly bemoaning the thawing surface.

Pascal slowed the horses and Charmian

leaned out of the carriage thinking what fun she could have next summer with her father, who was a charter member of the Ripple Boat Club. I could be very gay in St. Louis, but how selfish that would be. It seems so silly only to dress for good times, go calling, and entertain, when you have twenty-four hours in every day.

Her father's friends were much older than she, and try as she did, she had never been very close to their children. Dennard Manley was persistent, though. He would be at her father's supper party tonight, she supposed. She frowned. Dennard nearly always bored her. There were few times that she could truthfully say that he pleased her. He came frequently to her home and she disliked pretending that he was welcome.

Thinking about the party tonight reminded her that Gabriella Danforth would be there as well as at the theater. She wished desperately that Gabriella wouldn't come, for whenever she was present Charmian felt like an interloper. Her father was so attentive to Gabriella on such occasions that

Charmian felt neglected. Even Gabriella chided him, saying, 'But Charmian, dear child! Llewellyn, we must not forget Charmian. Tell us what you are thinking.' Charmian seldom made any pretense now of answering such a question, for Gabriella, directing the current of conversation, would neatly snag it and send it back into its former channel.

As Pascal drove on, Charmian began to relax a little. She was thinking of how Ginger Blue had changed through the years. The stables had been enlarged and the string of racers and saddle horses grew each year. Charmian loved the horses. Although her first pony, Whistlejackets, had been gone many years, she always called her favorite horse by that name. Her father clung to the name 'Blue' in his horse's names, and some of the better known ones were Blue Belle, Blue Flame, Royal Blue, Lady Blue Bonnet, Blue Whippet, Blue Moon, and Blue Gypsy. The original stud, Ginger Blue, he had won from Cyrus Manley at Donnyleigh years before he named his estate after the horse.

The cold air stimulated Charmian and she began to look out of the carriage window with interest, but they were still in the poorer section of the city, and she sighed.

The past month has been especially difficult. The school she had estabished among the river bottom's poor residences was kept going by sheer patience. The two teachers she had hired to assist her had been ready to give up more than once, but she pleaded with them to stay on. Pascal passed the low, squat log building her father had reluctantly donated toward the cause, and with a sigh of relief she noted that it was past closing time and that everyone had gone.

They drove on, turning into Olive, and she sat idly watching the merchants' signs: E. Cutting and Co. — Ready Made Clothing; McGunnegle and Way — Whls. Groc. and Commission Merchant; Powell, Lamond and Co. — Wholesale Dealers in Domestics, British, French, and Swiss Dry Goods; Laborz and Shaffner — Tanners, Curriers, and Hide dealers; Nath'l Phillips — Sign of the Golden Eagle — Music and Military Store.

"Wait, Pascal. Pull up there, please." Charmian did not wait for him to come around the carriage to help her, but pulling the long skirts away from her ankles, she stepped down hurriedly. She went quickly into the music store. It had a dry, musty air, and she could smell the moth preventives used in the pockets of uniforms. Three army officers from Jefferson Barracks were not too busily engaged with their shopping to pause and look at each other with a gleam of interested surprise. She distinctly heard one of them whisper, "Where've they been hiding that doll?"

The clerk came forward. "Good evening, ma'am. Can I help you?"

"Yes, I want the new tune, 'St. Louis Polka.' For the pianoforte."

"I'm sorry, miss. I just sold the last copy to these gentleman. It's very popular. I'm expecting some new ones on the next eastern shipment. Probably arrive on the packet, the *Tagliona*, out of Pittsburgh next Friday."

"Very well." Charmian turned to go. "I'll come in again some time."

"Oh, wait, miss," said the young captain. "I hope you'll pardon me, but I can't bear to have you disappointed. Please permit me." he took a roll of music from under his arm and extended it to her. "Pardon me for being so bold as to speak to you," he continued.

Charmian looked frankly into his eyes. "Thank you, but don't bother, please. I can wait. There's no hurry." her clear eyes met his coolly. Oh, those young officers out at the Barracks were considerd quite excellent material for guest lists, but she thought most of them overbold. Hardly a party had been given which she attended without meeting several, for society in St. Louis had taken greatly to the military male, and it was a fad to include them. Charmian added, "Thank you," and bowed and hurried out.

The young officer turned back crestfallen, and the other two, waiting only until she was out of earshot, exclaimed, "How the mighty hath fallen!" They clapped him on the shoulder. "You're not losing your touch, Captain?"

He shook them off and inquired of

the merchant, "Do you know the young lady?"

"Only from a distance. She is Miss Charmian Saucier. Her father owns the Saucier Shipping Line."

"What are some of his boats?"

"*Ginger Blue* is one, *Swiftsure II* another, and the new one, *Charmian*, is a beauty. I often walk down to the levee at my dinner hour just for the exercise." He turned toward a desk at the rear of the counter and held up a steamboat timetable. "The *Swiftsure* is due this afternoon from New Orleans."

The young captain turned back to the door and, with closed fingertips, flipped a kiss after Charmian. "Until we meet, Miss Saucier!"

Charmian, unaware of being the topic of their conversation, wished a little later that she had accepted the captain's offer. That silly tune, 'St. Louis Polka,' kept going through her head, and she had hardly used the shining new mahogany pianoforte her father had bought for her last summer.

"Pascal!" she called on inspiration.

"That new song, 'St. Louis Polka.' do you know it?"

Pascal turned his head in surprise. "Oh, yes, Miss Charmian."

"Well then, whistle it!"

"Not right here on Olive, Miss Charmian!"

"And why not? I want to hear it now. I don't care if it's Olive or Lucas Place! Go ahead — whistle it!"

Pascal immediately obliged and she called out, "Louder, Pascal! Louder!" She began humming. It had splendid rhythm and she could almost hear the violins tonight at the supper party. She began to get excited. "Let's go faster, Pascal. Speed up the horses." She wanted to get home and sink into the froth of the big wood tub. Brigette would have her dress ready.

Pascal was still whistling loudly and passengers in the other carriages they met stared into Charmian's. One of them was Dennard Manley, going down to pick up his father at the docks. Like Charmian's father, Mr. Manley always went down to see the boats come in. He had retired, and his son Dennard had become Llewellyn Saucier's Associate.

Dennard caught a glimpse of Charmian in the Saucier carriage and tipped his tall hat with an elegant flourish. He frowned at Pascal and shook his head at him, laying his finger across his lips. They had passed him then and Charmian leaned forward. "Louder, Pascal, louder!" if Dennard Manely was of a notion to tell her coachman what to do, he could just get it right out of his mind.

In a few minutes they were turning into the road which led past Donnyleigh, the Manley estate. The countryside lay in patches of melting snow and black soil, with fence corners and thickets cutting the winter fields into neat patterns. The Manley mansion was close enough to the road for passers-by to see the tall chimneys of the Georgian structure and to catch a glimpse of the thick columns of the broad piazza. 'A poor imitation of Ginger Blue,' her father often muttered as he took Charmian out in the carriage on Sunday afternoons. Donnyleigh was much older than Ginger Blue, but the piazza had been added years after Saucier had built his house.

Two miles farther on Pascal slowed the horses to turn into Charmian's lane. Her father had had two big columns of brownstone erected at the entrance, and across it there arched a sign bearing the name 'Ginger Blue' in high, gaudy letters, against grilled iron work. The lawn had been terraced in the past year, and boxwood lined the drive, formally marking it off from stables to entrance. Pascal stopped at the side door and Charmian got down without his help. She stepped into a muddy spot between the flagstones and went around to the back of the house. Here the whitewashed bricks had mellowed into genteel age.

She wiped her shoes on a mat at the door and went in. The warmth of the kitchen embraced her and she sighed, stretching herself and moving her tired shoulders. Brigette came in at once from the dining room, her thin figure worn fine with responsibility.

"Charmian, I'd think you'd have had enough of this foolish whim. You look tuckered out. Sit here and let me take your gaitees. Mud on them, too! I suppose you've been calling on your friends in Battle Row again?"

"Don't scold, Brigette. I was tired, but I'm really rested now and excited about the play tonight. Is the bath water hot, and what about my dress? Is everything ready?"

Brigette's sharp voice softened. "I believe you are excited." One black brow rose triangularly. She held out a kitchen chair and stooped to unbutton the gaitees. Charmian had such pretty ankles, she was thinking, when Pascal came in. Brigette's eyes flashed upward and caught the look of appreciation in her husband's eyes. Oh, he still knew a pretty ankle when he saw one. She waved him away with the words, "off with you, Pascal, and see to it that the firewood's in for the evening. Blue is getting worse than no account since he's been chasin' that girl Phoebe. An' his poor wife no more'n cold in her grave."

Phoebe and Timkins had stayed on as servants, although Timkins had married a girl from the fields and worked little about the house. Blue's wife had died in childbirth only last month, and Phoebe had prepared her for burial,

Charmian remembered. She could almost see Phoebe's soft brown eyes hovering sympathetically over Blue. Saucier encouraged marriage among his slaves; it kept down trouble, he had always said.

Brigette stopped by the big kitchen stove and lifted the heavy lid off the black pot. She peered within and said, "Stir some butter in that pot liquor, Sabetha, and make it good. You know how Pascal likes it." The savory liquid was for Brigette and Pascal, not for the slaves, whom Brigette suspected of stocking their larders with provisions from the house. She kept the keys to the storeroom dangling from a heavy braided leather belt around her waist. She set the food out carefully for each meal, counting the very onions, Florry said, that went into the stews. "For if I didn't, the blacks would steal more than we eat."

Sabetha was as fat and placid as Charmian remembered her from the dim years of babyhood, unchanged except for the whitening of the kinky hair peeping out from under her bright turban. Florry was her daughter by a bright-skinned Florida Negro with whom Sabetha had consorted one happy summer before she came to Ginger Blue. After the advent of Florry, she had taken counsel with herself and married one of Saucier's Negroes. Her life had been a full and happy one, even after her husband died. Miss Charmian's homecoming had been gratifying. The master had been cheerful in anticipation and had had the whole place renovated. Sabetha was proud of her Big House, and proud of her fine cookery.

She disliked Brigette's presumption in telling her how to prepare the pot liquor, but that was Miz Brigette, always having to have her hands into everything. Sabetha went back to the pot disdainfully and peered into it as Brigette and Charmian left the kitchen. She spoke sharply to Blue coming in with an armload of wood, and he stood before her awkwardly, his big feet clumsy in a pair of his master's cast-off boots.

"Did you light the fire fo' Miss Cha'meen?"

Blue nodded, his dark eyes rolling toward the corner of the kitchen hallway which still resounded to the young mistress' footsteps. He was thin, but he had lost a little of the strained, unhappy look which he had worn such a short time ago.

Sabetha motioned him toward the wood box. "Clean up an' I'll give you a bite."

She filled a steaming dish from the pot and, taking the lid off a heavy black skillet, cut a dodger of corn bread, golden-centered and brown-topped, to flare his nostrils wider with its tantalizing fragrance.

"Co'n pone and po'k and greens. Pot likker fo' dat white trash Pascal!" Sabetha set it down hurriedly, meanwhile keeping an eye on the hallway lest Brigette come back and catch Blue eating at the kitchen table. Pascal would not be coming in until later, after seeing that the horses were properly taken care of. Pascal was leaving more and more of the stable work to the Negroes, and had already urged Mr. Saucier to hire Mr. Ryan as trainer for the Ginger Blue racers.

Sabetha left the kitchen and went to stand in the well of the back stairs for a moment, thence to the foot of the circular staircase from which she could hear the murmur of Charmian's and Brigette's voices. She crept back to the kitchen, satisfied that they were deep in the intricacies of Charmian's costume for the evening.

Charmian stood by her canopied four-poster on the step-stool she used nightly to climb up on the high feather mattress. Her new dress lay on the white coverlet where Brigette had placed it in the late afternoon. Her father had told her of ordering it soon after the Christmas season, but Charmian had been too concerned with work to give it much thought. Last week it had arrived from the same great Parisian couturier who had designed her mother's party gowns when Llewellyn and Marie Louise were first married.

The supple, rose-colored satin shimmered in the flare of the gaslight overhead, and the new logs blazing in the fireplace generally added their luster. The corselet waist was embroidered with tiny seed pearls and promised to embrace Charmian's waistline lovingly. The deep square neck was bordered with tiny waving plumes of soft feathers, and among them glittered four rare gems set in yellow gold: an amethyst, a ruby, a topaz and a diamond.

"They were your mother's," Brigette said softly, as Charmian stood looking down upon them. "Your father has always said they were to be a surprise for you, that some day you should wear them."

"They're beautiful!" But Charmian was not seeing them at all. She was back in a cold, untidy cabin, and the son of French peasants had come to see his sister and minister to her wants. She remembered the look of slight disdain upon his face and the contempt in his voice for the daughter of a wealthy man who had come for the same purpose. He thought she had come because she was playing at being charitable, perhaps because she was bored with the society which had bred and borne her.

She frowned and turned aside. She was sure that Pierre thought she would throw aside this new plaything when she was tired of it, that she was only seeking new excitement and thrill. She knew that he was aware of the difference in their worldly wealth, and that his sister, Emilie, had told him about her before this morning. Brigette touched her elbow.

"I'll get your bath ready and lay out your fresh wrapper. Then you can dress after supper."

Charmian moved about the room restlessly. It was spacious, and carpeted with soft pink roses on a green background. The shade of the roses was echoed in the buds of the chintz and among the green tracery of leaves and vines of the canopy and slipper chair. A rectangular mirror framed in dull gold hung over the mahogany dresser with its marble top. Portraits of her mother and father looked down from the east wall, and a miniature of her mother stood on Charmian's desk. She picked it up and studied the face; then, taking it to the mirror, she compared her own with it. They were startlingly alike; although there was more of her father about her individual features, the whole impression was like that of her mother.

Impulsively Charmian decided to dress

her hair as her mother had worn hers in the miniature, in high, soft rolls, sweeping back from a clear, wide forehead. Waves had been contrived within the rolls, and the whole was framed with soft curls covering the back of the head. Charmian took the pins out of her black hair and it cascaded past her shoulders.

As she was dressing later, she heard the carriage coming back down the drive. Pascal had gone to the levee for her father. A glow of satisfaction passed over her. He would be so pleased that she was dressing for supper, instead of wearing the wrapper as Brigette had suggested.

The white of her skin was as soft as the camellias which bloomed on the terraces in the summer; her eyes were bright and her cheeks flushed with the excitement of an evening out and the surprise she was going to give her father. Brigette was still working on her stays, pulling the laces tighter and tighter, until Charmian gasped.

"I'll not be able to eat a thing, Brigette. Maybe I should wait until after supper.

"But you're not to eat too much now, anyway. Your father has ordered a grand supper at the Planters' House. Oyster and lobster from the east and wines from Cherbourg, not to mention the fancy cakes and pastries. Mind, you remember to be a lady."

Charmian laughed. "All my born days you've reminded me to be a lady. It's not always been easy, Brigette." She was remembering the episode of running away from her father's ball many years ago in order to go to old Granny Popo's cabin. Pierre Gregoire had restored that memory to her this morning. Granny Popo was old and dried-looking now, with great cavernous pockets for eyes, and a blankness had settled on her moribund face.

Brigette adjusted the knots in the stays and handed Charmian the first petticoat. She disdained putting it on over her head and stepped quickly into it. Brigette shook her head. She had always quarreled with the seamstress about the plackets in Charmian's petticoats. They had to be made deep enough for her to get into without mussing her hair. There they lay in formidable array: first, second, third, and fourth petticoats, all bristling with starched ruffles, all elborately tucked and fagotted and embroidered. The corset cover was of thin white batiste, with a pink ribbon run through the eyelets in the beading. Charmian impatiently pulled her thin shirt deeper into the corset, and Brigette shook her head disapprovingly.

"Men don't like women to look flat-chested. Now, look at that bosom! It's stylish to show your charms." Brigette twisted her shoulders. *"Mon Dieu!* You Americans!"

"Brigette! Don't pretend you're French! Anyone with half an eye can tell you're not!"

"I have an Irish face and a French heart." Brigette sighed. Those familiar words belonged to Pascal. How she wished she had been born in France instead of only living there a few years; changing the spelling of her name from 'Bridget' had only mildly appeased her.

"The dress, Brigette, then I'll be ready." Charmian lifted her arms to run through the sleeves as the gown came down, Brigette murmuring all the while not to muss her hair.

"It's devastating, that's what it is! I'm

excited, lambie, for I have a funny feeling."

"So have I, Brigette. Something is going to happen tonight." Charmian turned about slowly. "I have a feeling that something strange is going to happen."

They heard Saucier coming up the stairs to his room, and Brigette closed the outside door of Charmian's suite. She didn't want him to see it open and call for his daughter, thus ruining the effect she hoped to produce.

Before he was ready to go down, Charmian was downstairs reading the *Daily Union*. Her eyes caught the arrivals and departures of steamboats and she knew she was searching for the Gregoire ships. The *Fresco* was listed, with its master's name and sailing orders. Her eyes dropped to the more impressive Saucier advertisement a few lines below. Each paragraph was indented with a tiny picture of the same steamboat, as the paragraphs of the news column were indented with the thumb and index finger of a hand. A new residential section was going to be opened, extending the city limits westward. The new gas lights on

Front leading up from the river were ready to use.

Another eastern steamboat explosion had occurred, sending more than a hundred people to agonizing death. Charmian shuddered. Her father did not allow racing on his line, but even so, there had been one bad wreck and two minor accidents last year. She tried to turn the page, but the fascination of the reporter's eyewitness account of last week's explosion on the Ohio held her. The overheated boilers had exploded, sending out a scalding stream of steam and boiling water on the passengers. It was not too unusual, but something should be done. Racing was quite common; there was hardly a boat on the river which would not engage in a friendly race, and betting ran so high at times as to give it a dangerous aspect.

Charmian heard her father's step on the stairs. She smiled and stood to meet him.

The brilliant lights of the candelabra, which now burned gas, shone on his dark hair, which still only threatened to whiten. Tall, slender, and aristocratic, his fine features regular in profile, he was as dashing as a young soldier.

Saucier saw his daughter moving to the parlor door and stopped abruptly. A smile died on his lips, and she saw the breaking up of his face as he stood there. Charmian was frightened.

His voice was harsh when he spoke.

"You must forgive me, Charmian." He brushed his hand across his face and it was almost as though he were wiping it clean of his emotion. For he smiled and in his normal tone he said, "You startled me, *cherie*. For a moment it was as if Marie Louise were standing there."

She went to him and touched his hand and lifted her face, and he kissed her gently. "The dress is charming, and you are beautiful in it," Saucier said.

"Supper is ready," Pascal said from the door of the dining room.

# 7

IT was late when Charmian and her father left Ginger Blue for the theater. They were wrapped in a fur lap robe to ward off the chill March air. As they neared the business section, they spoke of the new street lights, admiring the sickish yellow glare which fell within a small radius about each post. The moon, high above, gave more illumination to the street than the gas flares.

The theater, however, was brightly lighted and the street was crowded as the carriages and surreys discharged their occupants. The Sauciers were greeted by friends and Charmian and her father nodded and smiled as they walked across the entrance, entered the dress circle and went to their box in the first gallery. Four of Saucier's guests were already seated, and the adjoining box was filled with other friends who would join them later at the supper party.

Charmian's father helped her off with

her wrap, although the two young men had sprung to attention the moment the Sauciers entered. They were Dennard Manley and his assistant at the shipping office. Gabriella Danforth and her companion, obviously a chaperon, smiled, and Gabriella spoke sweetly.

Charmian's eyes drifted over to the next box. In it, sitting very straight and with a pleased expression on his face, was the young captain she had encountered at the music store in the afternoon. She gave a start of surprise. But if she was startled at the captain's presence, she was even more so at recognizing Pierre Gregoire, seated next to him.

Both men leaned forward, the captain smiling broadly, Pierre bowing with friendly restraint.

Charmian bowed slightly. Her eyes locked with Pierre's and held, and for a moment she forgot everything else. Gabriella's lovely voice recalled her.

"My dear Charmian, you look lovely. Your gown is a dream."

"Thank you, Mrs. Danforth. My father ordered it for me."

"Excellent taste. From Paris, I'm sure.

Really, Llewellyn, you've certainly a flair for beauty." Gabriella's voice was warm and flattering.

"Very kind of you to say so, Gabriella. You look entrancing yourself." Saucier leaned forward and smiled at her.

It did not seem possible for a woman to hold youth and beauty as long as Gabriella had kept hers. Yet she did not look, in the soft lights, many years older than Charmian. Perhaps Gabriella's eyes were a little less bright, her skin just a trifle less perfect, but her auburn hair was still thick and glossy, her expression animated. She and Llewellyn Saucier continued their conversation in subdued voices, although Gabriella burst into bright, ready laughter now and then and Charmian had an uncomfortable feeling that too many people threw more than an occasional glance their way.

"Sh! Sh! Curtain!"

"It's beginning."

The play, *Lucrezia Borgia*, was long and a little dreary to Charmian. There was no intermission, and the cast was called out again and again at the final curtain.

"Come, daughter! I'm glad that's over," said Saucier, rising. "Can't think they did so well tonight. What do you think Gabriella?"

"Not so good as the last time we came. Thank heaven we can get up and move about now." Gabriella consulted the small watch which dangled from her shoulder. "It's late. What time did you order supper served, Llewellyn?"

A tremor went over Charmian. Gabriella's casual voice gave the impression that she was Saucier's hostess. Charmian did not hear her father's answer, for the people from the other box joined them and Dennard was holding out her cape while her father helped Gabriella.

"Captain Whitlake," Dennard was saying. "Mr. Gregoire," he added, to Charmian.

"We have met," Charmian said in her clear voice, and she nodded, with another smile for Pierre and a stiff inclination of her head to Captain Whitlake.

There were three carriages: an elderly couple, Pierre, and the young captain in one, Dennard and Charmian in another, and Gabriella, her companion and Saucier in the third. Charmian disliked the arrangement; she was surprised that her father had not kept her with him.

"We'll meet our other guests there," he said as Dennard's coachman started up his carriage.

Dennard the man was so like Dennard the boy that Charmian was still irked whenever she looked at him. He was constantly being thrown at her, she thought rebelliously. Just because he was heir to Donnyleigh and to his father's shipping interests, which he had recently combined with Saucier's, did not make Dennard any more attractive to her. His hair, which had been white in his youth, had darkened only slightly, and secretly Charmian called him 'Pinky.' His complexion gave him a very young, frilled and babyish look.

"Warm enough, Miss Saucier?"

"Yes, thank you, Mr. Manley." He could call her 'Miss Saucier' after all thee years! How perfectly silly, when she had even slapped his face once, now to be calling him 'Mr. Manley'!

"And did you enjoy *Lucrezia Borgia*?"

"Not very much, I'm afraid."

"Ah, truly? I'm surprised, Miss Saucier. I thought it rather stupendous. But then, the interpretation may have lost some of its zest for you. The music before the play — I'm sure you must have liked that?"

"'The St. Louis Polka'? I adore it, if that's what you mean. I tried to get it at Phillips' this afternoon. It must be very popular, for the last copy had been sold. In fact, the young officer in our party had just bought it. He offered it to me."

"Charmian!" You mean you went into the music store unattended and talked with a strange young man?"

"Oh, don't be dull, Denny! Of course I went into the music store alone. Lots of young ladies shop every day all by themselves. There's nothing wrong with that!"

"But the young captain? I hope you put him in his place?"

"There couldn't have been anything very wrong about his offering it to me and, as far as the captain's concerned, I note that he is one of our guests."

"Of Mrs. Danforth's, you mean," Dennard said stiffly. "It isn't proper, as you very well know, to be addressed by a perfect stranger. Why, what must he think of you?"

That awful rocking feeling of wanting to slap Dennard came over her. Why must he continue to affect her in this way?

She did not answer, and they continued in silence while the coachman pulled up to the curb in front of the Planters' House. The other carriages had already arrived, and Pierre Gregoire and Captain Whitlake stood waiting at the rack in front of the hotel. Gregoire wore a long dark cape and a tall beaver hat. He was not so handsome as the captain but there was an awareness in his face, his body was hard and compactly built, his height superb; Charmian wondered what it might be like dancing with him. He, also, was Mrs. Danforth's guest, and Charmian wanted to ask how she happened to know him.

Gabriella had always known and entertained the most unusual people. She never seemed to care whether they were young or old; it only mattered that they were interesting. Charmian thought of her as struggling to retain her youth, for she was grown when Charmian was yet a little girl. Brigette had whispered that Gabriella used artificial coloring on her high cheeks, and Charmian was inclined to believe it.

They were going in now, and Gabriella was walking with Saucier. Charmian knew a moment of resentment, and then checked her feeling. After all, her father must have some companionship beside her own and that of his male friends. It must have been very lonely for him at Ginger Blue all these years.

She knew that she had been a keen disappointment to him this winter, when he had counted on filling the house with friends, music, and laughter again. But she had been so absorbed in her work that they had entertained hardly at all, and then she knew she had seemed disinterested.

Dennard addressed a remark to her and she rallied to be polite once more. Then they were inside the big dining salon, with its gleaming candelabra throwing brilliant light down upon the assemblage. It seemed as if most of the gayer St. Louis theater crowd had ordered supper here. They greeted each other, merchants and their wives, professional men, and a number of military officers from Jefferson Barracks with their ladies. The orchestra was striking up a tune for the supper group.

"We meet again," said Captain Westlake, as he seated himself next to Charmian at the big round table.

"Yes," she answered, knowing that Dennard Manley across the table was wondering how she had slipped through his fingers. For here she was, sitting between Pierre Gregoire, one of his business competitors, and the army officer he had censured a few minutes ago.

Charmian sparkled. Everything the young captain said seemed to please her, but she was more aware of Pierre. She knew when he smiled, when his dark eyes were regarding her, although he pretended more interest in Gabriella on his right. On a mad impulse for more of Pierre's attention, Charmian turned to him deliberately and asked, "Do you ever pilot your own boats, Mr. Gregoire?"

"Occasionally. The first year I owned the *Fresco*, I was the pilot." He picked up his goblet and drained it, not looking at her. That was not necessary, for she was already indelibly fixed in his memory. The piquancy of her face, with its deep widow's peak; her black hair; the dark eyes with their long lashes; the pointed chin; the high, rounded cheeks; the red lips; the smallness of her waist; and the whiteness of her throat which followed down to the upward curving of her bosom. She was captured within his vision, and although he had thought this morning it would be best if he never saw her again, now he knew his life would have been unbearable if he had not.

"Where are your offices?" she persisted.

"On Front. Next to the silversmith's shop."

"Oh, yes, I remember. I see the shop when I go to Battle Row."

"You are serious about your work, aren't you, Miss Saucier?" He turned directly to her for the first time.

"Yes. Yes, of course I am!" She lowered her lashes. So he thought she was society belle by night and a would-be-actress playing at charity by day!

"If you are ever in need of my help, I shall be glad to assist you in any way possible," he said.

Charmian turned surprised eyes upon him. "Oh, thank you, thank you, Mr. Gregoire! You can't know what it would mean to get some of the merchants and professional men back of our work!"

"Yes, I believe I can understand. Someone told me about your school today. That's a fine step forward." He had made inquiries about it this afternoon because of his sister's enthusiasm for Charmian's work.

Pierre was interrupted by the host, who had risen and was addressing his guests from the head of the table. He raised his wineglass and the guests followed suit.

"My friends," said Llewellyn Saucier, "I give a toast. I give a toast to Mrs. Gabriella Danforth, the future Mrs. Saucier."

A looked of amazement and unbelief flashed across Pierre Gregoire's face. Stunned by the impact of her father's announcement, Charmian saw that look on Pierre's face die into immobility.

She sat tensely, her face white, her fingers interlocked and strained together. She knew that her father had been seeing a great deal of Gabriella at her home recently, that Gabriella's attitude toward him had been possessive; but that he should ever marry her — A dozen impressions flitted through Charmian's head. The scene at home just before supper, when her father had recalled Marie Louise so vividly; the time he had linked his and Gabriella's names together himself when he had forbidden Charmian to go into the poverty-stricken homes on the waterfront; then a scene of long ago when she was a little girl, and had overheard Gabriella and two of her father's guests at a ball discussing the possibility of Gabriella's marrying Charmian's father.

She tried to tell herself that this must have been a sudden decision. Perhaps her father had had too much to drink. But she rose with a quick movement, and the faces blurred about her. She went over and kissed Gabriella and her father.

As she went back to her chair, something within her was crying. She was no longer her father's little rosebud. They were separated now, more than she had ever thought possible. And the thing which had driven that fact home was something in Gabriella's eyes as she turned a cold cheek to Charmian. Something in her eyes — a gleam of victory; and on her face, a look of smugness.

# 8

THE blazing Missouri summer lay like a shining wave over the yellow-brown of the river. The line of trees along the unbroken edge of the woods seemed like a vast fortress to Charmian, shutting her off from the intangible thing which was threatening her. This small clearing here on the bluff made a refuge for her. She had started coming here in June after her father's marriage to Gabriella, to get away from the feeling of strangeness which had invaded Ginger Blue.

Gabriella was having the house done over. Two new wings were built, one on either end of the house, which gave it a rambling, cluttered effect. The clean, clear-cut architecture was now gone. There were too many porticos, too many cupolas, too much gingerbread, too much of everything, Charmian thought rebelliously.

"Think of it, Brigette," she had said

one day early in the summer when the buildings was first started, "twenty-four rooms! What shall we do with twenty-four rooms?"

"I'm sure I don't know. Fourteen was all your poor mother needed to set her wild with worry that everything was properly cared for. I don't like to speak ill of the new mistress, but she has uppity ways for one who had so little before now."

Charmian had not answered. It was not surprising that Gabriella wished to have the house done over, to have more rooms added; but there was also the wholesale entertaining which the building and renovating had not interrupted. It was almost like living in an inn. The Sauciers' lavish hospitality was becoming the talk of the city. It seemed almost as though Gabriella and her husband were trying to crowd into their first summer together all the gaiety they had ever missed. Charmian, alone in her secret haven, probed deeply and ruthlessly within herself.

Perhaps I'm only jealous, she thought, jealous of Gabriella.

133

It had been weeks since her father had kissed her, and he never called her 'little rosebud' in front of Gabriella. She knew that her stepmother only tolerated her, that she contrived to keep Saucier by her own side, shutting Charmian into an unhappy state of loneliness and making her feel an intruder in her own home.

Today she recalled the time the Mother Superior had found her wandering in the convent garden. Although it was against regulations for her to be there, Charmian had been treated kindly. The Mother Superior had talked about the good which would be done in this world.

'You can be what you will make of yourself.' Mother Superior's words came to her back across the years. 'The poor and needy — you can give succor to the poor and anoint their weak flesh.'

They had had a long talk together. Charmian, who had always loved life for the sake of living, had grown more serious after that conversation.

Llewellyn Saucier had not known that sending his daughter to the academy had actually contrived to help separate them. He had wanted his daughter to be taught something about religion, but more about being a lady.

Charmian knew it would have been easy to bow to the wishes of her father to carry on with the brilliant and never-ending confusion of entertaining and being entertained. The Review of the Militia, the Midsummer's Day program at the city park, the Ripple Boat Club at Chouteau's Pond, horse racing, the outdoor garden restaurants and their orchestras, moonlight excursions on the Mississippi, dancing until early morning, shopping for clothes, reading the latest books in the fine leather-bound volumes her father brought to her and Gabriella — Oh, life could be so very easy, so very, very easy if she would just resign herself to their way of living.

But if she did give up her work, what would become of Myra Clancey's new baby, whose father was killed in a saloon brawl last month, before its birth? And who would look after the Brewster children, whose mother and father were lost in an explosion in one of the ghastliest steamboat wrecks of the year? And the Brownes and the

McGintys, the Forresters, the Smithers, the Radcliffes, the Malones, the O'Haras, and the Nikolopokous?

She made her calls on the houses of them all, just as regularly as a doctor in attendance. She had inveigled her father into permitting her to buy a little cart to drive, rather than using the carriage and taking Pascal from his work. By now she was a familiar sight, with her dark blue, fringed, one-seated trap, going through the thoroughfares of the city. Summer had brought new problems to her, for when the winter's cold was dispelled by the sun, it seemed no time at all until the epidemics of diarrhea and summer complaint swept over the poor cabins along the waterfront and the bottom lands.

Charmian had not seen Pierre Gregoire since the night of the theater supper party, not even at his sister's home, for Emilie was soon able to be up and Charmian had no further excuse for going there. Pierre was helping Emilie more and more financially and the new baby had grown like a robust little animal. Sometimes Charmian reminded herself that Pierre had forgotten about the help he had promised to her.

She read that he had acquired another new boat, the *Redwing*. She knew that he was working harder than ever, and that the Gregoire Shipping Line was using more space in the advertising section of the *Daily Union*, her father's favorite city paper. Pierre's name had been on the list of business men who were sponsoring the new series of lectures at the Mercantile Library this fall, and now and then Gabriella had mentioned Dr. Sydney Gregoire in her conversation. Sydney had been 'poor dear Lewis" physician.

Charmian had driven Whistlejacket today and he now stood tethered with the cart in the byway which she had discovered late in the spring. It was nothing more than a wagon track leading out of the main road, but it afforded her the solitary refuge she wanted. Someone had built a log house here, but it had been destroyed by fire during the winter. The clearing stood on the high brink of the river, looking out over the water and giving a clear view up and down the opposite shore. From here, Charmian could see the activity of the boats as they came into the St. Louis wharves. She was apart from the noise and confusion, and she loved to see the passenger steamers coming into dock. Here she could see without being seen, could think without being interrupted.

She stayed for almost an hour, then suddenly realized that she would be late for supper and that Gabriella would not like it. Hastening to her cart, she patted Whistlejackets' sleek back and untied him. She had stayed much longer than she had intended, having one more stop to make before she could drive on to Ginger Blue. The sun was still high and hot above her fringed umbrella. She couldn't remember another summer so hot. Perhaps that was because she had never spent a summer like this before. Her fine white hands were not so fine nor so white now. Hands which before had never been in water except to bathe them had washed and wrung out heavy clothes in strong homemade soapsuds, had hung those clothes on wind-whipped lines in muddy backyards. For a time it didn't seem to matter that they were work-worn hands, but she had tried of late to take better care of them, wearing white knitted gloves when she went to bed and when she drove in the hot sun.

She recalled her errand with a start as she saw Dr. Sydney Gregoire's carriage at McGhinty's door. With an exclamation, she pulled Whistlejackets to a stop and, stepping down from the cart, tied him beside the doctor's horses. She hurried across the dusty chicken-littered yard and tapped at the door.

It was thrown open by Laurie, McGhinty's oldest girl, white-faced and big-eyed. "Oh, it's you, Miss Saucier," she whimpered.

"Come in!" shouted the young doctor. "Now, you, stop snivelling and go keep up the fire," he commanded the young girl. "And you, Miss Saucier, lend me a hand." The room was hot and bright with sunlight. The woman on the bed was having a convulsion.

Charmian and Dr. Gregoire worked together silently. She saw the beads of perspiration on his face grow into rivulets and drop on the rough bed.

"I don't know why I should try to save her, except that the half-dozen she already has need someone to look after them."

Dr. Gregoire ordered Charmian sharply to do his bidding, never really looking at her, and Mrs. McGhinty's labor began to draw to an end. Charmian was faint with nausea but she worked on by the doctor's side, handing him the things he called for, holding the woman's hand when she wasn't busy and gripping the edge of the rough table with her other hand to steady herself.

"Your first one?" the doctor asked presently.

Charmian looked as though she might have borne the child herself, as she nodded.

"You're a little green about the gills; get out into the air." He took the baby from her shaking hands and wrapped it in the flannel she had brought out to the cabin just the week before.

Charmian crept silently out of the hot room and found that the sun had gone down and that the heat had died down a little. She had arranged for Mrs.

Lane, the midwife, to take care of Mrs. McGhinty, but during the hour which had just passed, Laurie told her that the midwife wasn't at home when she ran to get her. Seeing the doctor's rig in the next block, Laurie had gone to him for help.

Charmian stood leaning against her cart, her hand straying along Whistlejackets' shining coat. She still wore the big apron that the doctor had ordered over her dress. She was lost in the bewilderment of the past hour and did not realize that a carriage had stopped and that someone was getting out until her name was spoken.

"Miss Saucier! Is anything wrong? Can I help you?"

She turned slowly, her face white, the green still faint about her lips and temples. She looked at him for a long time before she realized that it was Pierre Gregoire.

"What is it? Are you ill? Please let me help you into my carriage and I'll drive you home."

"No. No, I can't go. Not yet. The baby — " She broke of. "Your brother's in there. I helped with Mrs. McGhinty."

"Oh, I see." His voice was mixed with admiration and sympathy for the embarrassment which would be forthcoming as soon as she had regained herself. She was still too deep in the recent activities of assisting in childbirth to be anything but dazed. But slowly the color was coming back into her white cheeks and there was no sign of embarrassment on her face. She turned her dark eyes upon Pierre and within them was only deepest compassion for the woman inside the little house.

Pierre stood helplessly watching Charmian. The girl he had seen at the Planters' House surrounded by wealth could not be this girl who had just assisted with a difficult birth in this squalid house! It helped bear out the testimony which was indignantly voiced by his sister, Emilie, when he had protested that Charmian must be only toying with the idea of charity work. This girl had not been merely playing a few minutes before his arrival upon the scene. She had gone through a difficult experience without any previous conception of all that it meant.

"Here," Pierre said roughly, "let me give you a bracer." He took a flask from his pocket and uncorked it. Charmian shook her head, but insistently he held it up to her lips. She swallowed a little and her eyes opened sharply.

"Better?"

"Yes."

"You don't have to say anything." His voice softened. "Let me drive you home. One of the boys can come back after your trap.

His words brought back the remembrance that supper must be waiting at Ginger Blue, and the cold anger that Gabriella must mask because she could not let Saucier know how she really felt about her grown stepdaughter.

She sighed. "If you'll only give a message to someone to take to my father, it will be very kind of you."

"But you're not going to stay here. Someone can come."

"Yes. Mrs. Lane, the midwife, has promised, but she wasn't at home when they needed her."

"I'll drive to her place and see if she's there now. I'll be right back. Where does she live?" He paused by his buggy wheel.

"Two squares over on the next street, the house next to the blackmsith's shop."

After he had gone, she went back into the house. Dr. Sydney Gregoire was gathering up his things and putting them into the satchel.

Charmian was still tidying up the rough little house when Pierre came back for her. He had picked up some fresh brown bread at the bakeshop, and carried a basket of food from the market. Mrs. Lane held her long nose in the air as she entered the room. It was about time someone took over the McGhinty household and straightened it out. She was good at that and delighted in scouring places that needed scouring.

"They'll be in safe hands, Miss Saucier," Pierre said as Charmian took off the big apron she wore.

"An' where are the little ones? Down at the crick, I s'pose?" asked Mrs. Lane as she plumped down the basket on the old table.

"Yes," murmured the oldest girl, her

eyes greedily fastened on the basket. "A-wadin' and a-catchin' craw-pappies." She brushed her drab hair out of her eyes with a thin hand.

"I'll come and see you tomorrow, Laurie," said Charmian kindly.

The girl hardly looked up. "Yes'm."

"Can't you say thanks to the good lady, Laurie? Pity no one ever stops to thank you for your good works, Miss Saucier," sniffed Mrs. Lane, her hands clearing away a place to set out the food. "Go wash, Laurie, Fust, bring in a bucket o' water. We can use a-plenty of *that*. And whilst you're about it, bring in some cobs from the shed and — "

Outside, Charmian took a deep breath. She paused and Pierre stopped with her at the edge of the tiny, bare brown yard. The chickens had gone to roost now, and the place was quiet except for their cluckings from a makeshift hen house in the side yard.

Pierre helped her into his carriage. Whistlejackets could stand for a while longer, until she sent Blue out to drive him home. Better to leave him here than to take him to the livery stable down the street. It would cause less comment, Charmian knew.

Pierre kept to the street they were on for a few squares. Everywhere along the way children stood hanging on the gates, or stopped from the play to watch the elegant carriage go by. "Howdy, Captain Pete!" called one urchin.

Pierre waved his whip in greeting. The other boys took up the first one's cry. "Howdy, Captain Pete!"

"Howdy, Miss Saucier!" That was the Brownes' oldest girl, brazen as Brigette had always said she was, hanging on the edge of the hitching rack in front of the general store.

They turned down the Alley and were soon through the small pack of shouting children who were chasing a shaggy-haired mutt. "Poor dog!" murmured Pierre. One or two of the children stopped long enough to gaze with interest at their carriage, and Pierre remembered how he used to stare after the Saucier's long ago.

"I remember the first time I saw you, Miss Saucier," he said suddenly after they were out of the squalid section. "You

146

were with your father in his carriage on the way to the wharf. I had not been here very long from France. Everywhere people were unkind to me. But you smiled to me from your carriage."

"I thought you were very brave, I remember."

Pierre's voice stilled within his throat and he kept his eyes on the black manes of his horses. Charmian's eyes were veiled by her long black lashes. They were silent then, driving through a quiet side street, with the dust swirling about the carriage wheels. Pierre drew the horses down to a walk, as though to make the drive last longer. They passed young Father Dennis Carmichael as he stood on the terrace at St. Patrick's watching the pigeons fluttering about the stone urns on the parapets. He waved at them and Charmian smiled at him and nodded. Pierre touched his hat respectfully.

"A great man," he said.

"Yes," she agreed. "So young to be so great," she added.

It seemed much cooler now, and Charmian knew a sudden reluctance to go home. Home to her room where she might take a tepid sponge bath and change into the cool wrapper which Brigette must have laid out at least an hour ago. Then supper on a tray because Gabriella would not have waited dinner. Later, she would perhaps go out on the big front gallery which opened off her room to sit in a porch chair and look down upon the lawn. There would be laughter and voices floating up from the piazza below. The moon would be white and full tonight, and the keys of the pianoforte would respond to the fleeting white fingers of Gabriella.

I don't want to go home to that again tonight. Last night, the night before, and the night before that — it made a kind of pattern. There would be callers, as usual. Every evening brought callers unless there were some social function in town which Llewellyn and his wife would be attending.

Charmian smoothed the wrinkles out of her big square of lace-edged linen and adjusted her hat. She was tired, she felt unkempt and in need of freshening, but still she did not want to go home. Her eyes fell upon the *Missouri Barnburner*, the daily paper her father abhorred, folded in a neat square on the leather seat. She scanned the columns under the notices of *Steamboat Arrivals, Port of St. Louis*. The name, 'Montesano Place,' caught her eye.

# 9

**M**ONTESANO PLACE was a hotel situated in the village of Carondelet, on a high bluff overlooking the river in the southern suburbs of the city. It had become very popular, and Charmian had been there several times with her father and Gabriella. Her eyes closed briefly to remember the cool garden where they had been served a festive dinner especially prepared for Lewellyn and his bride.

Pierre turned the horses toward Compton Hill, and impulsively Charmian said, "Let's go to Carondelet! To Montesano Place." She gasped as she realized what she had said. What must he be thinking of her boldness?

"I'm sorry — it just sort of burst out."

"Why not? I'll be most happy to take you there, Miss Saucier, if you will permit me."

A tremor ran up her back. They'd be

sure to run into someone who knew her, someone who would take great pains to tell her father that she had been seen unchaperoned with a strange young man. She would be no better than the girls you saw out riding in the evening with their beaux, unchaperoned. Brigette still accompanied her and Dennard Manley unless her father or his were along, but she would be the only one of the household who would not be shocked. Brigette still secretly took great pleasure in affairs of the heart that were not carried out in the strictest good form.

"You understand that my father will be perfectly furious?"

"I have seen your father furious once before."

Charmian laughed, and Pierre joined her. All of the strain between them disappeared magically. She felt exhilarated with one cleansing sweep of gaiety. Brigette would doubtless call her the hoyden she was, and she would not care a tittle.

Gabriella would pretend concern over her tardiness at the supper table, thus bringing Saucier's attention to Charmian's inconsiderateness.

Pierre flicked the tasseled end of the whip across his horses' backs and they broke into a light trot. The breeze, the first she had felt today, passed over Charmian's face, cooling her burning cheeks, washing out fatigue, and excitement blazed within her.

"Mr. Gregoire, do you know the song, 'They Tell Me Thou Art the Favored Guest?'"

Pierre's brow puckered. Of course he knew it, but he could pretend that he did not. "Will you sing a little of it?"

"I don't sing. However, it goes a little like this." She hummed the first few bars softly. She knew the words by heart, for it was one of the younger crowd's favorite songs this summer. She hummed them again and stopped.

Pierre picked up the tune in a soft whistle. How many times he had heard it during the summer, floating on the river breeze as he piloted the *Redwing* downstream. Negroes in the cotton fields left off whistling 'St. Louis Polka' to croon the new song.

"Oh, it's very pretty," she said as

152

he stopped on the last note. "But my favorite is still 'The St. Louis Polka.'"

He whistled the opening notes and her eyes danced.

Now they were out in the country, leaving the last of the residences behind them and bridging the short distance to the little village of Carondelet. A church spire rose in the distance; they could barely see it in the dusk of the summer evening. They heard the sound of a horse approaching before they reached the next bend in the road, and Pierre turned his carriage carefully to the side. Charmian recognized at once the star-faced mares that Dennard Manley drove in his carry-all.

She sat rigid in the seat beside Pierre.

"That's Manley, your father's assistant, isn't it?" Piere asked.

"Yes." Of all people in the city of St. Louis, it would have to be Dennard Manley whom they would meet! She could almost see him start as he recognized her. He bowed stiffly, and she barely inclined her head. The road was narrow and he gave quick attention to his vehicle. Pierre offered no vocal greeting, and Charmian did not look to see if he had bowed.

When she spoke again, there was a new quality in her voice. There was something about Dennard which always made her feel daringly anxious to overstep the bounds of propriety.

They were coming into the village now, and they crossed a narrow bridge before reaching the wide drive which led past the two-acre flower garden surrounding Montesano Place. The drive leading to the hotel was lined with carriages and traps, making the roadway hard to manage.

Everyone is here, Charmian thought. She glanced down once more at her dress. It was blue *mousseline de laine*, with ruffles around neck and hemline. The night air had cooled her until she no longer felt hot and ungroomed. Life surged through her, glowing and anticipatory. The sound of music drifted out from the ballroom of the hotel, Christy's Band playing 'Canderbeck's Quickstep.'

Pierre drove slowly, carefully, to the only vacant place along the hitching rail which ran parallel with the famous rose garden. It was almost dark now, but a brilliant moon was coming up in a great orange ball above the trees at the cliff's edge. Candlelight flickered in the garden where customers were being served, and voices and laughter rang out from the small chairs and tables.

"Shall we go inside to the dining room, or do you prefer the garden?"

"The garden, please. That is, if you'd like?"

Pierre handed the reins to the first of the little black boys who had come running out at the crunch of the wheels. "Here, boy, mind you tie them good."

"Yassuh, Mistah Cap'n."

Pierre leaped down and, going around to Charmian's side, held up his hand. She gathered up her skirts and stepped out. Her wide straw hat, with flowers matching the blue of her dress, had slipped back on her forehead, and she reached a white hand to straighten it.

"Here, or over by the garden wall, Miss Saucier?" Pierre asked as they started in.

"By the wall, please. You can see the

river from there, I believe. That is, we may see it if we should stay until the moon gets high."

"It will take us some time to eat dinner if you are as hungry as I am."

"I'm starved, to tell you the truth. I've not touched food since lunch."

Pierre stopped beside a table overlooking the stone wall. Other late diners lingered, talking and laughing in the garden. Only a few tables were empty. Charmian was glad for the dimness of the light, although she knew that several people were highly interested in watching their progress through the garden, and some of the chatter had ebbed for a moment only to begin again in subdued murmurs.

Pierre had scarcely seated her when a waiter appeared. Pierre asked, "What do you have tonight?"

"The very finest sherry to begin with, sir."

"Right. And the bill of fare?"

"Fried spring chicken that melts in your mouth, sir, and green, tender corn fresh from our gardens. Melons that were iced since morning, sir, and French pastry, of course, and fresh bread and butter. There's roast of venison, too, and catfish still sizzling in the spider. Barbecued ribs, sir, that would make you forget you were ever hungry, you'll eat so much, and a whole young lamb still on the spit, sir. Then there's blueberry tarts, and mint jelly and — "

"Your choice, ma'am?" said Pierre to Charmian.

The naming of all the foods made Charmian's mouth water, and she said faintly, "Let us start with something that is ready."

"Bring wine and venison and barbecue. And then two tender young chickens put in the pan right now. No fooling around, mind you. We're hungry, The corn and the freshest bread you have, right out of the oven, and butter that's made today."

"Yes, sir. 'Twill take only a minute, sir." Bowing and walking backward, the waiter reached the path and hurried toward the kitchen-way of the big building.

Charmian leaned back in her chair, feeling the stiff rounds of the wood comforting against her back. In the excitement of the last hour, she had forgotten her fatigue, and now with the knowledge that food and wine were near, a warm, steady glow of happiness stole over her.

Both were silent, Presently the long wailing sound of a steamboat, blowing for a landing, cut the air. Deep and loud, its echo resounded against the bluff of the river. There's nothing like that sound in the whole world, thought Pierre.

"Do you like the river, Miss Saucier?"

"Oh, yes. Always. As long as I can remember, Father has taken me down to see the boats come in. When I first learned to ride my pony, Whistlejackets, we'd ride to the bluffs by our own secret path and stand our horses on the bank to watch the river traffic."

"I remember Whistlejackets," said Pierre. "You and your father have always been good companions."

"Yes, we always were."

If he noticed that she emphasized the word 'were,' he did not let her know. She went on presently, "Of course, now that he has married again, he and Gabriella are together constantly."

He had seen them, of course. Gabriella and Llewwellyn were at all of the social gatherings of any importance in the city. Gabriella was always beautifully dressed, he remembered, and Saucier very well tailored. He had a striking figure and the impeccable tailoring emphasized it.

Someone spoke to them and they were startled out of their thoughts. Charmian recognized Captain Whitlake, the young soldier she had first met at the music store and later in the same day at the theater and supper party at Planters' House.

"Good evening, Miss Saucier and Mr. Gregoire! I thought I recognized you as you approached the table, and felt that I must come over and pay my respects." He held out his hand to Pierre, after bowing low to Charmian.

"Thank you, Captain."

"How do you do, Captain Whitlake," said Pierre, remembering that the only other time he had met Charmian socially before this evening, he had been handicapped by this same captain from Jefferson Barracks.

The tall young officer stood erect by the table. "Isn't it a beautiful summer evening? And the music? By the by, Miss Saucier, did you ever get the copy of 'St. Louis Polka' which you were anxious to purchase?"

"No." Somehow, after that evening when her father had burst the bombshell of his marriage to Gabriella, she had not remembered to call again at Phillips' for the music.

"I shall send you my copy by tomorrow's post," said the young captain.

"Oh, I pray you, please don't bother."

"No trouble at all, I assure you. The pleasure would be entirely mine."

Pierre said casually, "But, Miss Saucier, then you have not completely sorted the stack of music I brought you when I called last?"

"How perfectly careless," she said. "I was so enthralled over the new song, Mr. Gregoire, that I must have played it over and over. You'll pardon my carelessness?" her voice was a soft entreaty. "You see, you really need not bother, Captain. Mr. Gregoire has already anticipated my wishes."

"Which new song is that?"

"Oh, you know, 'They Tell Me Thou Art the Favored Guest.' Everyone's singing it."

"I supposed it was the latest one, 'Oh, Think Not Less I Love Thee,' or perhaps, 'My Heart Is Like the Silent Lute.'"

Captain Whitlake's voice caressed the words in the two titles.

Anger shot through Pierre. He saw the waiter approaching. His voice harsh, he said, "Here is our wine, Miss Saucier."

"*Au revoir*," said the captain. "until we meet again, I bid you good evening." He left them as suddenly as he had approached.

"My stepmother said Captain Whitlake came to call one evening soon after I met him. But I had gone to my room and did not come down," Charmian said.

"Here is your wine," said Pierre.

"He probably thinks I am overbold to come to Montesano without a chaperon."

"Here is your wine," Pierre said again, holding out her unnoticed glass. "Drink your wine."

She took the goblet and sipped slowly

from its edge. "What," she asked, "did you mean by that stack of music that you brought me the last time you called?"

"What," he countered, "did you mean by being so enthralled playing 'They Tell Me Thou Art the Favored Guest'?"

The laughed together again, and the tension was broken. The wine was good. Charmian could feel a tingling sensation through her body. She reached up and took off the wide-brimmed hat, which was made only for a sunshade. She looped the blue satin riboon over the high-backed chair, tying it so that the hat adorned it prettily. The candle the waiter had brought sputtered in the passing breeze and threw its light upon her pale face. Her eyes were shining with excitement.

The waiter brought the first course, and they began eating as soon as he had served their plates. The corn was succulent and the spicy tang of the barbecue was wonderfully satisfying. Charmian ate heartily. The nicest thing about being with Pierre, she realized suddenly, was that she could pick up the ribs with her fingers and eat to her heart's content. With Dennard Manley, she would not have dared eat ribs.

She picked up the huge linen square and wiped her lips. "Good, isn't it? Oh, dear, I hadn't known how hungry I was until it came."

"I have not eaten since morning. The *Redwing* docked late this afternoon, and I was at the office getting some papers ready for tomorrow's trip." Pierre was eating slowly, enjoying every morsel. Eating was one thing that he never rushed. He could remember too well meals when he had not had more than a crust of bread. To see Charmian eat with a very real appetite was most pleasing to him. They made a long, leisurely meal of it, watching the moon change from a huge orange ball into a white glowing disk which lit up the garden and silhouetted the forest trees about it.

They lingered, and the waiter replenished the wine in the goblets and the candle in the bracket. The music had stopped from within the hotel, and the carriages left one by one.

"We'd better go," Charmian said at last. "It must be very late." She would not yet think about the reception waiting her at home. Gabriella would be in bed, but Charmian's father would be still seated out in the big porch chair nearest the porte-cochere, waiting.

Pierre paid the waiter in gold. She could see the glitter of coin as it passed hands. Remembrance of a little shabby boy, scrupulously clean, flashed through her mind. No matter what his trials, Pierre Gregoire must be wealthy now. He must be very proud to have earned everything with the sweat of his brow and the brawn of his strong arms.

They drove rapidly going back into the quiet city. Once Charmian's eyes closed and she fell soundly asleep, awakening to find that Pierre's arm was supporting her, and her head was on his shoulder. For a long while she did not move; she could excuse the first few minutes with having to think where she was. It was as though she were recovering from the effects of a strong drug. She could scarcely believe that she had spent the evening with Pierre Gregoire at Montesano Place. A swift, tingling sensation swept through her, and she knew this was the happiest evening of her life. She stirred, raising her head, and Pierre's voice was excusing himself.

I thought only to keep you from falling. You were so quiet, and then I saw you had gone to sleep."

They were coming to Compton Gill. Charmian sat up straight, and Pierre removed his arm and gave full attention to his horses. They could not see the house at Ginger Blue until they were around the bend in the drive, and then they saw that the double parlor was brightly lighted.

Pierre stopped in the shadow of a giant tree. He flipped the reins around the whip in the dash and, turning, put his arms about Charmian. She felt the rough surface of his coat, noted the faint smell of tobacco, felt his hair brushing her forehead as he leaned forward to kiss her. His lips pressed gently against hers and she moved slightly, then returned his kiss.

She sat up sharply. "Please."

Pierre let her go. Abruptly he took up the reins, then dropped them again. "No, I can't let you go just yet." he kissed her again.

"Please. Please don't."

After a moment, he drove on silently.

"Let me out here," Charmian said as they approached the house. She was trembling from head to foot.

"Indeed, I shall escort you to your door, Miss Saucier."

"My father will be in an outrageous mood."

"I have seen him outraged before." Pierre's voice was grim. He drew up beside the stone hitching block. Blue came forward from the rear of the house and took the reins.

"Hitch them, please."

"No, no! You must not stay, Pierre!" Charmian's voice was high in alarm. His name slipped out unheeded by her. She heard a movement on the piazza. "Are there any guests, Blue?" she asked in a low tone.

"Dey's one new one, Miss Ch'meen. An' the same ol' ones what's been heah. Yo' pappy's in a te'bble tempah. Tak Blue's advice, suh, and go long lak Miss Ch'meen say."

"Is that you, Charmian?" her father's voice, sharp and curt, demanded.

"Yes, Father." She whispered frantically to Pierre, "Do go home, please, I beg of you. He'll order you off the place. He'll tell you to stay away from here."

"On the other hand, I think he will be relieved to see me," Pierre said calmly. "If I ran away, then he'd think there was reason for my going." He slipped his hand through her arm and turned her resolutely toward the house. "Good evening, Mr. Saucier," he said pleasantly when they were within speaking distance.

Charmian had never heard her father's voice so cold.

"It is a very late hour for you to be bringing my daughter home." Saucier had risen and stood at the edge of the stone steps. "Do you know, Charmian, that we have been looking for you tonight? Hunting for you like a small child who has run away from her nurse. We found the trap with Whistlejackets. What do you mean by going out for the evening and not letting me know?"

"I'm in disgrace, Mr. Gregoire, so please leave me now," Charmian said sweetly. "Good night. It was a very pleasant evening."

Pierre stood there not knowing exactly what to do. "Please, sir — "

"The lady asked you to leave."

"Good night," Pierre said. Without a backward look, he turned and went toward his carriage. He was remembering another night, the night she had run away from the party years before. He had waited behind a thick cluster of bushes at the corner of the garden path that night long after he was ordered off the place. Yes, her father had been furious that time, too.

Charmian stood on the top step and watched him going. She sighed audibly and then, turning casually, said, "Good night, Father."

"Is that all you have to say?"

"I'm not a child."

"You've overstepped the bounds of decorum. You very well know that. Out with a common steamboat pilot! And to Montesano Place!"

"Pierre Gregoire is no common steamboat pilot. He owns a small shipping line, as you probably will become more aware as time passes. It was kind of Dennard Manley to let you know where I was spending the evening. *And so like him.* Since you found my horse, and you have known most of the evening where I was and in whose company, I'll say good night."

Her father remained standing as Charmian turned toward the hallway and the spiral stair case. The gas was still lighted in the glittering chandelier in the front parlor, she saw through the open door. She paused at sight of Gabriella. her stepmother, sitting in her favorite chair, as leaning forward, her slender white hand reaching out, lingering caressingly over the cheek of a young man as he gazed up at her ardently from his position on a low stool at her feet.

# 10

IT rained during the night. Charmian was restless, and heard the water dripping from the heavy foliage of the big tree outside her window long after its beating on the roof had stopped. She lay on the high four-poster bed, her eyes open, thinking about Pierre Gregoire and the evening at Montesano Place. Her face burned with the memory of his kiss. After a long time she fell into a deep sleep, to dream of him until morning.

Later, in a half wakeful doze, she tried to recapture some of the feeling which had stolen over her last night in the garden among the flowers. She realized suddenly that it was late, and half rose; then, remembering that it was Sunday, she sank back among the fluffy pillows. The room was flooded with bright yellow sunlight. Brigette had been in her room straightening things. Charmian's lilac-sprigged lawn negligee lay folded neatly over the arm of the small chair near her bed. The water pitcher had been filled recently, for a drop still lingered on the handsome rose painted on its side, like a drop of dew.

She heard voices outside and, climbing down from her bed, she crossed to the east windows. Gabriella, dressed smartly in a green riding skirt, stood with a crop in her hand, snapping off blades of grass near the mounting block. As though engrossed in this occupation, she seemed surprised when she heard a masculine voice.

"Oh, it's you, Tom." The husky quality which was always noticeable in Gabriella's voice was deeper than usual. It grated unpleasantly in the jeweled morning.

Charmian withdrew quickly. She hated eavesdropping. But Gabriella's voice carried, and she heard her asking Blue for a horse for Mr. Benson. That was Tom Benson who had been with her in the drawing room last evening! Charmian despised herself for her quick suspicion that this early morning meeting was a planned rendezvous. Gabriella had the reputation for being much sought after since 'poor dear Lewis'' death, and among the suitors most frequently mentioned had been Tom Benson, a bachelor of means from Vicksburg, whose reputation for gambling was common gossip.

The little French clock on the marble mantel struck a silvery note, and Charmian pulled the velvet cord which called Brigette to her wing of the house. Brigette was stiff-lipped and drawn this morning. She entered the room without a word. Charmian had finished with the washbowl and stood in front of her dressing table, arranging her hair.

"Good morning, Brigette," she said a second time.

"And what, pray tell me, is there good about it?" snapped Brigette. "Your father has tramped a creaking floor board the night through, and just went up to bed in time to miss his wife going riding with Mr. Tom Benson. Nice goings-on, right in front of his very nose. And you stay out half the night, until we think we will have to get the Guards to hunt you, and thus have your name bandied about by all the trash in St. Louis."

"I'm sorry about Father. That was

quite unnecessary."

"Don't go to bemeanin' him, poor man. He must be half out of his wits, with you not even botherin' to send us a message." She turned mercilessly to Charmian. "An' if you were ten years younger. miss, I'd turn you over and, I warrant you, I'd blister that little bottom of yours."

"Since my last blistering, Brigette, you'd find that it has grown considerably."

Brigette turned a shocked face. "Mind your talk, Charmian Saucier. It's plenty rough speaking you've got since you started out on your charity work."

"Oh, come, Brigette, it's much too beautiful a day to be cross with each other. However, you should remember you brought up the subject in the first place." Charmian threw the lawn wrapper about her shoulders. "Now, get down off your high horse and listen — as I know you're very well dying to hear." She whirled over to the thin, sharp-eyed Brigette.

"Brigette, he's as handsome and nice as can be. Just what I thought years ago."

"He's nothing but the son of French peasantry."

"Then you do know who I mean. But of course, Pinky told you — the tattler."

"You should be ashamed of yourself, going off like a common — "

"Coquette?" Charmian's laughter trailed out. She had supplied a word that she had often heard Pascal call Brigette.

"That's light talk, and I won't have it!" Brigette snapped.

"All right, then, *hoyden*."

"You're just as much of a problem as you always were, an' I'd been in hopes the academy would make a lady out of you."

"My mother was a lady." Charmian picked up the oval miniature of Marie Louise Saucier and studied her face. "Tell me, Brigette, didn't she ever do anything which could have been critized?"

"Nothing that I ever knew. Not unless you'd call bringing yourself into the world — the hoyden you are," she amended. "Maybe 'tis a good thing she didn't live to see how you'd turn out!"

"You've a sharp tongue, Brigette. You

may bring my breakfast."

"An', my little lady, you may just march right down and get it yourself. Ol' Brigette climbing the circular again in this hour? No, my lady." She gave the pillows an extra thump. "Florry may bring it, on second thought. That lazy — "

"All right, Brig, I'll go." Charmian turned as if to leave, knowing that Brigette was dying to hear all about last evening's excursion to Montesano, and that more than likely the tray was ready to come at this moment. It made Brigette feel good to order people around.

"Better untwist that hair of yours and give it a good brushing; going to bed with it like that, you'll never get the tangles out. Looks like a bird's nest this morning." Brigette picked up the silver-handled brush with its old English letter *S* on it, and said sternly, "Sit down."

Charmian smiled as she obediently sat on the low stool where Brigette always brushed her hair.

"He hasn't changed very much even in all these years, Brigette. You'd know him," she said, as though she'd never been interrupted at all.

175

"Fine goings-on, I must say, you goin' to Monestano Place with that man unchaperoned, and getting in so late. You'll be the talk of the town, young miss, just mark my words."

"Oh, Brigette, don't be a fussy, old-fashioned old maid. You'd think you were really shocked, when you know very well that you'd have done it yourself if you'd had the chance."

"Frenchmen are such wonderful lovers, I always say. I remember he was a dark little boy, with bright flashing eyes and a wave in his hair. Pascal must have looked a lot like that." Brigette's voice was soft for just a moment, in memory of the first days she had spent at Ginger Blue. Pascal had been so handsome and so slender, so gay and so headstrong. He was the only man who had ever been able to handle her, although she'd die before she would admit he could. Life had been a happy whirl in those days.

Her voice changed with her thoughts and she spoke harshly as she heard Florry opening the hall door. "Set it on the piecrust table, Florry," she ordered sharply, crossing over to inspect the tray. She ignored the mulatto after a peremptory frowning glance.

Florry wore the look of haughtiness which she had in late years cultivated for Brigette's benefit. Tall, slender, lighter than most mulattos, a touch of color on her high cheek bones, Florry had recently become one of the best-groomed servants St. Louis had ever known. She wore a dark blue dress this morning, with a touch of lace at the throat. Her hair was black and lustrous and brushed into a deep bun at the back of her neck. Her eyes, bright and slightly slanting, were still and fathomless. She made no sound, quietly setting down the tray with its perfect appointments, attending to each detail with accuracy.

This was the thing which irritated Brigette the most. If only Florry would do things in a slovenly way, as she once did, or was lax in one small detail, it would give her a chance to 'rip her up one side and down the other.' But if the new mistress demanded perfection among the servants, then they must be perfect.

"The coffee should have more cream.

Miss Charmian likes it a little lighter."

Florry did not answer, but gently lifted the cover of an extra plate which she had not yet removed from the tray. The popovers were golden brown, the small piece of pink, lean ham curled tenderly at the edges, just as Charmian liked it. The golden yolk of the egg was thinly veiled from the basting which Sabetha had given it in the kitchen. Brigette pursed her lips, for the breakfast was perfect down to the tiny square of red jelly which sparkled on the thin white china.

"Very well," Brigette pronounced. "Mind you be quiet when you go into Mistress Saucier's room to redd it up. Clean sheets every morning, and leave the room to sun for one hour. Pull the drapes back good."

"Yes," Florry said patiently, turning to go. That one short word was the only one she had spoken, and now she paused briefly to curtsy to Charmian.

"Good morning, Florry. The breakfast looks wonderful," said Charmian.

Florry bowed and disappeared.

"The airs that girl gives herself!" It makes me sick."

"Brigette, you are too old to continue that nonsense. Florry is one of the best servants in St. Louis. Really, you should leave her alone. She hardly speaks except to give you a civil answer," Charmian said placatingly.

"No, she doesn't say much, but then the empty vessel makes the greatest sound."

"Do you or don't you want to hear about Pierre Gregoire?" Charmian sat down at the table and spread the huge white napkin over her lap. She was beautiful this morning, and Brigette was thinking what a lot of good the evening before had done her. Charmian took a bite out of one of the muffins. It was good to be alive this morning. She ate hungrily, and Brigette watched her after she had turned down the sheets.

"That Dennard Manley drove up in a huff about eight last night. I remember the time, for the old clock that your Grandfather Saucier gave your mother when she was married had chimed the hour. He rapped on the front door, and I opened it. We had waited supper for you, and your father had just sat down

179

to the table. Your father's wife had just flounced out of the dining room, angry." Brigette sat down on the low stool by the fireplace, crossing her arms over her flat bosom and frowning. "She stopped at the door when she saw young Mr. Manley and asked him to come in."

"Of course, I knew that Pinky would come straight here. We met him last night on the road. He saw me with Mr. Gregoire on the way to Carondelet."

"Your father's wife knew that he was upset over something, so she came back with him to the dining table and ordered only a bit of cake for her sweet. She did it a-purpose to hear what he had to say to your father."

Charmian was suddenly weary of Gabriella and silenced Brigette by rising from the table and motioning the food away. "I shall want the carriage as usual for St. Mark's at eleven o'clock. Will Father go? And what about Gabriella?"

"She won't be back in time. Pretty out — her ridin' off through the hills and hollers on a Sabbath. Your father will no doubt sleep until afternoon. But you, my lady, can go for the family." Brigette

180

sniffed again. She picked up the tray and started for the door. She stopped briefly on the threshold. "You haven't forgotten the races next week at the Gallatin farm, have you?"

"Almost," admitted Charmian.

She still had an hour to wait after she had dressed for the cathedral. She wandered around her room for a while, her gaze resting now and then on the portrait of her mother, which had been painted by a great Eastern painter in Baltimore the year before Marie Louise's marriage to Llewellyn Saucier. Charmian sometimes wondered about her mother's family. Somewhere back in the Barre family, which came from New Orleans, there had been a handsome, winning scapegrace named Zenon le Duc, who was given a royal land grant in Louisiana embracing three thousand arpens. Zenon ran away from trouble, seduced pretty young girls of nice families, and cared not a tittle whether he disgraced the family name or not. Charmian would never have known of this blot on the family escutcheon had it not been for Brigette's threatening her when she was

181

naughty: 'Do you want to grow up to be like Zenon le Duc? No shame, no face?' For a long time Charmian had thought that the young man had been literally without a face, not knowing that that was Brigette's way of saying he was without family pride.

The portrait of Great-grandmother Charmian Saucier still hung in the gallery in the left wing of the house. It was placed like a museum piece in a conspicuous place so that guests could see her beauty. Feeling an urge to see it today, Charmian left her room and crossed the floor to the circular stairway and walked softly down. She crossed the downstairs reception hall and then mounted the few steps which led to the gallery at the other end of the hall. The portrait was that of a truly beautiful young lady. Yet once when Brigette had been furious with her, Charmian had learned that her Great-grandmother Charmian had been involved in a scandal when she was sixteen.

This morning, gazing at her picture, Charmian was wondering, if that other Charmian had been in her place last evening, whether she, too, would have overstepped propriety? Great-grandmother Saucier had outlived the scandal and married an elderly widower to whom she had patiently borne ten children, only two of whom had lived. Something within that look on her face held Charmian's attention. There was more than just beauty; there was that same expression in her eyes that all of the Sauciers wore — *You can do anything. You can be what you wish. You can defy the rest of the world.* But that was what Mother Superior had said to her in the convent gardens where she had trespassed. Charmian stood resolutely before the portrait.

Her father's anger last night — A tremor of unreasoning fury went through her. She had not done anything really wrong. He seemed to *want* to misunderstand her. She had not been able to please him since his marriage to Gabriella. She felt cold and unwanted, in a world that once had been filled with warmth and love. She had been headstrong, she knew, in carrying on her welfare work, but of course, she had always told herself, his concern over her in that was perfectly silly.

Her thoughts turned to Pierre. What, she wondered, was he really like? In a way, he was still a stranger, yet she felt closer to him than to any other person she had ever known. Her senses began to sing, just thinking about him, here in the quiet gallery. Her lips trembled, and the keen edge of intoxication which had touched her last night swept over her again.

She turned to go, her eyes bright with quick, unshed tears.

# 11

THE rain had cooled the morning air, and the grass was still wet as Charmian crossed a strip of lawn to get into the carriage which Pascal had brought up. Blue was holding the horses, and she spoke to him before Pascal helped her up the carriage step. She spread the full white swiss skirts about her carefully in the carriage. They had just the right amount of starch in them to stand out beautifully over the fine muslin petticoats. The full draped sleeves and the square neck were faced with pink net which reflected on her delicately colored cheeks. Her basque was fitted with a high corsage, and her bonnet was edged with the same pink of the trimming of her dress.

Charmian always enjoyed the drive to St. Mark's Cathedral. As they went down Compton Hill, they met a carriage now and then, headed for the same place. She nodded and bowed and sat up very straight this Sabbath morning. There would be a few questions asked about her father's whereabouts. He had seldom missed Mass in the past, but since Gabriella's absence made him conspicuous if she did not go, then neither did he.

Pascal drove up to the front of the cathedral. Charmian had always admired it. The portico of the church followed the Greek revival style, after the fashion of the ruins of Paestum. Flanking the structure were the orphanage and the priest's house. The baroque reredos, the architectural perspective on the sanctuary wall, the transparent decorations, all made it a truly beautiful edifice — a Greek revival church, laid out by American architects, modified and embellished by Italian trends, and decorated by a French painter! It had a basement chapel, there were stone candelabra on the parapet, and there was a clock on the tower.

On this Sunday, the young priest from St. Patrick's Father Dennis Carmichael, who only last year had received his ordination to the priesthood at the hands of Archbishop Kenrick, was substituting for St. Mark's pastor. It had lately been the talk of the parish that young Father Carmichael would shortly be assigned to St. Mark's. He was a well known figure in St. Louis, and had recently been appointed editor of the *St. Mark's News*, a Catholic weekly. He was a romantic figure, having traveled up and down the Mississippi, but especially because of his writings of Indian lore and Missouri scenery and anecdotes. Some of the liveliest portrayals of steamboating in the West were written by the young priest. He had a large and interested congregation this morning, Charmian noted at once. All of the box pews were occupied.

A dark head above a white collar attracted her gaze. Pierre Gregoire had followed his favorite young pastor from St. Patrick's to the cathedral to do his worshipping today. She knelt, the only figure in the Saucier pew.

She had no chance to speak to Pierre when she left the cathedral without deliberately waiting for him. Father Carmichael was speaking with him, she saw when she looked back. Then there was only one thing to do, and that was to enter her carriage.

When she arrived home, Gabriella and Tom Benson were back from their morning ride. Her father and they were having a leisurely breakfast, and Brigette was sent to bring Charmian to join them as soon as she had freshened up a bit. Charmian walked down the stairs unhappily, but anxious to make up to her father any hurt she might have dealt him the evening before.

The table was cheerful with its bright ruby tumblers. The white linen was snowy and the overhead gas lights were burning brightly, although it was well past the middle of the day. Melon, creamed kidneys, fresh white bread, gold-brown fried chicken, hot corn muffins, and fried hominy grits sent up an appetizing aroma.

"Good morning, everybody," said Charmian as she entered and took her place.

"Good morning, dear Charmian," said Gabriella gently. That voice held within it tolerance, patience for a child who has been infinitely naughty, and loving, tender forgiveness. It made Charmian forcibly restrain a quick, hot retort.

"Did you enjoy church, daughter?" her father asked quietly.

That was something she could answer. Charmian told of young Father Carmichael's celebrating today, mentioned a few of their friends who had asked about them, and thanked Florry for serving her plate.

"And how was the morning ride, Gabriella?" she asked, turning her eyes not on Gabriella, but upon Tom Benson, who, under her gaze, turned a dull, brick red.

Llewellyn Saucier remained absorbed with his melon and his thoughts about the behavior of his daughter last night. She was no longer a child, but as long as she remained under his rooftree, she would be accountable to him for her actions. He was unaware of the tension in the room, and did not notice the coolness of Gabriella's reply.

"It was glorious, as usual. Bonny Blue took the row of hedges that Whistlejackets fluked out on last week, just like a jackrabbit leaping over a weed." She turned a still, warning glance on her stepdaughter.

"Of course, Ryan, the new trainer, is devoting a great deal of time to Blue Gypsy and Blue Whippet for the fall show, and I don't mind much if he neglects Bonny Blue. I can keep her in good form." She turned to Benson. "Do have some more chicken, Mr. Benson. You've hardly touched a thing."

Coming out of his reverie, Saucier added his hospitable insistence. "Yes, do, Tom. Gabriella doesn't like to fuss with a big dinner on Sunday, you know, and we won't eat again until tea." He liked to be tolerant of his young bride's whims. After all, she was gay and beautiful, and if she liked to have Sunday evening tea take the place of the heavy dinner he was accustomed to, he would not complain. It was so much more fashionable, Gabriella insisted. Several members of the Home Circle had decided to make it customary at their homes, so that calling in the evening was getting to be quite the thing in their social group. For them, the Sabbath closed at sundown.

As soon as the meal was over, Charmian went back to her room, and Saucier did not try again that day to engage her in a conversation about her activities of the night before. It could wait until another time when he had had a chance to investigate young Gregoire.

Benson returned to the room he had been given upon his arrival from Vicksburg. He had not liked the clear-eyed stare of the young daughter of his host.

He had known Gabriella for a long, long time, even before her marriage to Danforth. Once when she was visiting in New Orleans, he had met her at a house party. He had been very wealthy then, inheriting his father's estate when he was only twenty; in late years it had dwindled to a few paltry acres, barely enough to support him, and then only if he was not too generous with his own money and willing to accept the hospitality of other more fortunate friends.

He sat gloomily looking out of the window. It had been foolish for him to come here. Gabriella has been insistent, though, in her last letter to him:

*We are having a house party as soon as the redecorating and building are finished. Really, you must come, Tom, dear. There'll be lots of fun, plenty to eat and drink, and riding. You remember those long rides we used to take, don't you, Tom?*

Did he remember them? Gabriella could outride, outshine any of the young Vicksburg belles, even though she was from five to seven years older than they.

He had written back to her:

*Dear Mrs. Saucier,*

*I do honestly thank you for your very kind invitation to join you late in August. Unfortunately, I shall be unable to attend at that time, as I shall be in the east. I know you and your husband will congratulate me upon my forthcoming marriage to Miss Antoinette Reaves, which will be held in Vicksburg the tenth of next month. We shall spend our honeymoon in Baltimore and New York.*

He had received a pleading little note in answer:

*Tom, dear, come at once. Please don't stand upon ceremony. Mr. Saucier joins me in extending a cordial invitation to our very dear friend.*

Tom Benson never really knew what compelled him to take the next boat to St. Louis. He told Toinette that he was going on business. She pouted her pretty red lips and shook her yellow curls at him, and he kissed her ardently as he left her. She was still such a child. Sometimes he felt guilty when he thought of the difference between their ages.

"You are a little coquette, my darling, and if you're not careful, you shall pay dearly for it!"

"How dearly?" she countered.

"Very dearly. You will be married to an old man and you will want to play up to the youngsters, and it won't do you a mite of good, because your husband won't allow any nonsense from any of those young blades."

He had thought constantly about her answer to that, since last evening when Gabriella and Saucier had made such a to-do over Charmian's being out with a steamboat man. For Toinette had lifted perfectly frank blue eyes to him and said:

"There's only one other man besides you that I have ever really thought I could love, Tom. Of course, you'll forget the times I've been *engaged* to other young men — that didn't mean a thing. But this one man — I'd better tell you now since it's all over and done with long ago. I saw him only once, when I was younger. He was, of all things — a pilot! Papa saw him again later, but I was in New Orleans visiting. We've lost track of him now because Vicksburg is not on his course."

She was so innocently serious, so desperately bent on making a clean breast of her first love, that Tom had kissed her and playfully demanded his rival's name so that he could shoot him on sight.

She had laughed a little and said, "Gregoire. Pierre Gregoire." There was something serious in her eyes, even though she answered lightly.

Tom wished he had not come to St.

Louis. He wished, too, that he had never heard the name Gregoire. Nor that he had gone riding this morning with Gabriella.

He wished only to be on his way again. He had had to make his appearance at the table so that it would not look strange to Saucier that he must leave suddenly after having made a promise to stay for the races next week.

I thought I was madly in love with Gabriella once and that I should never marry anyone but her! He could hear her scornful voice down through the years: 'Tom, you're fun, but I want to marry someone who knows how to take care of his money. When your money is gone, I shall be rolling in wealth!' He had been gambling heavily then. The man she had meant was Llewellyn Saucier, and she had finally married him.

If he hadn't gone to Paris that year — the year that she suddenly married Lewis Danforth — he might have been married to the vain woman who, from what she had said to him today on their long ride, obviously wished to dull the shining happiness of his forthcoming marriage. He asked himself in bitterness, Could she be jealous of Toinette?

He felt sick as he packed his case and prepared to leave. He felt deeply sorry for Saucier and he remembered Charmian's searching look. If only he could tell her that anything which might have been between him and Gabriella was now over! He was going to take a boat — any boat — whichever left first going toward New Orleans. He pulled the bell cord and asked Pascal to have a trap for him in half an hour and to present his regrets to Mr. and Mrs. Saucier and to say that he must leave a little earlier than he had planned.

The message sent, he was finishing the packing of his clothes when he heard a light tap at his door. He opened it to Gabriella.

"You're leaving?" she asked, swiftly crossing over the heavy rug and standing close to him.

"Gabriella, you shouldn't have come to my room. You know that someone may see you."

"It doesn't matter. I do what I like. But then," she said coolly, "I took the precaution to see that no one was around. He," meaning Saucier, "has gone down to the wharf on business. She," meaning Charmian, "has gone to call on some poor river rat's wife who has just had a baby and whom, it seems, she helped deliver." Standing by the foot of the heavy mahogany bed, she went on mockingly, "Seriously, Tom, I do wish you happiness in your marriage. Tell me more about the beautiful Toinette. I remember Colonel Reaves — such a gallant gentleman. You remember, he was at that house party. I can see him now — tall, handsome, and just beginning to be a little stout."

"Yes," Tom said quietly. "I remember. I saw him kissing you on the stair — at the landing."

Gabriella laughed, and the sound was not good. The room reeked of her exotic perfume. It was not sweet like the breath of lilac from Toinette's sachets, but something wild and intoxicating. Tom's face grew white.

"I must finish my packing." His hands trembled on the handle of the bureau drawer. He was fighting for composure which was crumbling fast. Gabriella laid her white hand on his. Her fingers curled up over it possessively, invitingly.

"Don't bother to hurry, Tom, my darling. I've already told Pascal that you have changed your mind, that you are not leaving until after the races as you had planned."

# 12

AUGUST was hot and sultry with the temperature soaring day after day into the nineties. The nights gave but little relief to the heat-parched earth. Patches of green lawn faded and browned into dry stubble; dust lay thick upon roads to swirl in endless clouds after buggy wheels had passed over them. Babies sickened and many died of 'summer complaint'; citizens getting up tired in the mornings turned only a desultory hand to the day's tasks and sat and fanned whenever possible.

Social activities dropped to the mere passing an hour or so in the coolest retreat available. The Ripple Boat Club was the most popular organization in town, and evening found a few couples on Chouteau's Pond, drifting over the quiet waters in hope of catching a slight breeze.

Old Granny Popo, the voodoo woman, died, and the Negroes at Ginger Blue held a funeral for her. The ritual was not so much in respect for the poor old crone, but rather for the love of their own peculiar, primitive mourning. Their weird chants and haunting songs filled the night air. Charmian, hearing the sound, knew that Granny Popo had gone, as had been expected for weeks.

Florry seemed different. "The old heathen's charms on her are broken," Brigette said several times that week. "She probably won't be so hoity-toity now."

"Nonsense, Brigette! Old Popo had nothing to do with Florry."

"Don't you ever believe it. I went through Florry's cabin once when she was gone. It wasn't a pretty sight, let me tell you! I wouldn't touch the stuff, but made Blue take it out and burn it."

"What was it like, Brigette?"

"Fine thing! You don't believe in voodooism, and yet you want to know about the charms she used."

"Weren't you afraid?"

"Me! Indeed not! I had that trash cleaned out in no time. She was mad as a hornet, and, of course, I know she got fixed up again. It was a miserable stinking mess of herbs and snakeskin and an owl's eye. She had a little shrunken head of a baby she carried around on a cord run thorough the eye socket."

"Brigette!"

"Very well, my little lady, you were asking me!"

Charmian didn't answer. Her thoughts shifted abruptly. She was thinking that if she had not been at Emilie Vigo's house that day late last winter, she might not have seen Pierre until she met him later at Planters' House under entirely different circumstances. Although she had not seen him since the Sunday at St. Mark's after the evening at Montesano Place, she had received a message from him delivered by Pascal without Brigette's knowledge.

Pierre's writing was fine and precise. The message said briefly:

*I am sorry if you had any unpleasantness due to our evening together. Today I leave for New Orleans on the* Redwing. *I shall hope to see you early next month when I expect to remain in the Port of St. Louis several days.*
　　　Respectfully yours,
　　　　　　Pierre Gregoire.

It was a long month.

Charmian did not go to the races. Instead, she turned her attention to the possibilities of a school for the slum section known as Shepherd's Graveyard.

In all of her work, she had found this part of the city to be the most neglected by city authorities. Fights were common, and several bodies which had lately been washed ashore along the wharf were identified as people from this community. The St. Louis Grays were called out often to subdue drunken belligerents.

"That, my fine lady," cautioned Brigette sharply, "is one place I forbid you to go. I set my foot down! You are not to ask Pascal to take you there, and if you do, I warn you, I'll do something drastic if he dares carry out your orders."

"Save your worries, Brigette, for something more worthy."

"The slops are thrown into the streets and the whole place reeks of filth. It's no place for a lady to even drive through, let alone step down in the muck of the street. If Pascal takes you there, I'll bash in his head, you may be sure."

This was the place that Charmian had the most difficulty in getting Pascal to take her.

"It's not that I'm afraid of my old woman, Miss Charmian, but I am afraid for you. This ain't no place for you. It's the disgrace of St. Louis. Nothing but trash lives there." He did not need to add that the house of Mary Simms, which had burned last week, was burned purposely by police to get rid of the source of some of the nightly brawls.

The *Daily Union* had recently been carrying many items about disturbances which seemed to stem from this notorious section.

PERFECTLY TERRIBLE RIOT, ran headlines in one of last week's papers.

An Irishman with a terrible temper, which had been inflamed by immoderate drinking, with not so much as by-your-leave, mixed last night with a German immigrant who came in on the *Swiftsure* yesterday afternoon. The common brawl took place in Maguire's Saloon in the neighborhood known as Shepherd's Graveyard. Before the disturbance could be squelled, the German's head had been bashed open, and the Irishman suffered severe cuts and bruises about his person. Several bystanders joined in the affray, and Maguire's Saloon was the scene of one of the worst riots taking place lately in the city. Such disgraceful actions should not be tolerated by the peace-loving populace of St. Louis. Chairs were thrown, windows were broken, tables overturned, and beer and wine kegs were split to spill their contents upon the filthy floor.

Your reporter happened to be passing along the street, bent on going to the wharf to meet the *Tamerlane*. Soon the entire surroundings were enveloped in hysteria. Men joined in the melee for the pure fun of taking a poke at someone. The St. Louis Grays were called out, and a few shots in the air soon quelled the disturbers, letting them know that the Grays meant business.

The editor of the *Union* had followed the story the next day with a flourishing editorial on the deplorable conditions existing in Shepherd's Graveyard. He was too kind to mention any names, some of the young men involved being from good St. Louis families, but he concluded by saying:

It is the duty of city officials to carry out law and order in this disgraceful community, the duty of each noble Christian citizen to do his bit toward alleviating the distress of the indigent, and the duty of the various churches in our growing city to work toward the betterment of home life of the poor little children whose plights are unfit to consider.

Charmian was stirred by the comment of the editor. The next day she went to young Father Dennis Carmichael. He was telling of one of his excursions up the Missouri to a group of young boys who sat around in a circle with their mouths open.

Charmian was left standing in the vestibule of his home while the housekeeper went to announce her.

"Don't keep her waiting, Mathilde, send her on in," said Father Carmichael's soft voice. "And now, lads, be off with you and I'll continue the tale tomorrow. That is, of course, if I hear no more of the Widow Lane's complaints about her chickens being roasted at the river. And you, Tommy Silvers, I'll be looking for that basket of grapes you promised me. Todd, you'll sweep the walks tomorrow before the bishop gets here, and you, Paul" — he put his arm about the little cripple — "I'd like another sketch of the cathedral. Put some shrubbery in on the east side. I know there's none there, but it'd help its looks to add a bit, and who knows, the bishop may order some to be planted just because you drew it there."

Charmian waited while the children passed her. Little unwashed faces grinning back at the young priest, among them Tommy Silvers, who had been released from custody last month because of Charmian's protest to the hatchet-faced judge of the juvenile court.

Father Carmichael watched them out and closed the door after them. "I'll be at them to wash up a bit in another week or two, Miss Saucier. I couldn't afford to scare them off with too much of a change in the beginning."

Charmian laughed, and the sound brought a smile to the priest's lips. He was youthful in appearance, his face smooth and clear, his eyes a vivid blue, his hair fair and curly. Charmian was thinking, He has an almost angelic face, it is so beautiful and *good*. He was tall and slender, but his shoulders carried strength in them. His long black robe seemed to bother him when he crossed the room, as though he were unaccustomed to wearing it. He folded it about him impatiently as he sat down after having seated Charmian on the stiff little sofa in his study.

They made a few desultory remarks about the August heat, the sinking of the *Rowena* a few days ago, and the number of German immigrants who had come in recently by steamboat from New Orleans.

"I'm sure that you are wondering why I came to you, Father Carmichael."

"On the contrary, I think I know. Perhaps if not the exact good works, then at least I can venture just generally that you have something in mind which needs the Church's attention. Say, for instance — Shepherd's Graveyard?" His blue eyes twinkled. "I see," he added, watching her face, "that you must have read the *Union*'s editorial. I wondered whom it would bring to my study today. You are the first to come."

"Shepherd's Graveyard, yes." She paused. "But more than that."

He waited for her to continue while he observed her closely.

"Father, do you know how little is being done toward the establishment of public schools in St. Louis? I believe that if we had schools to educate the people in right ways of living, we should not have as much trouble as at present."

"You're far-thinking, Miss Saucier. You are not only considering the present generation of adults, but those coming along after." He stood up and walked over to the rough stone fireplace which rose to the ceiling.

"Ignorance is the greatest curse of civilization. It retards progress, it breeds distress and sickness, both mental and physical. No city can be truly great without education. St. Louis is already a great city in population. It can be even greater. It must have more schools. But denominational schools are not enough."

"Private schools and seminaries are only for the wealthy," said Charmian. "Our state set up a program for the public schools, and what has happened?" She paused dramatically. "We have only a few ward schools. What about districts without *any* schools? We have had a few meetings of public-spirited citizens who have talked about it. *Talking* doesn't do any good. *Actions* are what count."

Father Carmichael stood watching her. Here was the impatience of youth, the drive of an intense interest.

"I have been in St. Louis one year and three months; in your state of Missouri only two years. Even in your America, *my* America, three years — and I shall never go back home. This is my land. Missouri is raw and new but ahead, there are many changes, some we have never yet dreamed. The steamboat on the river has helped, but more than that, a great system of roads, and the railway — they are yet to come."

He strode back to his chair and then crossed over to look down upon her face. It wore the same inspired look as his own, but he was unaware of the vision which lay in his eyes.

"The people must be ready for these changes. They must be a healthy, intelligent people, or they cannot adapt themselves. The newspapers are right. Some of the conditions are deplorable. Education is the first step forward, and more public schools is the answer. Every child must have his opportunity to learn."

He stopped suddenly. Here was one of the most beautiful girls he had ever seen, the daughter of one of the wealthiest men in this part of the country. It was surprising that she should even be here today. It was unbearably warm outside. A row of small perspiration drops outlined her upper lip, and now and then she wiped her forehead with a small lace-edged handkerchief. This America was indeed surprising. Miss Saucier was speaking his own kind of language. She was a lady in every respect of the word, and yet he knew from the stories he had heard that she was undaunted by the notoriously dirty and dangerous sections of the city, and she proceeded in her own quiet way to carry out her errands of mercy, through all kinds of weather, and against the wishes of her father.

"Miss Saucier," he said, "you inspire me to go forward in setting up a new committee for furthering education and public health in our city. Not long ago, a young man — Mr. Pierre Gregoire, of whom you may have heard — and I were talking about these things late into the night."

At the mention of Pierre's name, Charmian started, and the priest saw the pleased look which came into her eyes.

"I see that you know of him. He mentioned your charity and said that he thought the business men should set a fund at your disposal and, more than that, should offer assistance in other ways."

Charmian flushed with pleasure. How could she have thought had Pierre had forgotten his promise to help her? She became eager and her voice rang with excitement.

"I discussed my work with him very briefly, but he knows some of the things which need to be done. He seemed enthusiastic, but he has been gone. He is away, you know, some of the time."

"Yes, I know. I've traveled with him. One of the best pilots on the Mississippi. A man who knows his business and is alert. I shall, with your kind permission, put your name down on the committee, Miss Saucier. I shall add that of Pierre Gregoire and my own, also the young editor of a weekly paper published by two of the protestant churches, perhaps two or three business men. Mr. Hartner and Edgar Lee would doubtless be willing and able to assist us. Some other ladies — perhaps Mrs Saucier?"

"Gabriella!" she said incredulously. "Oh, I'm sorry, no. No, I don't believe that she would be interested enough to give it the time it deserves." How could he have thought that Gabriella would be a suitable member of such a committee!" She would scorn the suggestion, would make fun of it behind her fan, or even right out in the open at her next dinner party.

"I see. I thought she might be interested in this work. But then, I understand. There are others who have more time at their disposal. It is so good of you to call, and I shall certainly make it known that you are responsible for the pursuance of the idea."

"No, please don't. I shall be glad to help on the committee, but I don't want any publicity." Charmian rose and reached for her parasol.

Father Carmichael took her out to her waiting chaise. He bowed low to her as Pascal started up the horses, and she smiled and was gone. He stood in the small courtyard for a long time, gazing at the street and the corner where the chaise had turned, as though by watching it he could still see her.

# 13

ON her way home, Charmian thrilled with a singing triumph. The days had dragged along, but now they were to be filled with thoughts of seeing Pierre again, and of what she should say to him, and some of the things which he might say to her. She had Pascal drive by St. Mark's slowly, taking in the beauty of the church with hungry eyes. The grass was burned and dead-looking, but the caretaker had early this morning washed the walks, and pigeons were fluttering above the roof top, giving it an air of quiet restfulness.

She had one or two calls to make: one to see the McGhinty baby, who had been named for her, and another to the new family of French immigrants who were living in Emilie Vigo's cabin.

By the middle of the afternoon, she was worn and hopelessly wilted with the heat. She drew out a mirror from her reticule and, while Pascal drove down the street, she made a few attempts to pat her hair into place before reaching Compton Hill.

Arriving at Ginger Blue, she found the house filled with activity. Gabriella was having an evening garden party. The servants had been stormed out of the indolence of the past two weeks and were furbishing the big house for the arrival of guests in the late afternoon. Supper was to be served on the terrace and Christy's Band had been hired to furnish music.

Two little darkies were manipulating push brooms in a leisurely fashion as Pascal drove up to the porte-cochere. They stopped to stare with big eyes at the chaise.

"Here, you ninnies, come and hold the horses whilst I help Miss Charmian. Where are your manners?" Pascall cuffed the ears of both in one sweeping gesture, grinning broadly at Charmian as they squealed and shied to the front of the bays to told them steady as he helped her down.

"Little black rascals! Your pa would do well to be rid of half the mouths he feeds."

"Ginger Blue could feed three times as many and never miss it, Pascal." When Charmian was smaller, her father had often spoken of the slave market in New Orleans where he preferred to buy his Negroes. Of late years, he was more inclined to buy them from his associates who wished to sell, for he encouraged family life for his slaves, and thought that those already acclimated would be less likely to run away than those who came from the deep South, leaving families behind them. He was using Negro roustabouts on his boats as well as the white men, he employed as crew. Saucier's slaves were faithful to him, for he fed them well and housed them decently.

"What's going on, Sabetha?" Charmian asked, walking through the kitchen door. Cakes and tarts stood at one end of the long table; baked chicken and hams sent up mouthwatering odors and the kitchen was filled with the bustling attendant upon a big party.

Sabetha hardly looked up. "More comp'ny. Seems like the new Missy cain' be content less'n we uns havin' comp'ny underfoot."

Charmian made no comment, although she knew that Sabetha's complaining was justified. Up long before the break of day, she would work this night until the last of the food had been served and the leftovers returned to the kitchen. Then she would take up her 'totin' pail' and fill it with scraps from the various plates to carry home to the youngest of the pickaninnies.

Charmian stood by the table looking at the food. She picked up a fork and twisted a little skewer of chicken liver away from the giblets and ate it with relish. Gabriella came into the kitchen at that moment, her white swiss dress fresh and cool in contrast with Charmiman's.

"Good gracious, my dear Charmian! You look worn out with the heat. Sabetha, how did the last pan of tarts turn out? And did Blue get back from the store? Those new confections are just the thing, don't you think, Charmian, to top off the supper? And the wine, did Pascal bring it up from the cellar? Move about, Sabetha, and get things well on the way. It will soon be four o'clock. Charmian, my dear, don't you think you'd like a bath and rest until time to come down?"

"You are so considerate, Gabriella," Charmian said, unmoved by the thoughtfulness of her stepmother. "I think perhaps, if you don't mind, that I shan't come down at all tonight. I have some writing to do and I have been planning all week to finish reading my new book."

"I don't see why you aren't more observant of your father's wishes, Charmian." Gabriella moved toward the kitchen door. "Won't you come along and let us discuss this?"

Charmian followed her. She knew that Gabriella would much rather she didn't appear tonight, but for her husband's sake, she must seem concerned over his daughter's nonappearance.

"I'd rather not come down," Charmian said, stopping at the foot of the stairs.

"Really, Charmian, I see no reason for your stubbornness. You are a trial to your poor dear father." Gabriella sighed. "Of course, it has been terribly warm of late, and I know that you have been busy with your charity cases." She withdrew slightly as though the mere words might contaminate her. "I don't see why you bother. You could have so much fun, my dear. This next season will prove to be most interesting. Never has St. Louis had so many intriguing things planned. A new theater is to be opened, and another new hotel, and the winter promises to be gay. Professor Quenton is coming from New York to teach ballroom dancing, and they say he spent part of last year at the English and French courts, so that he can teach us all the latest steps." Charmian made a movement toward the stairs. "Of course, it's just the way you feel about things."

"But I love gay times! What makes you think that I'm just an old stick?" Charmian's face flushed. "My father and I went everywhere together, you know, until this summer."

"Yes, dear, but you should be thinking of beaux of your own. Why, at your age, I was married!"

That was an unfortunate thing for you to say at this point, Gabriella, but I won't pursue it, Charmian thought. "Oh, there's plenty of time for that later!" she said, desperately trying to be pleasant, as she went up the steps. Her skirt tripped her a bit and she almost lost her footing just as she got to the landing.

"Charmian! Do be careful. Those stairs will be the death of someone!" Gabriella admired them almost as much as Saucier, although she used to grow dizzy looking at them when she first came to Ginger Blue.

She had gotten used to them by now, and she sometimes ran up them lightly as though to prove to herself that she had not lost her youthful grace and agility. She stood now for a moment looking up the stairs after Charmian had disappeared into her own wing at the other end of the upper hall.

Sometimes she was afraid that Llewellyn would see how little she cared for his daughter. Even while he had been courting her, she had been jealous of Charmian's youth and beauty and the fact that her father seemed to enjoy her companionship as much as he did her own. She stood quietly looking up, until the steps seemed to fuse together, making a straight oblique line which ran up into the quarters above to the intimacy of the Saucier home life. She had never quite broken into it, she was perfectly aware. Tears of quick rage came into her eyes and she saw the line of steps wavering dizzily as she continued to stand there, her white hand clenched into a tense fist against the newel post.

I hate her. Sometimes I feel that I hate Llewellyn. He built a circle around himself and Marie Lousie that I've never been able to enter. His first wife was his first love. 'I love you, Gabriella,' patiently, even tenderly, Saucier had said to her, but with an air of *compassion*, rather than *passion*. It infuriated her.

Llewellyn would be withdrawn tonight if Charmian did not come down and join their guests. Gabriella had taken such pains to invite Captain Whitlake and, of course Dennard Manley, although she knew that Charmian did not like him. But it went against her grain to have to beg her stepdaughter to help entertain guests. She should be grateful that someone else took enough interest to keep some life in the house.

Until I came, Gabriella liked to console

herself, there was no style about Ginger Blue. The place just ran itself, with a parcel of poorly trained Negroes and that impudent white housekeeper, Brigette, looking after it. Llewellyn had been sweet to her, giving her unlimited funds to build onto and redecorate the old part of the house, It had fallen into almost shameless ruin. The roof over the old wing upstairs leaked in places, and the ceiling had to be replastered. In another year or two, she supposed, it would have fallen in over their heads, and it was not an old house at all. Thank goodness, in another few weeks summer would be over, and then they could settle down to a life of enjoyment. Tom Benson was trying to slip out of her life now for good, she knew — but then, Tom was not the only attractive male.

Always popular, Gabriella in the old days had laughingly waved aside any of the hints of scandal which were sometimes whispered to her by Dr. Sydney Gregoire. "Better marry me, Gabe; the old ripsnorters are after your hide again."

"They can't prove a thing, Syd, as you

ought to know by now."

"You don't think we've been indiscreet, do you?"

"Indiscreet?" She laughed. "Or do you mean indiscreet so that someone would find out?"

"You are a minx, you know, Gabe. Some day some man will kill you for the cheater you are."

"What about yourself? Cast not the first stone. Why don't you be honest with yourself, Syd? You don't want to marry me. It wouldn't be a wise move on your part at all. There's many a little belle who would be more than glad to trade her mamma's apron strings for your very handsome self. And could bring you a nice dowry, besides."

"I suppose I'll wind up marrying a simpering little slow-wit one of these days, but I'm going to have some fun first. You can't know what it's like not to have money. Lord, when I think of how hungry we used to get. You've never known the feeling of your stomach gnawing at itself."

"Haven't I? You just don't know the feelings I've had. We're too much alike,

Sydney. We both want too much for nothing."

"Don't ever think you won't pay for what you get. Your beauty, your everlasting charm, my dear — "

"Don't be nasty, Syd."

"See me tomorrow, darlin'? Same place, same time."

"Maybe. It's according to my mood by then."

"You know you'll be there. Here!" After his kiss, which always left her breathless, Gabriella was ready to go anywhere, any time.

# 14

THE first days of September were blessedly cooled by a driving rain. The clay roads turned into bogs and the earth had a washed, living smell again. The foliage took on new life and the grass which had been burned a dark brown seemed almost overnight to develop new green shoots and reach out for new roots. The Mississippi, which had fallen to a record low, swelled again to a muddy and respected width and went over its banks into the lowlands. It swept on down toward the Gulf, carrying debris which caused pilots to keep a wary eye for snags. It made the crew of the *Redwing* nervous and taut, Pierre Gregoire saw, on their way back to St. Louis from New Orleans.

Gregoire was proud of his new boat. It was one of the finest on the Mississippi. Its present cargo was the most valuable it had ever carried, for besides its usual quota of passengers, it was carrying a fortune in court gems and silver which were going to the American relatives of a French nobleman. It made Pierre uneasy to have this precious cargo; better boats than the *Redwing* had sunk in smoother waters than this treacherous stream.

Pierre stood watching Natchez recede into the distance. In a way, it was here that the Gregoire Line had been born. His thoughts turned back through the years. He had gone to see Colonel Reaves as he had promised, on the first trip back to Vicksburg after he had rescued the colonel from the hijackers at Natchez-Under-the-Hill. The colonel was responsible for the acquisition of his first boat. The *Fresco*, an old boat owned by one of the colonel's relatives, had originally been purchased by the colonel with the idea of hauling his own cotton to market. But it had not proved to be worth the trouble to keep up a crew for it, and it had fallen into disuse at a private dock.

After discussing it with Colonel Reaves, Pierre offered to buy the boat for a small sum, repair and paint it and equip it with a crew and haul the man's cotton to market that season and the next. The bargain proved beneficial to both. Gregoire had made enough on the return trips hauling freight to pay for the renovation of the boat during the idle winter months which followed.

The *Fresco* gave him a start in the shipping business, and not long after the second season opened he bought a small dismantled passenger boat and restored it to its original value. Freight rates were high and the demands many, so no boat need lay idle during navigable seasons.

Pierre was going into his sixth year now as owner of the Gregoire Line, and he had done very well indeed. The *Redwing* was his fourth boat, and he had already begun casting about trying to find another to buy, and was also weighing the advantages of building a new one. For the present when in St. Louis he was living at the Southern Hotel, which was not too far from his office, a hotel where many of his clients stopped on their stay in port.

Pierre had hired an excellent accounting clerk. He labored at his desk hours daily adding long columns of figures which eventually turned into banknotes. He also took care of orders and requests which came in by mail on the stage and by other steamboats. From the first the *Redwing* was popular. It was a fast boat to begin with, and it was known as a safe one. Reports of steamboat disasters were swelling the newspapers these days, and a boat with as excellent a reputation as the *Redwing* was in demand. Besides this, Pierre, employed only the best of cooks and the cuisine was considered excellent. His prices were high enough to be prohibitive to the immigrant trade and to cater mostly to the wealthier Southern gentlemen and their ladies who were in gala and lavish spending moods.

A hint of an early fall was in the air, and the goldenrod had started showing their yellow heads along the distant roadsides which led down to private landings along the water's edge. Black-eyed Susans sprang up in profusion almost overnight to bloom for the ecstasy of bumblebees and purple asters covered the grazing meadows. Cotton fields were white and stretched for miles along the banks above the levees. The morning was perfect. Pierre stood by the rail long after he should have been at his table for his usual early lunch.

"How do you do, Mr. Gregoire." A soft feminine voice brought him back to the present.

Turning, Pierre saw in surprise that the girl was Antoinette Reaves.

"Good morning! I did not know you were on board the *Redwing*, Miss Reaves, or I should have come at once to welcome you. Is everything satisfactory in your cabin?"

He found her more beautiful than he had remembered. On first glance, he saw that she had matured a little, and the challenging look she had worn when he met her six years ago had settled into quietness. The roving quest for gaiety seemed gone. He remembered that she had chatted easily of life on her father's estate at Vicksburg and of parties at other homes of the South's wealthiest families. But the breathlessness seemed to have flown. She was a charming young lady, frankly pleased to find an old acquaintance.

"Oh, yes," she was answering, "everything is quite nice. We didn't know until last night that you are the *Redwing*'s master. Father could hardly wait to see you, but he had to meet with one of his old friends in the saloon just now. He's most anxious to have a chat with you to see how you have fared through all these years. He said for me to be sure to give you his regards. He often speaks of you."

Pleased that the colonel should be so cordial to him after all this time, Pierre smiled and said, "That's kind of him, indeed. You may be sure that I've not forgotten the colonel's thoughtfulness in helping me get started in shipping. But I mustn't keep you standing, Miss Reaves. Would you like a chair on deck?"

She came over to the rail and stood so close that Pierre could see the clear whites of her eyes which were slightly tinged with the reflection of blue. Her lashes were unbelievably long and golden. Her hair was the same bright aura he remembered, a gold that caught the sunlight and stole its radiance to embellish its own. Curls caught up at the back followed the perfect swirling shaping of her head and the front waves dipped into a swirling pompadour.

They stood silent, watching the water and the scenery along the river banks. Pierre saw Toinette shiver a little and asked, "Are you too cool?"

"Not at all," she answered. She was not cool at all. She was frightened because after all these years she had found the man — the only other man besides Tom — who she could love. She was not proud of all that she was thinking. Tom was a substitute for the man she might have had. A flash of the old childishness came back in her defensive thought: It's not fair. I promised to marry Tom because I thought I'd never see Pierre Gregoire again. She was trembling and thought that Pierre would see. With an effort she said, "Shall we find shade? I'm afraid the sun will give me freckles!"

She put her hand through Pierre's arm and motioned toward some chairs placed forward. "There's so much to talk about. I want to hear all about you."

"It's lunchtime. Would you care to join me at my table?" As he spoke, Pierre remembered his timidity and confusion at their first meeting. A picture of the elegant dining room at the Natchez House came back to him. He had eaten in much finer places in these past few years but that had been his initiation to elegant dining. It was almost strange that he should now feel so at ease with Miss Reaves.

"Oh, yes, I'd love to. I'm terribly hungry!"

But when they had been served, it seemed that Toinette's appetite had flown with their conversation, for she toyed with her fork, pushing aside bits of delicately brown fried chicken, and making only a pretense of eating.

"So now you own the *Fresco*, two small freighters, and the *Redwing*!" She gave him her brightest smile. Remember, we told you that you'd be successful. I knew you could do it!"

"Your father gave me the first opportunity when he let me buy the *Fresco*. I'm very grateful to him for that. I might still be only a pilot if that chance hadn't been given me."

"You earned your opportunity that

night in Natchez. Papa might have been killed. Tell me more about yourself, and I want to hear about St. Louis. I've always wanted to go and stay a month or two there and really get acquainted, but Papa prefers New Orleans." She sighed as though she had found New Orleans dreary.

"My fiancé spent a few days there recently and then he went on east. Perhaps you know the Sauciers at Ginger Blue whom he visited? Tom is an old friend of Gabriella Saucier's. She used to be Gabriella Darby before she married Lewis Danforth." She stopped short, as though she realized that she was talking too much. He did know them, she could tell before he answered her.

"Yes. I've met them, I knew Mrs. Danforth before her marriage to Llewellyn Saucier. She is a friend of my brother, Dr. Sydney Gregoire."

"Tell me about Mrs. Saucier," she said. "I've always wanted to meet her, and Tom has promised me that some day I shall. She is a woman of the world, very smart, and a wonderful hostess, I've heard. Especially since she has all of that money to spend. Tom said once that she was the most interesting person he had ever known — until he met me," she added quickly, and blushed. "Of course, he just said that, for there's never been anything very interesting about me. Do tell me about her. Is she very beautiful?"

She was watching him closely, he knew, and he hastened to answer, because he realized that he might take time to analyze Gabriella's beauty. "Yes and no," he said. "She holds a sort of strange fascination for most people." Yes, even me, he added to himself. "You can't make that definite, for I truly don't know how you measure beauty. She is — "

"Yes, go on!"

He shrugged helplessly. "I can't describe her. Slender, yet she's not too thin. I can't even tell you the color of her eyes, and that may seem strange to you, for one notices them. They have a tiny slant at the corners, giving her a rather foreign look. Her skin is a sort of golden tan. I'd say her eyes are green." They must be green; he remembered that she had a habit of wearing green and it seemed to him that it reflected the color of her eyes.

"Well! For a man who couldn't remember just how she looked, you do rather well in describing her. Yes, I know now that I'd like to meet her. Tom had an invitation to go there in August, but we were to be married early this month. Then something came up, and luckily we had not sent out the invitations, and I told him to go ahead East. We will set a new date when he returns." She wanted to let Pierre know at once that she was going to be married to Tom.

"Congratulations, Miss Reaves. I wish you the greatest happiness. What is your fiancé's other name?"

She started. "I do rattle on," she said ruefully. "Papa sometimes tells me I'm not even coherent. Tom Benson — have you met him?"

"No, I regret to say that I have not. Won't you have something more? I'm afraid that you've not eaten very much."

"Thank you, no." She was glad that she had asked him about Gabriella. Gabriella should no longer worry her since her marriage to Saucier, yet there was always something rather queer in Tom's voice when her name was mentioned. He semed to want to avoid speaking of her, and Toinette often wondered if they had been engaged long ago. She might never have known of Gabriella at all, except for a mutual friend who had chided both her father and Tom about Gabriella in the same breath. She remembered so well how her father had tried to brush the teasing aside, but Mr. Hamilton had kept at them until Tom broke out in a frenzy of swearing. She had carefully refrained from mentioning Mrs. Saucier to Tom until more than a week later, and in the meantime she had a chance to ask her father about Gabriella. Tom still tried to avoid the discussion, and Toinette was left with the feeling that there had been something serious between him and Gabriella. But St. Louis was a long way from Vicksburg, and it had been a long, long time ago, anyway.

Pierre recalled her to the present by saying, "if you'll permit, I'll take you back to your deck. It's time for me to go on duty. I spell the pilot on this return trip."

"Oh, of course. But it won't be

necessary for you to go with me." She rose and smiled at him, and Pierre almost caught his breath. She *was* beautiful. He wondered why he had not seen earlier that she had lost none of her breathtaking loveliness.

He did not realize that just talking with him had brought back the radiance to her. The coquettishness which she had thrust aside when she became affianced to Tom was challenging her now to be used as a natural asset. She held out her slender white fingers, and he saw how pretty her hand was in its white lace half-fingered mitt. Their glances met and she held his eyes for a moment. He stammered and blushed, but she was coolly poised despite the tumult within her.

"I'll see you late, Mr. Gregoire," she said, and it was like a promise.

Toinette walked back to her cabin, her long skirts swishing against the stiff petticoats underneath. She knew that Pierre was watching her and was glad that she had put on one of her prettiest dresses.

Darn Tom for going east, she thought.

It's almost like being left waiting at the church. If anything happens to our marriage, it will be his fault. This could have been our honeymoon if he hadn't allowed himself to be caught up in this silly old business trip!

She scowled. Tom's letter had been a little stiff, she remembered. And it was disappointing not even to be able to talk with him before he left. He had simply said that he had suddenly found it necessary to go to New York instead of coming straight back to Vicksburg. She had cried half the night. She supposed that was one reason her father had planned this trip. She tossed her head. They would not arrive in St. Louis for more than four full days, perhaps longer, since the river was high and navigation would naturally be slower. This was Monday and she had almost a week to be with Pierre Gregoire. The steamboat was isolated, a world in itself.

She knew there were aboard the usual planters from the South, a few government officials, some manufacturers, sightseeing Easterners, grocers from the Middle West, and growers from the

West who had come to market their produce and whose wallets were well padded with banknotes.

Toinette felt restless and turned from her cabin door without entering and went back on deck. She heard the Negro roustabouts, who had just had a hearty dinner, 'patting juby,' slapping their knees and clapping time. One of them had a very good voice and she could hear the words:

"*Oh, Adam he was de fust built man,*
*Dat's just what de Good Book say;*
*And Eve come next! Den sin began,*
*Dat's just what de Good Book say.*
*Eve bit de apple right in two,*
*A wicket thing fo' Eve to do;*
*Yes, dat's what de Good Book say.*"

"Fine thing, puss, for you to be listenin' to a bunch of black roustabouts." Colonel Reaves came up beside her.

"Oh, hello, Papa. All through with your meeting? Guess who I took my lunch with."

His big eyes twinkled. "That's easy,

daughter. A certain young steamboat owner, name o' Gregoire."

*"Dere was a man, his name was*
  *Lot,*
*Dat's just what de Good Book say,*
*An' he hab a wife an' daughter*
  *got,*
*Dat's just what de Good Book say.*
*His wife she balk an' make a halt,*
*An' de Lord he turn her into salt;*
*Oh! Dat's what de Good Book say."*

"Listen!" She was laughing openly. "Oh, Papa, isn't it wonderful that we came? I wouldn't have missed this trip for anything!"

He looked at her sharply. Where was the subdued young lady of day before yesterday? She was looking even prettier than she had last night when they were waiting for sailing time. He leaned against the rail beside her and they listened to the warm voices of the black men.

*"Oh, Cottonhook Jim, come pat yo'*
  *time,*

*Oh, Sandbar Joe, come shake yo'*
  *heel,*
*Oh, Yallerback Bill, come shout yo'*
  *rhyme,*
*Ontwill we make her tremble to*
  *de keel,*
*Oh, shuffle out and cut an' walk*
  *aroun'.*
*De coon in de holler an' de corn in*
  *de' grown',*
*An' possum fat an' taters and Betsy*
  *Brown,*
*Twell eben de captain j'ines de*
  *reel.*

*Backstep, frontstep, set 'em down*
  *agin,*
*Sachez to de left and swing to de*
  *right . . . "*

"Come along, or you'll be cuttin' capers yourself directly." The colonel moved his daughter along with him. "Don't you think it's time for you to take a little cat nap so you'll be looking your prettiest tonight?"

"Oh, don't make me go in yet, Papa! It's such a beautiful day."

He laughed, his laughter plainly indicating how well he knew she could wind him about her little finger and do exactly as she pleased. She always had, she always would.

"Tell me, Papa, how much money will the *Redwing* actually make on this trip?"

The colonel stared at her in amazement. He chuckled. "So that's how the wind blows, worrying about the finances of young Gregoire! Well, daughter, I don't think it's a female's place to worry about figures, but it's an interesting fact, nonetheless, that these blasted boats practically pay for themselves in their first month. Let's see now, the *Redwing*'s a right handsome boat, probably cost your Gregoire a cool forty thousand. She's a good stern-wheeler, about two hundred feet long, thirty in the beam and with five foot in the hold. I'd say about two hundred tons measurement, but would carry about three hundred tons of freight. There's about a hundred and fifty passengers in the cabins and a hundred on deck. Well, for the round trip, I'd figure he'll take in twenty thousand dollars."

"Why, that's wonderful, Papa. He'll be as rich as Croesus!"

"Well, he has expenses, you know, but I venture to say he'll clear something like fifty thousand a month."

"That's a lot of money, isn't it, Papa! Even to you, it's a lot, isn't it?"

"Of course, puss. Now let's forget all about the financial situation of our friend, and you run along and get that nap."

"Very well, Papa."

So Pierre would be rich some day. Richer than Tom Benson — not that that would make any difference to her! Toinette undressed and got into bed in her cabin.

There was a perfectly marvelous brass band on board the boat. She had overheard some of the young men talking this morning as they came on board. Ned Kenall's cornet was known the country over, and it could make any boat popular. She wondered if she could get Pierre to ask her to dance.

She couldn't sleep. She kept thinking about Pierre. She knew she mustn't think about him; she should concentrate on Tom Benson. She was rebellious against her conscience and admitted to herself that she was fighting a losing battle with it. She turned on her pillow. The embroidered rosebuds felt rough again her ear, and restlessly she turned the pillow over. She sat up and looked about her. More ornate than their own comfortable parlor back home, the cabins were bewilderingly beautiful. The wooden filigrees stretched down the aisle outside in the little hallway in a tapering vista illuminated by cut-glass chandeliers. There were soft oil paintings on every stateroom door, and every carpet was thick and lush underfoot.

She closed her eyes again and presently she slept.

# 15

**P**IERRE was at the wheel in the pilot house. The current had shifted old sandbars in the night, and it was sheer madness to get out of the deeper channel. The leadsman was on constant duty. Pierre heard his call as he measured the depth. The *Redwing* stopped only long enough at the next landing to take on more wood from the great pile on the wharf, and to unload some barrels of molasses. Then they were off again, followed by the cries of onlookers, who were always at the docks to see them cast off.

Pierre tried to keep his mind on his task. As fast as a vision of Toinette appeared, he substituted the glossy surface of the river and found to his dismay that *that* changed into Charmian Saucier's image. It was most disconcerting when the river was as treacherous as it was today. He filled his pipe, holding the wheel in place with his feet while his hands were occupied. It had been a busy month for him. Tobacco warehouses were bursting with produce, and cotton stood boat-high on the piers waiting for transportation. He had not spent more time than just overnight in St. Louis since he had seen Charmian last. He would almost welcome the idle season this year, although he knew that much of his time would be spent in the boatyards.

He was planning on staying in St. Louis until the middle of next week and he hoped to see Charmian. His friend, young Father Dennis Carmichael, and he would try to get their committee together while he was in town. That wasn't merely a pretext for seeing Charmian, he told himself, but it would give him the opportunity to ask her permission to call.

The pilot returned on duty at four and Pierre was relieved to give him the wheel. "I'll take it again this evening," he said as he left.

"The old man's on a rampage all right. Not but what I've already given him his t'baccy."

"I'll throw him some for good measure,"

Pierre said. It wasn't that he believed a word of the old legend, but he walked to the rail and, grinning to himself, took out his worn leather pouch, lifted out a good portion of tobacco and dropped it down into the water. He waved a hand at the pilot and turned toward his cabin. When he was graduated from stevedore to cub pilot, he had heard the tales of many a pilot as they sat around the tavern tables. His first lessons had been hard ones.

Yes, he knew the river and he knew the river man's life, from cabin boy to roustabout, from pilot to owner, because he had lived the life of each, and the experience had given him an uncanny knowledge of how to handle his crew.

He felt uneasy about Miss Reaves. She's a dangerous little coquette, he thought as he shaved that evening. His dark beard always sprang out during the course of a few hours, so that to keep his face clean-shaven, he shaved twice daily. It was irksome to keep up the appearance he had lately maintained as owner of the shipping line. Sometimes he thought he had been happier as a pilot with a stubby beard and a good book in his hand after a long day at the wheel.

He took his time about dressing, selecting a new blue satin stock from the last he had purchased in New Orleans. Almost a fop as far as fashion goes, he thought as he eyed himself critically in his mirror. His lean waist was emphasized not only by the cut of his trousers, but also by the striped waistcoat which was nipped in sharply just below his ribs. His black hair was brushed with a few drops of perfumed oil and glistened with a luster akin to the high polish on his boots. They were high-heeled and made him appear taller than he actually was. His shadow bowed and scraped as he quirked his lips in an oddly humorous fashion and bent sharply, dramatically, as if he were at the French court.

"Yes," he told his reflection, "she is a little coquette." Just as though his summing up of Toinette's actions had never been interrupted at all.

Pierre made a last critical scrutiny of himself from every angle and then went to the dining room of the *Redwing*.

"Ask Colonel Reaves and his daughter if they will be good enough to come to my table," he directed one of the waiters.

It was a few minutes before they appeared, although the gong had rung its warning much earlier. Pierre saw the interest with which the girl and her father were watched as they crossed the room. She had a fragile, ethereal look, her sheer white dress seeming almost to float away from her slender body, yet clinging at her tiny waist and hips, and daringly exposing her rounded white shoulders and the white slender column of her throat from chin to her full, high bosom. Colonel Reaves, impeccably groomed, was wearing one of his inevitable white suits.

They stood for a moment and the waiter approached them and gave Pierre's message to the colonel. His rotund face brightened and he nodded a friendly greeting to his host from the doorway.

Pierre rose and held out his hand to them. "Good evening, Colonel and Miss Reaves. It's kind of you to join me."

"Not at all, my lad, the pleasure is ours entirely. I've been wanting to see you, my boy, ever since you bought the old boat.

You're looking happy and prosperous."

"Thanks to you, Colonel Reaves, may I say without smugness, I am both happy and prosperous."

"It's a great time. Nothing finer than owning a growing shipping line on the Mississippi." The colonel folded his large hands on his rotund stomach and looked from Pierre to his daughter. The little minx was sly tonight, looking downright demure in that disgracefully low-cut dress of hers. "Glad we came aboard the *Redwing*, Gregoire. If we find ourselves happily situated at the Planters' House, we may spend several days there. My daughter has begged me for years to spend a holiday at St. Louis."

"I'm so happy that we decided to come," Toinette contributed. She sank into silence. She had braced herself not to chatter on as she had this morning to Pierre. But it was a strange thing; being with Pierre made her feel voluble, as though she wanted to talk and wanted him to talk, also, telling her all of his life story, his past and his dreams of the future.

Their supper was deliciously cooked.

The dining room emptied slowly as though everyone were reluctant to depart from the pleasant atmosphere. The colonel offered a long black cigar to Pierre, who caught the warm, mellow tobacco smell which permeated the drawing rooms of prosperous homes and lobbies of good hostelries.

"Please go ahead and smoke," Toinette said as Pierre hesitated and made a move to put the cigar away in a breast pocket.

Pierre thanked her and the two men puffed away. The colonel deliberately took out his cumbersome gold watch and looked at it.

"Now Papa," said Toinette,.

"Now, daughter," countered her father. "You know very well that I would be most unhappy if I had to do without my evening game. If you children will have the kindness to excuse me, I'll be on my way."

"Of course, sir."

"That is, if you're free to take my daughter back to her cabin when she's ready to go — or do you have to take the wheel?"

"Not until midnight, sir. We can go to the saloon and listen to Ned Kendall. His band is to furnish music for the evening."

"Well, puss, I know you're in good hands," Toinette's father said comfortably, knowing her protest was not even half-hearted.

"Good-luck, Papa," Toinette called after his retreating figure. "He's crosser than a bear if he doesn't get to play cards every evening." She couldn't let Pierre know that it had all been prearranged before they left their rooms, although it was against her father's better judgment to leave her and Pierre together.

Toinette and Pierre lingered on deck a few minutes before going to listen to the band. They were on their way to the saloon when a low cry halted their footsteps.

"What was that?" Toinette asked.

A stateroom door burst open and a Negro woman rushed out. From the light above her they saw a long bloody streak across her dark cheek. A woman's angry voice cried, "I'll kill you the next time, you black thief!"

Pierre reached out a hand to stop the girl and she wrenched away from him. "She done lost it, suh. Allays losin' dat ring, suh, and I's to blame she say to Marse."

The woman came out of the room and, walking up to the Negress, raised her hand and scratched the other cheek. "Lying again? Won't you ever learn? Go below to your stinking pallet!"

She turned cold eyes upon Pierre. "I'll thank you not to interfere! Slaves are getting out of hand what with you Northerners taking sides." She turned and went back into her room, closing her door with a bang.

Pierre's face whitened. He turned to Toinette. "The injustice of it! That servant was telling the truth."

"Yes," agreed Toinette, "the woman was lying. But," she shrugged her shoulders, "there's nothing to be done about it."

"I'm not so sure," said Pierre, his voice tight. His hands clenched into fists and he stood looking after the retreating back of the Negress, whose drooping shoulders expressed despair.

The evening was ruined for Toinette. She could not recapture their earlier gaiety. Pierre sat silently listening to Ned Kendall, not hearing the music, seeing only the blood on the Negress' cheek, hearing her low cry.

# 16

INDIAN summer lay upon the land. A blue haze lingered across open distances, thin fog rose from the river, and the faint snap of a light frost had painted the sumac and smaller foliage in vivid tones. The air seemed suspended as if it were waiting. Summer was gone and fall was coming fast, but the earth was in a reluctant period of abatement.

The Reaves, father and daughter, stayed on at the Planters' House. The colonel had found companionable friends and he and Toinette had been introduced by the Sauciers to the elite of St. Louis. Toinette was one of the few new girls of the current season and was besieged with invitations. She accepted all of them, hoping to find Pierre at every entertainment which she attended, and feeling keenly disappointed if she did not. She had written Tom Benson of their prolonged visit in St. Louis and hinted that she was having a breathlessly wonderful time. He was gone east longer than he had intended, and by way of punishment Toinette deliberately postponed their marriage until spring.

"But daughter, you mustn't treat Tom this way," protested the colonel.

"Tom treated first, Papa."

"But that was business, my dear. You mustn't confuse the need of making a living with pleasure."

"It has been my observation that Tom confuses the two," Toinette said placidly, dismissing the feeling of guilt which struck only when her father was reminding her of it.

But Colonel Reaves was upset. What had begun as a simple flirtation seemed to gain serious proportions as time went on. When young Gregoire's boat was gone on a trip, Toinette was moody and unhappy. And on the day it docked, she made certain that her father and she, with Jamaica seated beside the driver of the hired rig, were on hand to greet him at the wharf. The colonel borrowed two of the Ginger Blue slaves whom Gabriella had graciously turned over for the duration of their stay at the Planters'

House. The Reaves went everywhere and became among the most welcomed guests in the city, for they were generous with their own hospitality, which took the form of supper parties and picnics.

Toinette was aware of Gabriella studying her several times on the occasion of their third visit to Ginger Blue. It was after dinner and the guests had moved from the dining room into the large front parlor. Gabriella caught Toinette's inquiring look, and realized that she had been staring at the girl Tom was going to marry.

She turned hastily to the colonel. "It's delightful that you and Toinette came to St. Louis, Colonel. Why do you have to be stuffy and go back to Vicksburg, when you know very well nothing's there which won't keep?"

"Such charming people as you, my dear," the colonel answered gallantly, "are making it hard even to think of going back."

"Then why think?"

"It seems best to return home for the winter."

"You would find St. Louis most

delightful this season. Isn't that true, Llewellyn?"

"Yes — yes, of course, Gabriella. Colonel Reaves and his charming daughter would be most happily appreciated by us as well as by our friends. The girls are getting along famously, don't you think?"

His eyes roved to Charmian and Toinette, sitting side by side on the rosewood love seat by the fireplace. Blue had lit the logs only a moment before they left the dining table, and they were burning merrily, sending out cracking staccato pops of the dry wood. Saucier was glad that they had asked no one besides the Reaves tonight, because they had been surrounded by such numbers of guests ever since the renovation of the house was completed.

He let his glance linger on Charmian now and then. She looked happier than during the late summer. He had not been able to understand why she seemed willing to settle into their plans so readily after her outburst of rebellion in going unchaperoned with young Gregoire to Montesano Place.

Saucier understood that Father Carmichael had formed some kind of welfare committee and that Charmian was an important member. It relieved him to know that she was no longer alone in her work. As long as it had the backing of business firms and St. Mark's Cathedral, then it must be worthy of his approval. His eyes fell upon his wife again.

Gabriella, only ten years older than his own daughter, had seemed to bloom again after their marriage. She reveled in the life they had been leading, although he had found it extremely tiring. Gabriella was a charming hostess. She was beautiful to begin with — a strange, exotic beauty — an important asset in a woman, in Saucier's opinion. It was different from Marie Louise's Madonna-like loveliness. He was beginning to find it easier to let himself think of the contrast between his first wife and his second. In the beginning of his marriage with Gabriella, he had let his generous indulgence overrule his good taste, not only in entertaining but in his mode of living. The past two months had opened his eyes to a number of things.

Gabriella, unless she had her own way about everything, would sulk for days at a time. It seemed easier and pleasanter to be agreeable about all of her wishes, whether they were trivial or important.

There was sharp tension in the air between the two women, his daughter and Gabriella. But since Charmian had met Antoinette Reaves, she seemed happier at home and was more considerate than usual to his guests.

There was an exciting week ahead. The fall horse show would be in full swing. The show tomorrow afternoon was one reason why Gabriella was content to be quieter than usual, for she was driving Blue Whippet and Blue Bonnet in the new carryall bought expressly for her by Saucier. The horses were well trained and Gabriella took great delight in them. She loved the exhilaration of driving the beautiful pure-breds in the show; it was something she had looked forward to doing ever since becoming Mrs. Llewellyn Saucier. The Ginger Blue stables were well known even before she had encouraged Saucier to build them up in the past two years.

Tonight she was terrifically bored. If Sydney Gregoire would only get back to town in time for the horse show this week, it would be worth all of this fuming around. Tom Benson should be here looking after his fiancée, although she was glad that Toinette had postponed the wedding. Gabriella had been thinking about Tom all day.

Did he think that she would really let him go after he had married Toinette? Their last good-bye was not good-bye at all. Although she had had just a stiff note from him after he went East, she knew that she was deeply imbedded in his mind. Why else would he have found it necessary to go East instead of going back to Vicksburg and marrying Toinette? The way men try to fool themselves! Was it his conscience? Or was he just not quite ready to give up his freedom?

"I'm simply dying to see your new riding habit, Mrs. Saucier."

"Call me Gabriella." She smiled warmly at Toinette. "Well, my dear, you shall see it tomorrow. It's a beautiful shade of green. Get last month's copy of Godey's and show her the pattern, Charmian dear."

"Charmian obediently sorted through Gabriella's magazines and turned the pages. She glanced up sharply. Someone was coming up the drive. She could hear one of the hounds tuning up.

"Someone's coming." Saucier stood up and then, as if to show he was not curious, he went over and stirred the logs.

They heard Blue's voice outside and then a tap on the front door. Florry's voice, low and musical, said, "Oh, come right in, Dr. Gregoire. Pleased to take your hat and I'll tell the mistress you're here."

Gabriella rose and then, as an afterthought, she sat down again and waited for Florry to announce the caller.

*Doctor* Gregoire? Toinette waited expectantly. He came in and she almost gasped. The living image of Pierre! There's practically no difference except that Pierre has such a clean, clear-cut expression, she thought. Dr. Gregoire wore his clothes dashingly, and very beautifully tailored clothes they were.

He was a little more slender, a little more taut and, all in all, a bit more the polished gentleman than his twin brother.

Gabriella was rising now and greeting him, and Saucier and the doctor shook hands. "Did you have a pleasant trip, Dr. Gregoire?"

"Yes, thank you. You've got a dog with a bad temper, sir." He bent down and rubbed his shin. "Almost broke the skin through these boots."

"I'll tie him up," said Saucier. He was not glad to see Dr. Gregoire. He did not particularly care for him, although Gabriella seemed to enjoy him. "I want you to meet our friends from Vicksburg," he said, after Sydney had bowed and smiled at Charmian. "Miss Reaves and her father, Colonel Reaves."

Sydney's eyes lit as he looked at Toinette. He gave her a swift, intimately searching glance and a flush mounted her cheeks and her eyes closed in confusion. He shook hands with her father and took the chair offered him after a moment of standing by the fireside. The chair was next to the sofa where the two girls were sitting and could not be moved without being obvious, Gabriella saw with annoyance.

Charmian, dear, will you please ask Florry to bring some chocolate," she asked.

"Please don't bother," said Gregoire.

"It won't be any trouble," Charmian said hastily. "I'll go call Florry." She was out of the room, glad to escape for a moment. Sydney was so like his brother in appearance, and yet they were not alike in any other way. Seeing him made her think of Pierre.

She paused in the darkness of the dining room and leaned her head against the door casing. Her hands reached out and felt the smooth soft surface as she stood against the wall. She remembered feeling Pierre's arms about her, the hard surface of his jacket, the faint smell of tobacco, the brush of his hair against her forehead, the feel of his lips against hers. Her heart began to pound. "Pierre." She whispered the word. "Oh, Pierre!"

Bitterness assailed her as she went to the kitchen. He should have had the privilege of coming and sitting in her parlor and courting her like any other young man. But she had not dared as yet give Pierre permission to call upon her. He had been almost angry with her the last time he had seen her.

"But I don't have young men callers, Mr. Gregoire."

"Not even Dennard Manley?"

"He's my father's business associate." She could have added, Pinky is nothing to me, absolutely nothing.

She found that Sabetha had gone, but Florry was setting out the thin chocolate cups in anticipation. As long as Florry had the good will of the new mistress at Ginger Blue, she need have no fear for her position. Since early fall, she had been occupying a small room in the house and was no longer required to keep a cabin.

"Oh, that's fine, Florry. Miss Gabriella wants chocolate served, and it would be nice to cut the white cake and put some of the cookies on a tray, too."

Florry nodded. "I thought she'd like some of the preserved ginger and candied peel." Florry, trim and neat, expertly ran a thin silver blade through the thick white frosting of the layer cake. "That young doctor is certainly a purty man." Her lowered eyes stayed on her work. "He's the spittin' image of that brother. Take two peas in a pod and you've got the same thing."

"Not quite, Florry. They're not exactly alike."

"I wouldn't turn around for the difference."

I would, Charmian said to herself. I certainly would. "As soon as it's ready, bring the tray in, Florry."

"I don't see how that colonel man can eat any more. I don't recollect ever seein' any man enjoy his supper more than him."

Charmian went back to the parlor. Gabriella had changed places with her, and she quietly took the chair formerly occupied by her father's wife. Toinette, Gabriella and the doctor were engaged in a lively discussion of coming social events. The colonel and Saucier were talking about the cotton crop and river transportation.

"Mark my words, Saucier, the steam

locomotive will some day replace the river freighter."

"Not a chance in the next fifteen years."

"I don't mind paying freight rates for my cotton, but you shipping men are really cleaning up. I heard that the *Peter Marken* made seventy thousand on her last trip."

"I don't believe it."

The colonel shrugged. "Well, you ought to know."

"There's a few boats earning as much as fifty thousand a trip, but seventy thousand's a lot of money."

"Yes, I know. But I heard from a reliable source that the *Peter Marken* made seventy thousand, and I'd like to make a bet with you."

Saucier laughed. "Gambling's in your blood, Colonel. I'll take that bet. I know the master. He used to operate one of Manley's boats. What are the stakes?"

"You'll haul one load of my cotton to market next season without charge. Or if I'm wrong, you can have that load of cotton."

"Done," said Saucier.

The room had grown quiet. There was a little quirk of smugness around each man's mouth and Charmian smiled to herself to note how alike they looked.

"We'll be the witnesses," said Dr. Gregoire.

The two older men broke into laughter and Gabriella stood up quickly. "Here's some refreshments. The table over here, Florry."

"My brother's not so dull," said the doctor. "I thought I'd make a better living in medicine. But they tell me that even a good pilot can take in as much as seventy-five dollars a day for some of these trips. Actually, I think that's too much to pay a man for piloting a boat. And, since he owns his own boats, my brother's getting rich. The charges are too high!"

"You're wrong about that, Doctor," Saucier said. "The life of a boat is short, and the season is short. The hazards of navigation are high; if you knew about the sinkings and the burnings on the Mississippi from St. Louis to New Orleans, you wouldn't talk like that. A pilot has a boat one day and a good cargo of freight, money in his pocket, and a dirty pack of cards in his cabin. He's happy when he lands because on his next trip his boilers may blow up. If it doesn't send him to Kingdom Come, he's lucky, but his boat is gone. It may be next season before he gets another berth."

"Llewellyn!"

"I beg your pardon, my dear. I didn't mean to bore the guests."

"Not at all, my dear sir," said Dr. Gregoire. "Boats and the river should be of interest to all of us. We can't talk about horses and clothes all of the time." I'll pay for that, thought Sydney.

"Nor pink pills," murmured Gabriella.

"Right on the bull's eye, Gabe," Sydney whispered.

"Naturally. Will you have some chocolate, Colonel Reaves?"

"No, thank you, Miss Gabriella. Although I do think it looks enticing in that thin cup and served by your white hands."

"Thank you, Colonel. You are a gallant gentleman." *But your stomach sticks out horribly in that lurid waistcoat.* "You'd better change your mind, Toinette."

"No. I couldn't possibly eat another bite, thank you."

"Here, here! Am I to eat all alone?" Sydney turned to Charmian. "How about you, Miss Saucier? You had a hard day, I know, if you're up to your usual stint in Clabber Alley. By the way, how's the child you helped me deliver?" The room exploded with silence. The colonel's face looked like imminent apoplexy and Saucier coughed.

"I beg your pardon! Truly, I forgot for a moment."

"It's nothing," said Gabriella. "Do have some chocolate, Charmian." *And don't look particularly startled that Sydney should make such a faux pas in this company.*

"Yes, thank you, I'll have some." Charmian stood up to take the cup and Saucier noted that her figure had seemed to fill out a little in the past month. The smooth blue satin clung about her long legs as she moved across the room. She's so like Marie Louise, he said to himself.

"Shall we go to the music room?" Dr.

Sydney murmured to Charmian.

"Why — yes," said Charmian, somewhat surprised. She moved forward across the floor and stepped into the lighted room used as the second parlor.

"I'm glad to be out of there," said Dr. Gregoire, taking out a white handkerchief to wipe his forehead. "Whew! Such a foul one! I assure you I was not thinking."

She smiled a little. He had shocked the colonel, and Toinette's blush had been like fire.

"You're not reproving me, Miss Saucier. Where's your sense of delicacy?"

"Perhaps I lost it when I helped you deliver the baby, Doctor."

"And a good thing, too. Nothing but nonsense, having to be so careful in front of the ladies. Have you seen my brother lately? Is he in town?"

Charmian's heart began to beat hard again. "I saw him last week at a meeting of Father Carmichael's committee. But your brother left on the *Redwing* last Friday out of St. Louis. I don't know whether he's back yet or not."

He glanced at her and saw the little pulse fluttering in her temple, and the pink rising high in her cheeks. He frowned slightly. The girl was in love with his brother!

That's good, the thought struck him. Here I am, letting Pierre get the best of me in everything. He's going to be rich — he'll make more from his boats than I, a doctor, can hope to make. Pierre is the smart one.

"I'll get the chocolate pot," he said, rising abruptly and going to the door of the other room.

"We usually let Florry do the serving," said Gabriella coolly as he reached for the heavy tray.

"It's a pleasure," said Sydney without looking at her.

The other two men were still talking about river trade and Toinette was sitting with the Godey book on her lap, turning the pages. Gabriella sat stiffly uncompromising.

"Have some more chocolate," said Sydney, returning to Charmian. "This is very nice of you to keep me company." He filled her cup again and sauntered over to the pianoforte. With one finger he picked out the tune of 'St. Louis Polka.'

Charmian's heart warmed.

"Finish your chocolate and come play for us. The evening's really sinking into a dreadful lethargy."

Charmian smiled and set down her cup. She stepped into the parlor and asked, "Will you all come in and sing?"

"I can't think of anything I'd like to do less than sing," Gabriella said, forcing gaiety into her voice. "But do go ahead and play." *When Charmian has to be sent to the pianoforte to save the evening for us, it is indeed a pretty out!*

Charmian sat down on the stool and began, her fingers white against the ivory keys. The pianoforte was in a far corner of the room, and the doors obscured the vision of the others in the front parlor. When she had finished the first song, Sydney said, "That was very nice, Miss Saucier, let us have another. Here, this is pretty. I heard Ned Kendall play it last week."

She played the song through twice at his insistence. "Thank you, Miss Saucier." He helped himself to another cup of chocolate while she played 'They Tell Me Thou Art the Favored Guest' and followed with one of her father's favorite hymns.

They went back into the parlor with the others and Charmian saw two red spots on Gabriella's cheeks, danger signals which she had learned to recognize.

Dr. Gregoire left a few minutes later.

"We'll see you tomorrow at the Gallatin farm?" asked Gabriella.

"I wouldn't miss the show," said Sydney. "Goodnight, Miss Reaves. It has been my great pleasure to meet you, and you, too Colonel. Thank you for the refreshments, Gabe, and you, Miss Saucier, for keeping me company." In another moment he was gone and the Reaves were also ready to go.

After they had all left, Saucier said, "I don't like young Gregoire calling you 'Gabe.' It's disrespectful."

"That's a stuffy word to use, Llewellyn, and Syd doesn't mean to be disrespectful. I've known him long enough for him to call me that."

Charmian escaped quickly, for Gabriella's voice had an angry warning note in it. Charmian walked to the staircase and, holding up her blue satin skirt, climbed the steps hurriedly. She paused on the landing and looked down into the parlor. The overhead chandelier cast a bright, hard light on both the Sauciers, etching them clearly. There was tension and strain in their faces and she heard her father say, "Let's go to bed. I find I'm very tired."

"Go ahead. I won't sleep much, I can assure you of that."

"You drive yourself too hard, my dear." He placed a hand on her arm, but she shook it off.

Gabriella did not answer but the look she gave him held scorn and petulancy. Charmian felt a wave of pity for her father. She went up the rest of the stairs very slowly. She stood for a moment just within her door and after her father had gone to his apartments, she crossed the hall and knocked on his door.

"Papa," she said.

His door opened and he saw her standing there.

"Charmian, my daughter." A soft expression lit his face. He stepped out into the carpeted hallway and saw the look in her eyes. "My little girl," he murmured. She held up her lips for his kiss. It was the first in weeks.

He drew her into the sitting room. "Your hands are cold. Let me light the fire."

"No, please don't. You must go to bed and get your rest."

"You'll go to the show tomorrow, Charmian?"

"Yes. Yes, I've planned to go. I think it will be great fun."

"I'm glad you're going, dear. We can be together when Gabriella is showing Whippet."

"That'll be nice. And now I'd better be running along."

He followed her to her own door and said, "Can I get anything for you, Charmian?"

"No, Papa, thank you." She kissed him again. She stood inside the door a long moment. Poor Papa. Poor, poor Papa.

# 17

CHARMIAN awakened once in the night from a dream which continued the scene of the evening before at the pianoforte. In her dream, Sydney Gregoire kissed her and Pierre challenged him to a duel.

"The idiots!" she murmured drowsily as she lay trying to go back to sleep. She was restless the remainder of the night, and finally got up before it was fully light outside.

She put a robe over her gown, brushed her black hair up high over her white forehead, and went downstairs for coffee. As she entered the kitchen, Brigette looked up from her own breakfast spread out on the able.

She was pale and drawn in the lamplight, and Charmian thought with a pang, Brigette is getting old.

"What are you doing down so early, Charmian?"

"I've calls to make before noon and

I might as well get started. I couldn't sleep."

"Anybody'd think you were a female doctor, the way you traipse around lookin' after the sick." Brigette stood up to clear away her dishes.

"Don't bother, Brig, I'll eat right here with you."

Pleased, Brigette smiled and sat down again. She moved the cream pitcher over a little. Sabetha, coming in from the pantry, made haste to set a place for Charmian and to get the coffeepot.

"Why don't you rest a little later in the morning, Brigette? You don't look very well."

"I have to come down and get things started. Your father's been getting out bright and early these past few mornings. I'll be setting his plate in another half-hour. That yellow hussy doesn't show up to work any more until after seven since she's been allowed the run of the house. And Phoebe's flat on her back the last week."

"I'll go see her before I leave this morning."

"You needn't bother," Brigette said

sharply. "We're looking after her, and you don't need to muddy your shoes on that path. Besides, there's nothing much wrong with her."

"I know about it, Brig, so you don't need to pretend with me. Besides, since she's married to Blue now, there's no reason to hide it. Sabetha, fix up a good hot plate for her in about an hour and I'll take it down to their cabin."

"You'll do no such thing, Charmian Saucier! I put my foot down. I put my foot right down, you hear me?"

Brigette stood up, and something in her tone compelled Charmian to stare perplexedly at her. "It's time you started looking after your own affairs, young lady, and keep out of other people's business!"

"Why, Brigette!"

"Don't Brigette me! I'll look after the darkies at Ginger Blue. You run right along to your sick and needy in Battle Row and Clabber Alley, and I'll take care of Ginger Blue."

"Don't be angry, Brigette. I only wanted to do something for Peebee."

"I'll take care of it," Brigette repeated.

"Very well." Charmian was sorely puzzled. Although Brigette had never allowed her to play around the cabins as a child, the Negroes had not lately been forbidden her ministrations when any of them was sick. She said no more but finished her breakfast quickly. Brigette, having put her foot down, left the kitchen. Sabetha moved heavily about the room, setting the black iron spider on the wood stove and starting the sliced ham to frying for Saucier's breakfast.

"May I have some more coffee, Sabetha?"

"Yas'm."

"Sabetha, is Peebee getting along all right?"

Sabetha walked quickly to the hall door and stepped outside to listen for a moment before she answered. "Seems lak she ain't, Miss Ch'meen. She's poorly."

"What appears to be going wrong?"

"Ah think dat woman" — Sabetha rolled her eyes upward — "gave de chile somethin'. She — " Sabetha, frightened, stopped.

"Go on, Sabetha. What do you think? You don't need to be afraid to tell me."

"Don' need to, no. No, Ah don' need to be, but Ah am. Miz Brigette's lak sumpin' gone crazy eve' since she sta't to suspect."

Brigette had not seemed well of late. She was thinner and sharper than usual, but the mere fact that one of the Ginger Blue Negro women was having another baby shouldn't upset her, even if the girl was Phoebe. Charmian shook the sleeve again.

"Ham's gonna bu'n!" Sabetha, ignoring her, went back to the stove and, picking up a fork, turned the meat.

"What does Brigette suspect?"

They heard a heavy step on the back porch and Charmian saw that it was Pascal coming in from the stables. She turned and left the kitchen, her mind still upon Phoebe and Brigette. Poor Peebee. Charmian decided to dress and go to see her, despite the fact that she promised Brigette to leave her to her care. But suppose something awful happened to Peebee? As a child, the pickaninny had tagged at Charmian's heels whenever the opportunity presented itself. Now that they were grown, she was always doing nice things for Charmian, pressing her dresses and ironing rows and rows of ruffles with infinite patience, cheerfulness, and anxiety to please.

Disregarding the danger of running into Brigette, Charmian hastily dressed and, hurrying down the back stairs, went directly to the path leading through the first field, the wood lot, and the row of cabins at the back. Blue's cabin was at the end of the second row, and he was standing beside the door, studying the distant sky. She came up so quietly he seemed startled when she spoke to him.

"I've come to see Phoebe. How is she, Blue?"

He shook his head and she saw that his soft dark eyes were filled with tears. The elongated black face drooped with misery. He stood there in clean, work-worn clothes, twisting his big feet helplessly in the dust. Charmian opened the door and went into the cabin. It was bright with knicknacks that she had given Peebee through the years, and a braided rug lay on the heavy wide flooring, which was spotlessly clean. There was a heavy, sickening smell about the room and Charmian shivered as she crossed to the rough-hewn bed.

Phoebe was unconscious. Charmian felt for her pulse and her face went white at its flickering, slow rate. She called to Blue. "How long has she been like this?"

"Ah don' know, Missy. She seemed restin' easy las' night."

"Go get a horse and ride to town for Dr. Gregoire. Don't waste any time, and don't tell him it's for Phoebe. Tell him I sent you to come at once to Ginger Blue." She was pushing him out toward the path. "Hurry, Blue, hurry!" She ran along, calling after him, "Tell Brig to come down and bring some whiskey. She stood an instant watching his long legs twinkling down the path; then she summoned one of the field hands to build a fire in the fireplace at the end of the room and filled the black kettle on the crane with water to heat. It seemed a long time before Brigette came.

"Young lady, you get right back up to the house," Brigette commanded.

Charmian stared at her, her eyes narrowing, her voice struggling.

"Brigette, if Peebee dies, do you know that you are a murderer? Don't try to get out of this, Brigette. What did you give her? What did you do to her?" She shook the woman's arm.

Brigette's colorless face seemed to shrink. "She won't die," she stated flatly. She stood looking down upon Phoebe. Then, taking a bottle out of the basket, she opened it and forced a little whiskey into the swollen, dried lips.

"If it will put your mind at rest, Charmian," she said wearily, "it wasn't me. It wasn't me who made her take it."

"Then who — " Charmian stopped.

Brigette did not answer.

She was busy with Phoebe, and warned Charmian to keep quiet. "Hush!" Charmian bit her lips and brushed at her eyes.

It was a long time before the doctor came, but they finally heard the horses' hoofs on the wooden culvert across the creek. Charmian knew that Dr. Sydney would be furious at being called for a Negro. Brigette urged her to go back to the house, but Charmian stayed on to

284

help Dr. Gregoire. And in the end, it was the older woman who marveled at the girl, Charmian.

"Will she be all right?"

"Just barely all right," Dr. Gregoire answered. "You caught her just in time, if I see the signs right. She'd have been gone in another couple of hours or so. Yes, she can thank you for saving her life. You know, Miss Saucier, you're not so bad at this business of assisting me. No, not bad at all. What made you call me, though?" He paused. "I'm warning you, don't call me again for a black woman!"

Charmian drew a coin purse out of her dress. "Your pay is just the same, Doctor, as if it had been anyone else at Ginger Blue."

He waved the money aside. "I won't be called out for a black woman, and I'm not taking your money so that you'll think you've made it all right with me."

"You mind your manners. You're speaking to a lady," Brigette said coldly. "Go on to the house, Charmian, and I'll settle this."

"There's nothing to settle. And as far

as Phoebe's concerned, she's as good as you are, Doctor." Charmian turned and went out the cabin door, striding angrily up the path. As an afterthought, she called back to Brigette, "Look after her, won't you Brig, until I get back?"

"I've plenty to do today, as you well know."

Charmian trudged on without answering. She heard the young doctor talking to Blue about getting his horse, and in another moment she began running and cut through the patch of woods so that he could not pass her on the wagon-track road. She didn't want another encounter with him today. He was really unbearably insolent.

Her father was still at his breakfast, she saw through the bay window in the dining room. She went into the house quietly, climbing the outside stairs at the back to the second story and entering through the wing that was seldom used by anyone but servants. She went directly to her room and dressed for the morning, wearing a dark green suit trimmed in rich brown beaver, with muff and hat to match.

She heard Dr. Sydney Gregoire's horse as he went through the drive to get to the main road and she smiled to herself. She wished she might have seen his face if he had realized that she had gone through the woods to avoid him.

A little later, she heard Pascal bring her cart with Whistlejackets to the carriage mount, and she hurried down the front stairs. Saucier, hearing her step, came out into the hall. "Good morning, daughter." He came forward and kissed her and she returned his kiss with warmth. He patted her arm and she reached up her small gloved hand and pulled his face down to kiss him once more.

"I'll be back early, Papa. What time shall we leave for the Gallatin farm?"

"By twelve sharp. It's a beautiful day, and we can take our time in this bright sunshine. You're looking very pretty this morning. By the way," he said sharply, "you've not had any breakfast, have you?"

She laughed at him affectionately. "Hours ago! Simply hours ago!" She patted his arm and hurried toward the door. "Take care of yourself, Papa."

She realized suddenly that her father had lost that look of youth which had always been with him. It had gone so gradually, she supposed, that she had never been aware of the change. Was it Gabriella who had caused it? Or was it partly her own determination to carry on her work despite his protests?

Pascal helped her into the cart and handed her the reins. "It's a beautiful day," she said.

"Yes. It's nice."

"When can we have another big bonfire, Pascal?"

"I'll have Blue rake the leaves on the east terrace today."

Something in his tone caused her to turn back and study him. It didn't seem right for Pascal to be spiritless.

"Are you feeling well, Pascal?" she asked as the wheels began to turn.

"Yes, thank you." He made an attempt at a smile, but there was no spontaneity in it. Oh, well, something between him and Brigette. Brigette's tongue was acid at times, particularly when she was not feeling well. Charmian frowned, remembering their conversation at the breakfast table. What was it Sabetha said after Brigette had gone? *Suspect.* That was it, Brigette suspected something. What on earth was it all about, anyway?

Charmian drove down Compton Hill, and Whistlejackets' hoofs clattered over the cobblestones of a side street as she turned off the main road for the first call. She was going to see Father Carmichael this morning before she went to Battle Row.

Pulling Whistlejackets up short to avoid an approaching carriage, she saw that it was driven by Pierre Gregoire.

He slowed his horse and tipped his hat. "Good morning, Miss Saucier."

"Good morning, Mr. Gregoire." her quiet voice belied the tumult that was playing havoc within her.

"A beautiful day, isn't it?" He wanted to prolong this encounter, and his words sounded inadequate for keeping her.

"Yes, a beautiful day," she agreed, seeing a curious face in the window of the house in front of her. "I love October," she added. Then, in a burst of intuition, "have you been calling on Father Carmichael?"

"Yes." He smiled, and she saw the flash of his white teeth between his red lips. Thank goodness he didn't effect a mustache like Dennard Manley. Pinky *would* want a mustache in spite of the fact that it was so pale that it hardly showed across a ballroom. "Yes," he was saying, "I had a report to make on the new school building plans." He saw faces framed by the window in front of her cart, and hesitated to get down from his carriage and come to speak with her openly. A girl had to be careful to preserve her reputation. Bother the nosy women who lived so close to Father Carmichael!

"I'm going to see him, too, although he's not expecting me."

"I'm sorry, Miss Saucier, but you'll not find him in. He left before we got through. Someone needed him; a death, I believe."

"Then I shall change my plans." Charmian was confused for a moment and Pierre knew that she dared not turn her cart around at this moment or the busybodies in the windows would think she was following him. "I shall see you at the show this afternoon at the Gallatin farm?" She gave a little slap with her reins and Whistlejackets took a step forward.

"Yes, indeed. Good day." he started up his horses and they passed each other on the narrow street, almost brushing their wheels together.

I shall see him this afternoon. Yes, I shall see him again today. The thought kept returning throughout the morning, and she was surprised to find how fast the time flew and that she must hurry back to Ginger Blue to eat lunch and join her father and Gabriella.

Her stepmother was standing out in the hall in front of her room, in starched petticoats and corset cover, talking furiously with Brigette, when Charmian appeared on the landing.

Gabriella caught sight of her and called, "Are you just getting in? We'll be late! Hurry, Brigette, and get everything attended to. Tell Florry we're having company for supper tonight. Charmian, do hurry, child."

"Oh, it won't take me long to dress.

Go ahead with lunch if I'm not down."

"Yes, we will." Gabriella went back into her room, shutting the door with a slam of exasperation.

"Brigette, how's Phoebe? I'm so worried about her."

"She's better. She'll be up in no time at all. Now, dismiss her from your mind and get ready for a bite to eat before you leave this house, young lady."

"I'll be ready before Gabriella," Charmian said.

She undressed and took a quick sponge bath. Brigette or Florry had laid out her new fall suit — dark red, with gray squirrel trim. She put it on, admiring the color, and anxiously peering into her mirror to see if it was as becoming to her as she thought it might be when she selected the material. The crisp air had given sparkle to the depths of her eyes and left her cheeks glowing and high with color, and her hair lay in thick, lustrous waves about her head. She dusted rice powder over her chin and on her forehead, touched a dab of perfume to her ears, and then picked up her new hat. It was olive green, with a dark red feather swirling down the right side of its upturned coachman's brim. She stood in front of the long mirror and turned around in a swift whirl, buttoned her gloves, and hurried to the spiral stairs. Gabriella was still in her room.

Downstairs, Saucier was reading the *Missouri Barnburner*, with a scowl on his face. Papa gets so provoked with that paper, I don't see why he ever reads it! "All ready, Papa?"

Saucier laid the paper aside and stood up, looking at his daughter appreciatively. "I must say that costume becomes you, Charmian. Or," he added with a touch of gallantry, "that you become the costume, my dear."

"Thank you, Papa." She pirouetted about him, as she used to do with a new frock as a child. He caught her and kissed her as she passed him.

He took out his ponderous gold watch and snapped it open in a gesture which indicated it was not the first time he had consulted it recently.

"I can't think what's keeping your moth — Gabriella," he said. "She was down once, and decided not to wear her new green riding habit, but to keep that for tomorrow." He shrugged, then smiled tolerantly, and she could see that the differences of last night had been settled. "Oh, by the way, there's to be company for supper tonight."

Charmian turned to sit down in one of the chairs. "Who's coming? I heard Gabriella telling Brigette there'd be someone, but she didn't say."

"Oh, you'll be pleased. The Reaves again, because Tom Benson arrived this morning."

Charmian's spirits dropped. She was not at all sure that she liked Tom Benson, but if Toinette was going to marry him, she felt that he must have his good points. She frowned, remembering the evening before he and Gabriella had gone riding together on his last visit to Ginger Blue — the scene in the parlor when Gabriella was caressing his cheek.

At that moment Gabriella came downstairs, and they all went in to lunch. Gabriella looked very young this morning. The green dress graced her fine figure. Charmian saw that she had changed her mind a second time, and wondered how much Tom's coming had caused her obvious indecision. Charmian studied her for a moment before she turned her gaze thoughtfully upon her father again. He was very handsome, she thought, with his profile turned to her as he spoke to Florry, who was offering him food from a heavy silver dish.

"Is Pascal ready with the brougham?" Gabriella asked.

"Yes, he's waiting," Charmian answered.

"What was all the commotion down at the cabins this morning?" Gabriella asked. "I heard Blue talking excitedly. He wakened me out of a sound sleep." She helped herself to the ham. "What was it all about? I should think the servants could be more quiet of a morning."

"One of the women was very sick."

"Were you taking care of her?" Saucier asked.

"It was Phoebe, Papa. Yes, I went to see how she was. I sent for the doctor."

"Do you mean Sydney?" Gabriella asked in amazement.

"Yes, it was Dr. Gregoire."

Gabriella laughed. "I'm surprised that he came. Or did he know who was sick?"

Gabriella laid down her fork. "I'll bet you played a trick on him! Come, child, why did you send for him,?"

"Because he could help Phoebe more than old Dr. Callen."

Gabriella laughed shrilly. "I'll bet he was furious."

"He wasn't very pleased, but I really didn't care much."

Saucier said nothing. There was a deep line between his dark brows. He had not forgotten about Dr. Gregoire's calling his wife 'Gabe,' and abruptly he changed the subject to the events of the afternoon. There were several things on his mind, among them the need to go to the boatyards later in the evening to talk with Dennard Manley about plans for the new boat which he was having built during the winter. Gabriella might not like his having business tonight, but with Tom and the Reaves there, she should have enough to entertain her. He pushed aside his plate. His appetite gone again, as it had been so many times of late.

# 18

IT was a rare October day, one of blue sky and beautiful coloring. The sturdy forest trees which had been left standing were bursting in riotous autumn. The brougham rolled swiftly along the streets and was soon out in the country.

Saucier and Gabriella and Charmian were quiet as they rode. Now and then they passed another carriage or trap also headed for the Gallatin farm. It was a gala day, and all of St. Louis' elite seemed to be going to the horse show. Gabriella appeared somewhat nervous as they approached the drive leading to the track. The meadow was littered with picnicking families who were making a real holiday. As the Saucier carriage passed along, they were greeted with cries of welcome. Gabriella's face remained serene, and she disdained more than a slight nod, her tense hands alone showing her uneasiness.

The amphitheater was already beginning to fill when they arrived, and Charmian recognized many of the prominent county families. Christy's Band burst into a lively tune, and faces were wreathed in smiles as latecomers hurried toward the stands.

"It's almost time for the first event, my dear. Shall we go to the paddock? Ryan will have Whippet and Blue Bonnet waiting for you. He says they're in fine fettle for the show."

"Yes. I'm ready."

"Come with us, Charmian."

"I'll go directly to our seats, Papa, if you don't mind."

Saucier nodded hesitantly. Gabriella's pursed lips indicated that she was not in the mood for an argument. Pascal stopped the carriage and let Charmian out and then drove on down to the arena.

Charmian heard a deep voice behind her as she walked toward the first row of seats which had been reserved for the contestants' relatives and friends.

"Good day, Miss Saucier," said Pierre Gregoire.

"Good day, Mr. Gregoire."

"Allow me to help you find a seat," he said eagerly.

"Papa is coming, but thank you so much."

"We've saved places for you, Miss Saucier, to tell you the truth," Gregoire said.

She paused a moment. "Why, that's most thoughtful of you, Mr. Gregoire." She thought, Papa'll be very angry. He'll be very, very angry. I don't care, though. She tossed her head a little and said aloud, "Yes, thank you. I hope there are three seats, because Gabriella will join us after her event."

"The seats are over here by the Reaves. Tom Benson is there, too. He came with me on the *Redwing* from New Orleans." Charmian's eyes followed his glance and she saw Toinette and her father and Tom Benson all watching them. She stiffened at sight of Tom, but seeing the eagerness of Toinette and Colonel Reaves, she stepped forward and Pierre followed.

The band began to play 'Canderbeck's Quickstep' and the entrance bell rang and the first roustabout entered the ring. The next entry was a high-stepping black filly, then two cherry-colored horses entered at a fast trot, pulling a spider-wheeled runabout. Their polished hoofs flashed in the bright sunlight, and one after another the six entries took their places in the circle.

"Oh, Charmian, I'm so glad you're here," said Toinette gaily. "Isn't it a perfectly gorgeous day?" Her blue eyes were deepened with excitement, her golden curls flashed, and a dimple bit in deeply at the corner of her pretty mouth.

The colonel and Tom Benson spoke to Charmian, Tom very politely, and the colonel with beaming cordiality.

Toinette settled herself beside Charmian, unfurling her yellow silk parasol and unrolling long green gloves and laying them in her lap. The clanging of a bell announcing that the gates were about to close cut into their conversation and now all eyes were upon the arena.

Christy's Band struck up 'Blue Juanatian' and the first event began. Charmian exclaimed over a perfectly matched pair of horses, and Toinette said, "My goodness! This reminds me of New Orleans!" The entries whirled around the show ring in almost perfect time, as though they had been trained to the music. They circled the ring several times and then were lined up in front of the judges' stand.

"Which one will win, Mr. Gregoire?" asked Toinette.

"I'd choose the two cherry-colored horses in the spider-wheeled runabout," came his prompt answer.

"I think so, too," said Charmian.

A burst of applause came over the grounds as one of the judges went forward to that contestant. The winner walked his horses around twice and then it was time for the next event. The bell rang out again as the ring was cleared and the murmur of voices grew in the arena. Saucier had not appeared in the amphitheater yet, and Charmian realized that he was doubtless waiting until Gabriella's event was over.

The crowd roared as the first vehicle for the second event started into the show circle. The music was drowned out as last year's favorite driver stood up in the seat and waved his arms in greeting.

"Cocky little devil," said the colonel to Tom.

Not any cockier than Gabriella, I'll venture, said Tom to himself.

The next three entries were beautiful. "I've never seen such handsome horse-flesh anywhere outside the downs at New Orleans," said the colonel. The crowd greeted each of the equipages with a roar of appreciation. Charmian found that she was trembling in expectation for Blue Whippet. Saucier was so proud of his stables.

The ringing of the final bell brought in Gabriella, the last entry. In the smart new trap she sat gaily, holding the lines perfectly. Blue Whippet and his mate, Blue Bonnet, were beautifully matched. They arched their high, proud heads, and the glossy manes fell brightly in a great depth. Ryan, their trainer, sat easily beside Gabriella, holding her rust-colored parasol and the long rust-colored gloves and purse. Now they were all in their places and the bandmaster silenced the musicians. Eight beautifully turned out vehicles and teams. The ringmaster snapped his whip, and the horses struck up a quick pace around the circle. The murmur started up again among the audience but Charmian and her group were silent. The pace went faster and faster, and still kept in perfect unison. The grace of the twinkling legs fascinated Charmian. The judges appeared to be having some trouble in making any kind of decision, for the equipages circled the arena twice more than was customary.

"Walk your horses!" shouted the ringmaster.

They slowed, and he lined them up in front of the stand. Attendants ran forward to loosen checkreins and give the horses a chance to rest a moment before they were expected to go into the final position.

The audience had grown quiet now, but each time a team took its stance, they burst for a moment into respectful applause. Charmian, unaware of her tension, had placed her gloved hand on Pierre's arm, and was leaning forward, intent upon Gabriella, who was obeying the signal to turn in. With queenly poise she turned at the signal and held the two horses at perfect stance. One of the judges was coming forward and the crowd burst into excited cries as he bowed at the waist and held out the ribbon to Gabriella. She gave one triumphant glance towards the stands and took the ribbon. Ryan received the purse and then they swept on around the ring. Charmian relaxed and was aware that her hands was clasped tightly on Pierre's arm and that his big brown hand was completely covering it.

They looked into each other's eyes and she bit her lips to hide the quick smile that appeared for a moment, before she hastily removed her hand.

"I — guess I got excited," she whispered in the rising murmur. Tom and Toinette were talking and Colonel Reaves was engaged in conversation with the man next to him.

The feel of Charmian's hand was still on his arm and Pierre's flesh was quivering from the contact.

"Charmian, I want to see you. May I call? You can't keep putting me off, you know. I must have an answer."

She felt a wave of emotion sweep over her from head to foot and her eyes lowered in confusion.

"Shh!"

"May I call?" he persisted. "May I call tonight?"

"I — I don't know," she said desperately, trying to think what to do. There wasn't any reason under the sun why he shouldn't call, not one. The rest of the present party would be at Ginger Blue tonight for dinner. Wasn't that a perfectly good reason for him to join them?

"If you don't let me call on you openly, as any man might, I'll come anyway and throw rocks at your window," he threatened.

She looked up at him, startled.

His dark eyes were gleaming. "I mean it, Charmian. I'm going to call on you, willy-nilly."

The bell rang in the judges' stand. The next event was about to begin, and Charmian saw that her father and Gabriella were approaching. They had to keep stopping in their progress across the grounds, for everyone was complimenting Gabriella, and her face was bright with pleasure. She caught sight of the Reaves and Tom Benson before her eyes fell on Charmian and Pierre.

"There they are — the Reaves, Llewellyn."

Saucier's gaze found Charmian at once and he nodded briefly to Pierre. His face lost its warm smile only to regain it a moment later as they came on to sit down with the party. Tom Benson greeted them quietly, and his eyes dropped for a moment before the searching, distracting look in Gabriella's. She was bubbling over with spirits now that her event was over, and she sat down beside Tom, leaving Saucier to sit next to Pierre.

"We'll have supper about seven, Llewellyn, if it's all right with you," she said presently.

"That will make me a little late for my meeting, but I think it will do," he said tolerantly. "All coming?"

"Yes, of course," Gabriella said.

"Papa, I'm inviting Mr. Gregoire to join us for dinner," said Charmian.

Saucier looked a little surprised. Always the perfect host, he said, "Fine." There was nothing more to say. Charmian had invited the young man to join the party.

It was a rather awkward situation, but none that couldn't bear working out later. After all, Toinette and the colonel found him an interesting person, and Gabriella seemed rather to like him. Fiddlesticks! he told himself, it's more than that. It's something in Charmian's eyes when she looks at the man that has me worried. He had never gotten completely over his anger at Gregoire's taking her out to Montesano Place.

Charmian sat through the remainder of the events with a warm glow upon her. There were many looks thrown toward them, the three pretty young women, the white-haired colonel, wealthy Llewellyn Saucier, and the two young men, Pierre Gregoire and Tom Benson. The party gave the arena their attention, but Charmian was not thinking of the events entirely. Once she turned her head and caught Dennard Manley staring at her. He gave an embarrassed nod at being caught, and she returned it coolly. He was not alone, she noticed; he also seemed to be in a party.

"Well, it's nearly over," her father said. The last ribbon and purse had been awarded, and some of the lower left stands had begun to empty. The ringmaster shouted for attention to announce the next day's events, applause rang out, and it was time to go.

"How shall we ride?" Gabriella demanded as though she would allow someone else to work it out, although she had the whole thing already planned. "Let me think a moment. Tom, why don't you come along with us, and the Reaves and Charmian can go with Mr. Gregoire."

Tom Benson hesitated. He looked at Toinette for an answer, but she was smiling at something Charmian had said, her eyes fastened on Pierre. The colonel, bless him, Tom thought, stepped forward and said, "Tom can go along with the young folks and I'll go with you, Gabriella."

"What does that make me?" Gabriella pouted her pretty lips.

"A charming young matron, married to the luckiest man in all of Louisiana Territory," said the colonel, lapsing historically in this enthusiasm to be gallant and yet win his own way.

"Come along, my dear," said Llewellyn,

knowing that to hesitate would be to give Gabriella the chance to show her displeasure at being ruled even through the medium of flattery. He looked into her green eyes for a moment and saw her smile harden into the fire of temper. He put his hand through her arm and she fell into step unwillingly beside him. She gave no backward look, and was handed unsmiling into the Saucier carriage.

She offered nothing in the way of conversation and made only one comment on the way back to Ginger Blue, and that, "The dust is unbearable. You wouldn't think this many people could afford to take the day off and go to a horse show."

The colonel chuckled, and Gabriella was so absorbed in her own thoughts that she did not notice. Saucier was busy with his pipe and drawing heavily upon it and he did not answer.

# 19

THE moment the party arrived at Ginger Blue, Gabriella hurried to her room to change. The colonel and Saucier went into the parlor and Florry served them with wine.

"Yes, sir," the colonel said, as though there had not been any interruption in his conversation, "I call that a bang-up fine exhibition of horseflesh. Blast me if I don't wish I was twenty years younger again."

"I'm afraid I've lost my taste for riding or exhibiting. My proper niche seems to be in looking on," said Saucier.

"Excellent wine," said Colonel Reaves, sipping from his glass. "Allow me to compliment you, Saucier. You have a beautiful wife and home. The gods have really smiled upon you."

Saucier hastened to answer, "Yes. Yes, of course." He got up from the love seat and moved restlessly to the broad window looking out onto the sloping terrace. "So you like Ginger Blue. I wish you might have seen the house before it was cluttered up with porches and gingerbread work. It had the simple, elegant lines of the old aristocratic places of the South. You remember the Livingston place at Charleston — the Easton Manor at Natchez? But time changes all things, tastes notwithstanding. Mrs. Saucier prefers the new trend. Here comes the rest of the party. Nice-looking horses young Gregoire drives."

"Strange that those two young men, looking so much alike, could be so different," Reaves mused, holding his glass up to the light and looking appreciatively at the rich color of the wine.

"The young doctor and his brother? Yes. They are different." Saucier's lips tightened. Outwardly, yes, perhaps, but they're the same blood.

"A bit unconventional in his talk," went on Reaves, referring to the slip of the doctor's medical comment of the evening before.

Saucier did not answer. Charmian and Toinette were coming into the reception hall and following close behind them were Tom Benson and Pierre Gregoire. Saucier went forward to meet them. Florry appeared and took their hats and Tom's cane, and the girls went upstairs to Charmian's room to repair the damages of the afternoon to their hair and faces.

Tom took the wine offered him, but Gregoire tactfully refused it. There would be wine served with the meal, of course, and he preferred to drink only that. He looked about him whenever the opportunity presented itself in lulls of the conversation. The chief discussion eddied about the new steam press in the newspaper building, the *St. Louis Daily Union*. From there it went to the projected railway that was shortly to be offered to the St. Louis district.

"The railroad will give the steamboat some stiff competition in another ten years," said Benson.

"Pshaw! Nothing can take the place of the steamboat."

"But railroads have ways of getting places that the boat can't overcome."

"You've been East and seen this great wonder, of course, Tom. But did you take a ride on one?"

"Yes. Yes, I did, sir. They're not developed, of course. Need some of the kinks ironed out, but they're coming right along."

Pierre offered no comment. He had small concern with the steam car at present. Time enough for that when in a few years they would be taking over freight that normally went by river.

His eyes roved over the luster of the rosewood table near him. A small decorated jar with candied sugarplums from a St. Louis confectionery stood near a handsome hand-painted lamp. A new leather book lay at one side, as though it had been read and put down in haste. The rose brocaded tapestry of love seats and chairs warmed the room pleasantly, and the soft gray of the heavy carpet echoed the color in huge roses scattered in big splashes. Draperies at the windows glowed with a rich luster as Florry came in and lit the gas chandelier.

All eyes in the room followed her, and she seemed perfectly aware of their scrutiny. She chose a footstool and placed it underneath the chandelier;

then, lighting the long taper from the fireplace, she climbed onto the stool and stretched up to ignite the gas.

Saucier broke the silence with his question: "Is supper almost ready, Florry? I have a meeting tonight."

"Soon's y'awl're ready, sir, it's ready," she answered. She blew out the glowing end of the taper and put it behind the open bricks by the fireplace. Florry's yellow face wore an inscrutable look tonight, and a strange rosy spot of color glowed high upon her cheekbones. Her dark eyes flashed momentarily at each man in turn, and she bowed and left the room. The amber glow of her eyes stayed hypnotically with them.

Colonel Reaves leaned forward. "Did you notice anything particularly strange about her?"

"Yes. I can't just yet put my finger on it," said Saucier.

She looks, Pierre was thinking, as if something extraordinary has either happened to her, or is going to happen. It was uncanny, that look she had thrown them. Almost as though she were above them, it contained supercilious arrogance;

she was completely, serenely indifferent, yet indubitably triumphant.

Gabriella, coming down the stairs, precluded further comment, and Saucier forgot about the incident in the next few moments. The two young girls were a study in contrasts as they came into the parlor: Charmian so dark, Toinette so fair, and both radiant from the crisp air of the fall afternoon.

Gabriella went into the dining room on the arm of Tom Benson, throwing her husband and his daughter together, with the colonel and Toinette and Pierre Gregoire bringing up the tear.

If I couldn't manage the ride home from the show, at least I can manage who is to sit next to me at my own table, Gabriella thought triumphantly. That little minx, Toinette! She should be pleased silly to have snared a man like Tom Benson, and yet she deliberately keeps him on edge. There was a slightly perceptive pause in her step as the thought struck her. Tom Benson and his postponed marriage to Toinette!

Why had Toinette postponed it? *When* had she postponed it? After she had come from New Orleans on the *Redwing* with young Gregoire in attendance! I've been stupid, utterly downright stupid not to have seen it before. I've heard plenty about Pierre Gregoire from her in the past few weeks. Enough that I should have seen through this more quickly. Pierre Gregoire and Toinette Reaves! I can take care of both situations with one stroke, Gabriella decided. That would pay Charmian back beautifully for all the trouble she's given me, for anyone can see she's in love with Pierre. Gabriella's quick laughter rang out across the room, and Tom looked at her questioningly, for a remark he had just made did not by the greatest stretch of imagination call for laughter.

"What is it, Gabriella?"

"Don't be silly, Tom. I have just thought of something very, very amusing." She then walked sedately to her place. She added to herself, If I manage right, Pierre will marry Toinette — and I *shall* manage right!

The food was delicious and served with the greatest aplomb by Florry. Her self-assurance faltered not once nor did her perfect-servant attitude waver. The puzzled looks cast a time or two by the men who had been in the parlor a few minutes before were lost upon her. Serve to the left, remove from the right. Automatically she held out the silver dishes and allowed the guests to help themselves. She removed the dishes carefully on a huge tray and substituted the final service plate for the dessert course.

"That will do now, Florry," Gabriella said in a low tone.

"Liqueurs for the gentlemen, my dear?"

"Yes, of course, Llewellyn, but I shall serve them myself. Do you girls wish to go ahead to the parlor?" she asked Toinette.

Toinette looked reluctantly at Charmian, who rose dutifully. "Shall we look over some new music, Toinette?"

Saucier coughed.

"I really must be going, Gabriella, dear," he said uneasily, looking at his watch. "Young Manley will be getting impatient."

"Oh, bother young Manley. He reminds

me of a parboiled lobster. I was thinking that very thing this afternoon when we encountered him after the show."

The colonel slapped his knee. "An excellent description, if you mean the florid young man we met at the gates. Although he looked like the kind of man who gets things done."

"Manley's very efficient. He's my junior partner, Colonel. We're thinking of building two new boats this season." Saucier turned for a moment to Pierre. "Anything new in your line this year, Gregoire?"

"Possibly," admitted Pierre. "However, we've not determined yet exactly." He drank a little of his liqueur and lapsed into silence. He glanced at Tom Benson, and a feeling of revulsion swept over him.

Benson and Gabriella! His speculations ceased abruptly as Gabriella paused by Saucier's chair.

"We'll excuse you, my dear. Of course, we know that you're simply dying to get back to your office, so run along." Her voice was deliberately soothing, as though she were giving a small child permission to continue his play.

"I hope that you do understand," Saucier said, looking at the three men.

"Of course, business comes first," said Benson.

"Off with you, Saucier. For myself, I prefer to let my dinner settle." The colonel shifted about in his chair and picked up his glass once more.

"Certainly, sir. Can I be of any help to you?" Gregoire asked.

Saucier gave him a surprised look. Blast him, Gregoire was certainly a courteous young fellow. He shook his head and bowed.

The others stayed on at the table, and Tom told a rather questionable story of an evening in Philadelphia. Pierre's face flushed, but Gabriella laughed unreservedly. "We'd better join the girls, or they'll think we've deserted them," she said finally, when the strains of the pianoforte came drifting in from the music room.

Charmian was playing. The overhead light cast a shining glow on her lustrous black curls. She bent to the keys, her attention undistracted as the others came

319

into the room. Gabriella's voice, low and warm, took up the words and she motioned for the others to join. "I Dreamt I Dwelt in Marble Halls," sang Gabriella.

Charmian stood up at the end of the verse and insisted that Gabriella take her place. Gabriella had to be begged a little, but Charmian, knowing how she loved to play, motioned for Toinette to join in urging her.

Toinette and Benson, aided in a moment by the colonel, came to her assistance, and Gabriella, with a flutter of her white hands, sat down in Charmian's place. Pierre and Charmian moved across the room together to the rose-brocaded chairs, leaving the others to sing to Gabriella's music.

"Let's go into the parlor," said Pierre after the second song.

Charmian's eyes met his and she nodded. The others were so engrossed in the singing that they were unaware of their leaving.

Charmian sat primly on the sofa by the fireside and Pierre took the other end of it. They watched the sparks shooting out from newly added logs and were silent. She finally started speaking about the work of Father Carmichael's committee, but Pierre interrupted her abruptly.

"Miss Saucier, you've made it very difficult for me. For weeks after that night at Montesano, I thought you were deliberately avoiding me. After refusing to let me call, you may be sure that tonight is a very pleasant evening for me."

"Papa was so angry that night," she murmured. "I thought it best to wait awhile."

He imprisoned her hands. "You won't hold me off longer? You'll permit me to come whenever it's possible?" His eager eyes held her. "I'm going to try to spend more time in St. Louis in the next few weeks, even if it will soon be time to dry-dock the boats for the winter. I should like to take you out to the theater — "

"Wait! Oh, wait! Papa was nice tonight, but I'd have to get his permission. You do understand, don't you?"

Pierre's hands were quickly withdrawn. Charmian had been reared so strictly. His ear caught the quick laughter of Toinette

Reaves in the music room. Toinette only pretended obedience to her father. She always did as she wished, anyone could see that.

"I realize your father must give permission, yet I see no reason why he should refuse it. Of course, he doesn't want you to marry a man of my background, and I must warn you in the beginning that I do want to marry you."

Charmian's eyes faltered from his and she toyed with her locket, outwardly calm, inwardly trembling. This isn't as I wanted it to happen at all. I wanted him to ask me to marry him, but not like this, not telling me ahead of time that some day he will ask me. The feel of his hands was still with her and she turned her face to look at him.

"Your father would always remember that my parents were French peasants," he said calmly.

"Pierre, I should not be marrying your parents, but you — "

He gathered her into his arms and for a moment she returned his kiss passionately.

"Charmian, my darling," he murmured. There was nothing calm about him now. "Pierre . . . Pierre."

Llewellyn Saucier precipitately tore his thoughts away from Gabriella and the dinner guests as he neared the long line of low one-story rock buildings which served as his office and quarters for the storage of goods from the Saucier freighters. The night watchman's lantern cast a dull flickering light against the inky darkness as the carriage approached. A light showed from the window of the office, indicating that Dennard Manley had already arrived.

"Pull up, Pascal, and wait for me," Saucier said. "I'll be only half an hour or so. If you get chilly, come into the building. There's a chair just inside the door."

"Yes, sir" said Pascal. Then, calling to the horses, he stopped the carriage at the hitching rack.

Manley opened the office door at the sound of the older man's footsteps. "Good evening, sir," he said pleasantly.

"Good evening, Dennard. Sorry if

you've waited long."

Dennard shook his head. "I found something to do. Been going over that last account of Chouteau's. I've got the plans for the new boat, sir. They're going to surprise you."

"When you're my age, you're not surprised any more." Saucier held out his hand for the long sheets of brown paper. They spread them out on his heavy mahogany desk to go over them carefully.

"What do you think sir?" Manley asked after Saucier had examined them. Dennard made a little church spire out of his index fingers and leaned back in his chair, waiting politely for his partner to express himself. He knew what he thought himself. He was thinking that it wouldn't hurt them any to stick with the conservative lines of the last boat.

"I'll sleep on it, if you don't mind, Dennard. By the way, I read that the *Peter Marken* docked late this afternoon."

"Yes, I know. I saw the master for you." Dennard unhooked his hands and let them fall idly to his sides. The old gentleman wasn't going to like losing his bet with Colonel Reaves. The loss of payment for hauling a shipment of cotton from Vicksburg to New Orleans was, of course, Saucier's responsibility alone.

"Well," said Saucier. "You don't need to tell me I lost. I can tell by your face."

Dennard shrugged. "I'm sorry, sir. I tried to get him to tone it down a little, and he said that seventy thousand was a little under what he really took in."

"It's all right. I'll tell Reaves when I get back to the house."

"The Reaves there again tonight?"

Saucier looked at him sharply. Sometimes Dennard irritated him. "Yes, the Reaves and some other guests — Benson and Gregoire."

"The doctor's getting to be quite a familiar figure around Ginger Blue, isn't he?"

"No," said Saucier, "not the doctor — his twin brother, Pierre."

Dennard's mouth opened slightly, but he closed it and it straightened out in a thin, firm line of displeasure; and then, without another word, he reached for his hat.

"Can I drop you somewhere?" asked Saucier.

"Thanks, no. I'll walk down to the Southern. My carriage is out front." Manley clapped his tall beaver down on his straw-colored hair. "Good night, sir."

"Good night." Saucier frowned as the door closed. He unfolded the plans to look at them alone. Yes, there were times when Dennard Manley irritated him.

He stood bent over the desk. He heard Pascal come into the outer hall, but he went on studying the plans and making notes. After another hour, he folded the brown paper again and locked it away in the desk.

"All ready, Pascal."

They went out together. The moon was almost totally obscured by dark clouds which had gathered since he had come. The air was close and heavy, as if presaging a storm.

The lamps on the carriage sent out only a dim light and Pascal let the horses pick their own way; they knew it well enough to follow it in almost pitch darkness along the river road where Pascal had turned. "Wait, Pascal! I want to get out a moment," Saucier called.

The sound that had first caught his attention was plainer now that the carriage wheels had stopped and the horses' hoofs no longer clattered on the cobblestone. "Tie the horses and come with me," he directed Pascal out of the darkness. Together they went down the terraced river bank, following the walks carefully to keep out of the heavy bog. Small craft tugged at their moorings below, and the rigging of a sailboat creaked. The long line of steamboats at the levee stood in semidarkness to the right. They were mostly darkened for the night, and the two men stood in silence for a moment.

"What is it, sir?" Pascal asked. Only the grip of Saucier's hand on his arm answered him.

The creaking of oars within their locks came to their ears. Someone was rowing out to a steamboat. All was dark on board, and both men strained forward and moved cautiously on the pier. The moon showed itself for the moment, long enough for them to see figures clambering over the side of the steamboat to the rowboat.

"Negroes!" said Saucier sharply.

Pascal exclaimed in the darkness.

They stood watching until the moon shone down on the water once more, disclosing the small boat and its cargo. The steamer lay revealed in the moonlight. The letters on the paddle box spelled out *Fresco*.

Saucier touched Pascal's arm as they walked back up the terraces to the carriage.

"The *Fresco* has carried the Negroes up from New Orleans and is helping them get away to the Illinois side of the river." Saucier grimly turned the last corner to his carriage and climbed into it silently.

So Gregoire's an abolitionist — helping slaves to escape — slaves, perhaps from the same masters whose cargoes of sugar, sorghum, hemp, and tobacco were the very basis of his shipping business. A word from Saucier to these plantation owners and Gregoire's business would be ruined!

Saucier's face was grim in the darkness. He had lost accounts to Gregoire this past year. Well, he would soon have them back! The Saucier Line operated a dozen steamboats on the Mississippi. And the Gregoire Line was still in its infancy — where it must remain or the Saucier Line would lose real money.

"Let us go," he said to Pascal. He would confront young Gregoire with his knowledge of tonight's performance. Just a word from him and the St. Louis trade as well would be ruined for Gregoire. Most of the shippers were slave owners, and had no sympathy with abolitionists. A strong word, that, and one not to be employed unless truthfully.

# 20

CHARMIAN was already seated at the breakfast table the next morning when her father came downstairs. She was waiting to pour his coffee.

Saucier had scarcely seated himself before he said, "Daughter, I want you to promise me not to see young Gregoire again."

"Why, Father?" Charmian said. "Why do you ask that?"

"Because" — Saucier hit the table with his fist — "he's a dirty abolitionist!"

"Father!" Charmian gasped. Her face was drained of color.

"An abolitionist," he repeated. "And I forbid you to see him again."

Charmian did not go out at all that day. The horse show would begin at the usual hour, but she would not attend. She went to her room and took her meals from a tray brought up by a bewildered Brigette

330

whose soothing tones proved to be of no avail. Sunken in apathy, Charmian barely touched her food, pushing away the choice tidbits Brigette had brought.

Gabriella tapped once at her door in the late afternoon, but Charmian refused to answer her knock, knowing that her stepmother was only curious about her decision to stay home.

What if Pierre is an abolitionist? she kept asking herself. If that's the way he believes, it's his own right to feel that way.

*I forbid you to see him again. I forbid you to see him again. I forbid, I forbid* — Her father's words were like a chant which would not leave her.

Papa won't go to Pierre. He can't go to him. He mustn't go to him. *Pierre wants me to marry him.*

*I forbid you to see him. I forbid you to see him.*

What if I agree with Pierre about slavery? What if I think he's good to help escaped slaves? That's my right.

Yes, that's my right. And it's my right to see the man I love and to marry him. You can't forbid my loving him, Papa.

You might keep him out of my sight, but you can't keep him out of my heart. You can't do the impossible.

She sat, toward nightfall, a tear-stained, disconsolate figure, peering miserably out of the dusk-filled windows. She heard the carriage drive up to the porte-cochere and knew that her father was at home and that Pascal would be soon putting the horses up. She rang for Florry and pressed her into service.

"But I can't go down to Pascal, Miss Ch'meen. Miss Gabriella say put supper on de table promptly. I gotta go right down and get busy, Miss Ch'meen."

"You do what *I* say for a change! I was mistress here many years before Miss Gabriella ever thought of having her chance of coming here!" Florry looked startled at the fire in Charmian's eyes.

"La, la!" Florry snickered. "Ah'll go dis once. But min' you, I won't tak de cons'quences."

"Tell Pascal to keep the horses hitched. I want to drive into town right away. It'll take me ten minutes. Run, Florry!"

The mulatto was gone in another moment and Charmian poured cold water into the washbasin and bathed her hot eyes. She looked aghast at herself in the mirror. What havoc her tears had wrought! But now that her mind was made up, her cheeks burned high with color and her eyes would clear up with the rush of the wind through the carriage. She tore with frenzied hands through her wardrobe, dressing quickly and pulling out a long gray cape and a hat with a heavy veil.

Fine thing for her to be going to the hotel alone at night! But she needn't go in. Pascal could take a note to Pierre. She must see him. She wouldn't wait another moment. She must see Pierre and warn him that her father would probably notify the Guards that he was helping runaway slaves.

Florry was gone longer than she should have been and was breathless when she came back into Charmian's room, her eyes wide, her hair disheveled.

"He say a' right. He jus' hep you dis one mo' time, Miss Ch'meen. He say you git into de mos' devilmentry dat any nice young gel could get into and stay nice!"

Charmian was hardly aware of Florry's recriminations in her hurry to finish the note she was writing Pierre. She finished but did not sign it, and, throwing the cape around her, ran down the backstairs and out the side door which led from the hall into the kitchen. There had been no sound in Saucier's room upstairs, and she supposed that he had not come up yet. She ran quietly through the terraced garden and out the back to the stable roads. Pascal had been instructed to hold the carriage at the rear entrance to Ginger Blue, which the Negroes used. He was impatiently waiting for her.

"Miss Charmian, this is bound to get me into trouble if you're caught."

"Oh, Pascal, you know very well that they'll be eating for the next hour, and that no one will miss you. You're supposed to be bedding down the horses. I told Florry to make sure that Blue stayed close to the house and for her to take my tray up as though I were there."

"One time won't make much difference now," said Pascal, his tone indifferent.

Charmian directed him to the hotel

where Pierre stayed. "Now, as soon as we get to the square just before the hotel, I want you to hitch the horses and walk on to the hotel. Ask for Mr. Gregoire and give him this note. I want to see him right away, Pascal. Make it plain to him about meeting me right here. You can drive us around for a few minutes."

"You're taking chances. It's light as day under those gas lamps. Anybody who knows you will recognize you."

"Hurry up, Pascal, and don't argue. It's a dark night and I have on a heavy veil."

Pascal drove fast and it was not long before they reached the downtown section. After one last burst of beautiful weather, as if for the fall horse show, the temperature had dropped, and Charmian shivered in the back seat of the carriage. The heavy storm curtains had been put up before Pascal drove to the docks for her father. Pascal slowed the carriage and stopped as she had directed him. She held out the note as he finished tying the horses and came up to her side of the carriage.

"Do hurry, Pascal. We can get back before they're through with supper, if you'll only hurry."

He was gone. It seemed a long time before he returned. "Mr. Gregoire's out for the evening. The attendant thought maybe his boat had left this afternoon."

"Well, couldn't you find out? Didn't the clerk know for sure?" she asked impatiently. "Pascal, you're exasperating."

"I bought a paper and checked it. But it didn't announce the departure of the *Redwing*."

She tried to think what to do next! She must see Pierre! Why had she stayed in her room all day instead of hurrying to him to warn him?

"Oh, bother! Did you ask the clerk if he had eaten supper there?"

"No, miss. Mr. Dennard Manley was buying cigars and I thought it likely he might listen if he thought I was anxious about something."

Pinky! He turns up every time I'm doing something I shouldn't. "Let's go, then, Pascal. Drive by the Planters' House. I'd recognize Mr. Gregoire's carriage if it were outside."

Pascal offered no remonstrance, knowing that once Miss Charmian had reached a decision, nothing could alter it. She must be blessed with a sixth sense, he thought, for there was the carriage standing in front of the hotel. The Planters' House door was opened suddenly, and out into the bright light stepped Pierre, gallant in attendance upon Toinette Reaves, followed by the colonel.

Pascal hesitated.

A choked voice came from the back seat. "Drive on, Pascal. Hurry, and don't let them see us!"

She was sure that they had not been seen, or that if Pierre had caught a glimpse of the Saucier carriage he probably thought it was occupied by another member of the family. Where could Pierre and the Reaves be going?

The next day Gabriella sat in the front parlor when Pascal came back from taking Saucier to his office.

"Build up the fire, Pascal; the room is getting chilly. And ring for Brigette, please, and have her get my shawl."

"Yes, Mrs. Saucier. As soon as I take

a note to Miss Charmian." Pascal bit his lips.

"Pascal! When I tell you to do something, do it immediately. You can give me the note for Miss Charmian. I'll see that she gets it."

Pascal's quick glance leaped toward the stairway. He had not seen Charmian at all since the day before. Reluctantly he handed Gabriella the envelope and left the room to get more wood for the fire.

Gabriella turned the letter over in her hand. She looked swiftly at the open doors, then quickly tore open the envelope, extracting the notepaper. It was from Pierre Gregoire, just as she had thought it might be. He was sorry that Charmian had not come to the horse show the day before, and he had thought she would attend the play last evening, as Gabriella had planned a supper party.

*I escorted the Reaves because Mrs. Saucier had said that you would all come together. I'm so sorry that your plans did not turn out that way. I shall hope to see you soon.*

Gabriella crossed the room and dropped the letter on the glowing embers in the fireplace and, picking up the poker, stirred them a little, igniting the paper. She smiled as it curled at the edges, then spurted up into a small flame. She settled down in her chair once more, her book half closed, and gazed into the fire.

It would have been a dull evening the night before, after Llewellyn had refused to carry out their theater party plans, if Tom had not still been here. Gabriella had pretended to be furious when Saucier dispatched a note to the theater saying that they would be unable to attend. But she had teased Tom until he had stayed with them, and she had rejoiced that she had gained one more point in her plans. Not only were Pierre and Toinette thrown together conspicuously, but she had had Tom to herself most of the evening when Saucier had gone back to his office to meet with Manley again about the boat plans.

Gabriella heard Charmian's step on the stairs and opened her book and began to read.

Charmian came into the room and, going over to the table, picked up a new magazine, not noticing Gabriella until she spoke.

"Are you feeling well, Charmian?"

"Oh, yes thank you."

"You look a little pale, dear. I'm so sorry that you missed the show yesterday. We had such a lovely time. You should have seen Toinette! Perfectly ravishing in a new claret-colored winter suit. Pierre Gregoire could hardly keep his eyes off her! It was a funny thing. Almost" — Gabriella paused, and her eyes caught the leaping of light in the fireplace — "yes, almost like a sudden leaping flame between them." She stopped abruptly.

Charmian's face had turned white. She fumbled with the pages of the magazine and turned to go.

"I was telling your father later but he had already noticed it. Tom didn't even go to the theater last night, throwing the two of them together! Ah, well, love is unaccountable."

Charmian's lips refused to move. She went out of the room and slowly climbed the stairs. She locked her door and would not admit even Brigette with her supper tray. She would not attend the horse show the rest of the week. She could not bear to see Pierre or Toinette.

In misery, she recalled every word of her conversation with Pierre the night before last. He could not have been playing with her emotions, he simply would not! Yet what had Gabriella said? 'Almost like a sudden leaping of flame between them,' Between Toinette and Pierre.

If Saucier had gone to Pierre to confront him about helping slaves to escape, Charmian was not informed of it, and she decided she would not mention it to him.

Father Carmichael called a committee meeting late in the week, and she learned that Pierre had gone to New Orleans on the *Redwing*. They missed him, but went on with the meeting, discussing immigrants, and transacting some important business connected with the hiring of teachers for a new school which was being opened in one of the river bottom districts.

The magic of the Indian summer days was spent, and the gloomy days of November came forward on gusty blasts of wind which whipped the leaves from the trees and sent St. Louis shivering about its way. The first snow lay upon the ground in thin patches before the *Redwing* returned. Charmian, watching the notices in the papers, saw the announcement of its expected arrival in the *Reveille*, and made a point of driving with Pascal down to the wharf. She had seen Antoinette Reaves only once since the night after the horse show, and noticed now that Toinette and Tom Benson were among others waiting on the wharf for the *Redwing* to dock. The two girls exchanged greetings, and Charmian, suddenly selfconscious, asked Pascal to drive back to the first street. The *Redwing* was overdue and she heard its deep-throated whistle as Pascal turned into Olive Street. Now that he's in town again, he can find a way to see me, she thought, ashamed of having gone down to the wharf.

She had one or two other calls which

she could make this afternoon, and she directed Pascal to Clabber Alley. The gutters were running with dirty clabbered milk again. She set her lips in a thin, straight line, determined to go to the city officials once more about the unhealthy condition in this section.

Finished with her work, she went back to Ginger Blue in time to permit Pascal to get back to the wharf to pick up her father.

She was finishing her toilet when they returned and she hurried to be ready when Florry rang the supper chimes in the lower hall. Immediately following supper she planned on running down to Phoebe's cabin to see how she was feeling. Her improvement was entirely satisfactory the last time she had inquired about her.

Charmian went downstairs on the first stroke of the chimes, and Gabriella looked up from her book in the parlor as her stepdaughter came through the reception hall.

"I've had a bad afternoon," Gabriella said as Charmian came into the room to stand by the fire a moment. "Sabetha was impudent to me and I sent her to her cabin. Brigette is finishing supper and I'm sure I don't know whether it'll be fit to eat or not. Florry has disappeared. Has she done this before?"

"Oh, Florry is unpredictable. I remember when I was a child she disappeared and was gone for two weeks, but she came back. Another time she was away for a month, but she always turns up again."

"You mean that your father put up with it? I can't imagine his allowing such a thing to happen."

"Father didn't allow her to leave. She just left. When she wanted to come back, she came back. He threatened to sell her but she promised each time that she would never run away again. Florry is a good servant — you know that."

"Well, yes. But I won't have this sort of thing!"

Charmian did not answer. If Gabriella could manage Florry, that would be something new. She asked, "Did you get your shopping done this afternoon?"

"Yes, and then I went for a drive. I ran

into Toinette and Tom. I declare, she is a charming girl! Pierre Gregoire seems smitten with her. They were at the docks, she and Tom, when his boat docked. I saw them all later at the confectionery on Olive." Gabriella imparted the news as casual gossip.

Charmian groped for an answer, but could find none. Saucier came in and after a few moments they went in to supper, served uneasily by a sullen Brigette. It was not a happy meal, although Sabetha had had the food well along the way toward complete preparation before Brigette had had to take it over.

Charmian offered to help clear the table, but Brigette would have none of her help. "Blue's comin' in directly," said Brigette from the kitchen pantry. "But let me tell you, if that woman sends Sabetha off again, she can just get the rest of the meal herself. I'm not takin' over Sabetha's kitchen work."

"Of course not, Brig. She'll be all right in the morning."

"I wonder what's keeping Pascal so long out at the stables? Ryan could look after the horses. With Phoebe still worse than no help in the kitchen, things have come to a pretty pass."

"Let me wipe the dishes for you, Brigette. You look worn out." Charmian tied an apron around her waist. "Here, let me get the water." She insisted because she did not want to spend another hour with Gabriella tonight.

Brigette grumbled on while they began the dishwashing. "I don't want your pa to catch you out here working. It's not becoming, and her in there just a-lookin' high and mighty."

"Brigette, how you do go on! You must mind your tongue a little."

"Oh, I hold it all right when she's about. But that don't keep me from thinkin' things. Pascals's goin' to eat a cold supper right here on the stove, a-stayin' out like that. I've got to set the yeast again and get the things out for an early breakfast."

Charmian was almost sorry when the dishes were finished. She untied the apron and washed her hands at the copper-lined sink. It was quiet in the parlor, she noted as she went through the vestibule toward the stairway. She glanced in and saw that Gabriella was absorbed in her book again, and that her father was reading the *Reveille*.

He laid the paper down and followed her to the circular stairs. "Charmian, wait a moment." He took long strides across the parquetry floor of the hallway. "I wanted to tell you that Pierre Gregoire called for you tonight. You were busy in the kitchen with Brigette. I told him that you were not at home to him now or in the future."

"Papa!" She threw her hand up to her lips and then, staring at him, she slowly withdrew it. "But, Papa — "

"Please, daughter. It won't be necessary to discuss it further. Pierre Gregoire is not welcome at this house, and I forbid you to receive him here. I do not care to hear any more on the subject."

"But what did he say?" she pleaded.

Saucier's face darkened. "Naturally, he asked why you could not see him."

Charmian waited for him to go on and then he added, "I told him that I had seen Negroes leaving the *Fresco* last week. It was not necessary to say anything more."

She turned without speaking again and walked slowly to the first landing, then she ran up the remaining steps without looking back.

# 21

CHARMIAN awakened soon after daylight and found that her room was cold and no fire was laid. Getting up, she went downstairs to get coffee. There was no stir in the big house and she was surprised to walk into the kitchen graying with only the dawn of early morning, no lamps lit, and the cook-stove cold. Sabetha might still be in her cabin, but where was Brigette? Charmian hurried up the backstairs to the housekeeper's quarters and knocked at her door. There was no answer, and she turned the knob and went in.

Brigette had not been to bed. She sat, a huddled, miserable figure, wrapped in a faded robe. The fire was out and the lamp chimney smoked. She did not look up as Charmian entered.

"Brigette, what is it? Why haven't you been to bed?" The star quilt that Charmian remembered Brigette working on for years when she was a child was neatly pulled up over the heavy bolster.

"I couldn't sleep," Brigette answered lifelessly.

"What is it, Brig?" Charmian put her hand on the older woman's shoulder and felt how thin it was through the thick robe.

"Pascal. He didn't come in at all. He's gone."

"Don't be silly, Brigette!" Charmian said sharply.

"No. He's gone. His clothes — his best ones are gone. He's gone with that yellow she-devil." There was no doubt in her voice, only the acceptance of something which had been on the verge of happening for a long time.

Charmian looked into the wardrobe. Pascal's things were gone, and the little wooden trunk which used to stand in the corner of the room was gone also.

"I nagged him. I nagged him too much."

"Oh, Brigette, hush! He needed it, just as I always have. Now, don't worry. You let me take care of you." Charmian felt the hot tears rising and coursing down her cheeks. She went to the window.

Someone from the Negroes' quarters must be stirring by this time. A thin column of smoke came up through the trees and she said, "I'll go down and hunt Blue to get things started. Now, just don't worry, Brigette, I'm going to make us some good strong hot coffee. I need some, too. Papa told Pierre Gregoire not to come back here any more." Charmian suddenly burst into tears.

Brigette's familiar calloused hand rubbed gently over Charmian's forehead. "Don't fret, child. Don't fret so. You're young. You've got your life before you. Why, there'll be a dozen more young men in your life before you marry and settle down."

Charmian stood up. "I'm not fretting. I'm not fretting after this, Brig. I'm going to see Pierre any time I can. Once he asked me to marry him — or told me he was going to ask me."

"There's a lot of difference between 'going to ask' and asking you, child."

Charmian stood up and walked to the door. "Hurry and wash your face, Brigette. I'll have your breakfast in a little while."

The day which started out so strangely progressed from hour to hour with no word from Pascal. Brigette kept to her room and Sabetha went about her work silently. Phoebe took over the cleaning and Timkins drove the carriage to Saucier's office. Saucier was grim about Pascal's and Florry's disappearance.

"Of course they're gone, gone together. It's not surprising. Good riddance to both!" he said.

The first days of winter were filled with dreary, hard work. Charmian welcomed the opportunity to occupy her mind. She stayed away from the next committee meeting held by Father Carmichael because she didn't feel ready to face Pierre yet. For hours at a time she denounced him for not trying to see her against her father's wishes. Then she felt herself filled with self-disgust because she didn't do something about seeing Pierre. Doubtless he felt that she had submitted to her father's wishes, or had even given him her own decision not to see Pierre.

To further upset her were Gabriella's expressions of delight that Toinette and Colonel Reaves were staying on at

Planters' House, and Charmian was not at all surprised to learn that Tom Benson had returned to Vicksburg without them. That meant only one thing to Charmian.

Under the new regime of Sabetha and Phoebe working together, things at Ginger Blue became slipshod, and they all missed Florry's well trained hands. Brigette took a severe cold the second day of Pascal's absence and kept to her room for a week. They had to call back the Ginger Blue servants whom Gabriella had loaned to the Reaves when they first came to St. Louis.

Gabriella invited the Reaves to dinner one night late in November. Charmian felt extremely ill at ease when she greeted Toinette, for Gabriella still talked incessantly about her, hinting that Pierre Gregoire was madly in love with her, and keeping his silence only because Toinette was engaged to marry Tom Benson.

But Toinette was as gay and friendly as ever, and Charmian relaxed her stiff formality and joined in the easy feminine chatter.

"You simply must come to dancing

class," said Toinette. "Last night we danced the quadrille and the lancers. The new steps are simply divine. The next lesson it will be the quickstep and the waltz. Do come to the next class, Charmian, you will love it." They were sitting on the sofa in the parlor after the meal was over. "Do say you'll come."

"I think that I will come, Toinette. I've been so busy!"

"Don't ever get too busy to have fun. What's life without fun?"

"It's a little dreary, I'm afraid."

"Captain Whitlake is simply gone on you." Toinette rolled her big eyes expressively. "You missed something by not coming last night. I could shake you! Pierre Gregoire — and he does cut a handsome figure, don't you think? — he was there, and his brother, Dr. Sydney, although Papa says he isn't very well mannered, using the kind of talk he sometimes does in front of ladies — And oh, lots of young officers from Jefferson Barracks!"

"Any girls?" said Charmian playfully, trying to act as though she had not even so much as heard Pierre's name.

Toinette made a moue at her. "Oh, but you know they don't really count. Charmian, I'm surprised at the lovely times you all have here in St. Louis. Why, the parties down in Vicksburg can't hold a candle to the St. Louis parties. I've talked Papa into staying until the weather gets hot. We ought to go back at Christmas time, and Papa's trying to get me to set a new date to marry Tom, but I'm having such a good time."

"But do you feel that you're treating Tom right?" Charmian asked, dismayed at Toinette's decision.

Toinette laughed merrily. "Most of the girls I know have been engaged five or six times before they get married, honey. It's nothing, being engaged! And besides, Tom understands, anyway. I'm just not ready to settle down yet and be an old married lady. Although," throwing a quick glance at the Sauciers, "I must say, if I could be like Gabriella, that wouldn't be so bad!"

Charmian did not answer, and Toinette prattled on about a series of balls which were being planned. "It will soon be the holiday season, and Christmas and New

Year's were made for gaiety. I'm dying to go sleigh riding. I honestly didn't try very hard to get Tom to stay, Charmian," Toinette confessed.

Charmian thought, Maybe Gabriella is right. Maybe Pierre is in love with Toinette. Anyone could see that Toinette was not too much in love with Tom, and she certainly mentioned Pierre frequently. They must have danced together often last night, and every night that they attended the class.

"You will come, won't you, Charmian?" Toinette asked again as she and her father prepared to leave.

"Yes, I'll come," Charmian said, and noticed her father's smile of approval.

"Of course, Toinette, she must go," Saucier said. "She stays in too much in the evenings." He laid an arm about her shoulders as they stood in the doorway.

Snow piled deep through the night, and boats scheduled to leave St. Louis the next day canceled their departures, Charmian heard at noon when her father came in to dinner.

She tried to take a nap in the afternoon, but she was too excited thinking about the dancing class. She knew that even if Pierre had planned to leave before, the chances now were that he'd be at the class tonight.

Phoebe laid out her clothes for her while Charmian bathed in the big wooden tub drawn up close to her fireplace. Her dress was soft red wool, draped low at the throat. She had not gone out in the evening for almost a month, and her cheeks burned with high excitement, her dark eyes blazed, and there was a glow on her face.

"My! You do look mighty puhty, Miss Ch'meen."

"Thank you, Peebee. Pretty enough for a dancing class?"

"Puhty enough fo' anything, Miss Ch'meen. Puhty enough fo' any man whut's eveh passed thu de doo's of Gingeh Blue."

"Miss Reaves is beautiful, and she'll be there."

"Yas'm, Miss Toinette sho am a puhty gal. But not lak you, Miss Ch'meen. You's got a shinin' iside you what comes out thu yo' face. It's jes' natchally somethin' nobody else got. Mammy say yo' ma had dat shinin', too."

"Go on, Peebee. You just like to make compliments. You feel sorry for me sitting here alone in the evenings."

"'Tain' right, Miss Ch'meen. Heah, let me pin dat cu'l up higheh. No'm, 'tain't right foh you to set heah alone. Not when dat man jus' natchally burnin' he hea't out."

"Don't be silly, Peebee. What man?"

"Ah members a dahk night, yeahs ago. Li'l white boy an' me a-peekin' thu de windows in de big house. You wan' us go to old Granny Popo's cabin. Dat boy done growed up and fall in love wif you. Dat man mean business. He gwine ma'ay up wif you. Cain' nothin' change dat, Miss Ch'meen. Florry say so."

"Oh, fiddlesticks! You're talking nonsense, Peebee. Florry doesn't know everything — Peebee, you don't know where Florry is, do you?"

"No'm, Ah don'. No'm, Ah don' know dat. Ah feels sorry foh Miss Brigette. Dat woman got all de fight taken right outen he'. Dat man powe'ful bad man, I reckon," Phoebe stated calmly, going about putting Charmian's clothes away.

Charmian tilted the pert hat down a bit more to the right and reached for her cape. Phoebe held it for her, and Charmian was aware of her gentleness as she adjusted the collar and her hand lingered lovingly on her young mistress' shoulder.

"Blue's holding the carriage, so I'll run." As she went downstairs, she was thankful that her father and Gabriella were in the parlor. Charmian avoided passing the door by taking the quick turn at the bottom of the stairs and going to the kitchen door. Sabetha was still washing dishes and did not look around.

Charmian went out into the white moonlight. She drew back into the lighted door at the sight of a dark figure standing in the leaf-stripped shrubbery at the bay windows looking into the dining room.

Her heart beat fast and she turned to go back. The man must have seen her because he ducked quickly into the shadows. Moonlight, almost as bright as day, silhouetted each shrub and bush against the white snow, but he was lost within the thickness of the trees.

Charmian sped around the corner of the kitchen to the waiting carriage. "Blue!" she whispered.

"Yas'm." He was standing, waiting to help her in.

"Blue! I saw someone looking in the window."

"Yas'm, Mist' Pascal. He come back."

"Pascal!"

"Yas'm. He don' want to come in. He don't know whut to do. I'm takin' him somp'n to eat down to de stables, soon's Ryan done wid de ho'ses."

Pascal! What should she do? What would Brigette want her to do? "Don't let him know I saw him, Blue. Give him something to eat and make him a pallet in the loft above the old carriage house!" Poor Pascal. Brigette had been nothing but a silent, hurt ghost since his departure. "What about Florry, Blue?"

"Florry not comin' back. She fond a yaller man she laks batte'n Mist' Pascal. Dey gone up norf to Noo Yawk. Gwine be real stylish and wo'k in a big hotel."

"Fine. That's the place for Florry."

"Dat woman too biggety wid fine airs fo' us."

Yes, Florry had biggety airs, too biggety for the rest of the Negroes, but Gabriella would be furious to know that she would never return.

"All right, Blue. I'll leave Mr. Pascal to you. Take good care of him, and he'll come around all right. Don't say anything to Miss Brigette yet, and I'll see about it all tomorrow."

"Yas'm," Blue helped her into the carriage and they were off down the drive. A great weight had lifted from her heart. Brigette would pretend she didn't want him back, of course.

# 22

THE ballroom of the Planters' House was brightly lighted. Charmian was late and the dancing had already begun. Professor Quenton stood, a funny little caricature of a man, with a baton in his hand, keeping time to the musicians' melody. He loosely described circles with his arms, and his silhouetted shadow against the wall looked like an animated scarecrow. Charmian felt an inclination to giggle as she saw it bob up and down, round and round on the wall. He whistled sharply, and the music and the dancers stopped.

He called for a review of the quadrille, and then saw that the new girl who had just come in was being surrounded by several men with reluctant girls trailing them. He clapped his hands together and shouted. "Order, order!"

Out of the sudden silence, Toinette's voice rang out, " — and you look perfectly beautiful, Charmian. We've been watching for you, haven't we, Pierre?"

"Order!" Professor Quenton called.

Pierre bowed, but Charmian had a quick, searching look thrown into her dark eyes which confused her and made her blush. She returned Pierre's bow, and then they stepped back to listen to the dancing teacher.

In another moment, Pierre had somehow managed to pass his partner on to someone else and was standing by to ask permission to dance with Charmian.

"But I don't know the steps."

"It's easy. I learned very quickly and you'll know in no time at all," he whispered back. "Just give me your hand, and count with the professor. I'll guide your step." He bowed elaborately, ignoring her protests and, reaching out, grasped her hand.

She marveled that he could be so possessive and yet make it appear as though they were little more than acquaintances. Out of the corner of her eye, she could see that Captain Whitlake had taken over Toinette and that they were already leading the line forming at the left. Toinette's cheeks were blazing with excitement, and the look she threw back over her shoulder swept Pierre and Charmian from head to foot.

"Don't hold yourself so stiff — I won't bite you," Pierre whispered.

She glanced at him from the corner of her eyes. He was looking very handsome. The dark broadcloth suit was well cut. His tan waistcoat nipped in his lean waist and flared outward to show a flowing white silk stock. His dark hair was shining and sculptured against the tan which had not yet left his skin.

"Count with him — one-two one-two . . . " said Pierre. "I've missed you. Why didn't you let me see you that night I came out?"

"I — I don't know," she said breathlessly. Then she added recklessly, "I didn't know you were there until later. It was Papa who decided."

"One-two, one-two." He pressed her hand. "Here, look at me. I'm glad you came tonight. Miss Reaves said that you might. One-two . . . "

"Watch your steps, Captain Gregoire!

Count like this: one-two, one-two, *one-two, one-two*!" Professor Quenton shouted. "Faster, one-two, faster, one-two — *faster*!"

Charmian was conscious of Pierre's arms as they swung and she felt them tighten once. It was like being held within them again as on the night they had gone to Montesano Place. She missed the step and said, "Sorry," and he pressed her a bit closer.

"You're holding me too tightly."

"I could never hold you tightly enough," he whispered back. "Charmian, I want to see you. Tonight. I've got to see you."

"All right," her answer slipped out before she could stop it. They changed partners then, and she was with Captain Whitlake for the next two dances. If she had thought Pierre was daring, she was amazed at the captain's quick advances; when they whirled, he took advantage to clasp her closely and look deeply into her eyes, scarcely loosening his hold when the next step demanded more dignity.

"Captain Whitlake! You forget yourself."

"I'm sorry. My apologies, Miss Saucier."

With another apology and a smile to

soothe her, he continued to hold her closer than the correct distance. She threw a look over her shoulder now and then to see the others.

"You're getting along famously," said the captain. "You've had a lot of dancing lessons. Or you're a very apt pupil."

"Change partners for the polka!" shouted Professor Quenton.

"Oh, botheration! Just when we were going fine!" fumed Whitlake.

Pierre was by her side in another moment, and the two men nodded at each other. Whitlake relinquishing Charmian slowly. The polka steps were familiar, and the music the favorite, 'St. Louis Polka.' Charmian was breathless after the first few minutes, for Pierre kept her whirling closer and closer to the exit. The professor was down at the end of the long room directing the musicians, and when no one was looking, Pierre danced Charmian outside the door. He snatched up a coat for her from the cloakroom, and they ran down the stairs laughing together.

"But you'll take your death of chill!" she exclaimed.

"Not I!" he said. "I had to get you away from the others. It's seemed like a year, Charmian. I never knew the days to drag on like these since I last saw you."

"The last time I saw you, you were helping Toinette into your carriage, preparing to take her to the theater."

"You're a little minx! You were jealous!" He grinned at her.

"I was no such thing! Toinette is a very lovely girl, and she is one of my best friends," she said sharply, hanging back a little.

"Come now, I didn't meant it, of course, but I had thought — " He stopped. He drew her into his carriage and she was grateful there were no passers-by to recognize her. "Here, let me put the robe over you." He drew it up, tucking it about her carefully.

She shivered. It was almost nine, she had noticed, when they changed to the polka in the ballroom a few minutes ago. Her father would be furious and the gossiping tongues would tear her to pieces if they knew that Pierre was driving her out in the country. He untied the reins and quickly got in beside her.

"But you'll freeze!" she protested. "Where are we going?"

"Just for a little drive, Charmian. I'm kidnapping you. It's your own fault, you can be sure."

"We'd better go back. I only came with you to avoid making a scene."

"I was hoping that you came because you really wanted to."

"It's a bad night to be out," she said primly. "Blue had trouble with the horses on the slick road. We must go only a few squares and turn back. They'll notice that we've left the ballroom. And this cloak — I don't know whose it is."

"Does it matter? Does anything really matter but that we're together again?" He let the reins hang loosely in his hand and turned his head to look at her in the white moonlight. His voice warm with happiness and triumph, he went on, "I'm not going on forever acting like a properly brought-up fashion fop, Charmian. I can't. I grew up in a rough atmosphere, and I'm going to take life as I want and need it. Your father doesn't want me to call on you. Then I shall see you without his knowing it." His hand stole under the robe and captured hers. "Tell me that you won't keep me waiting. I want to marry you, Charmian." he kissed her as he had before on that first night they were together. She stirred and murmured something, but it was useless to resist him, useless to resist herself. She gave herself up utterly to his kisses.

"We'd better go back," she said breathlessly. "We'd really better go back, Pierre. You know that we can't go further. We'll be missed and someone will tell Papa."

He turned the horses back toward town then, although they had gone only a short distance. "I can't do this, you know that, Pierre. I can't meet you out away from home just like — " She paused. She was about to say just like a common, ordinary daughter of the lower class, and wished bitterly that she could meet him under any circumstances he or she chose.

"When can I see you then, and where? Will you come to the next class? You know that it's not really seeing you, there with all the others. Marry me, Charmian — marry me now."

"I can't. Not yet, Pierre."

"Then you don't care. There's someone else."

"No, I swear there is not. But Papa — "

"Must you always think of your father? He didn't ask you if he could marry Gabriella, I'll venture to say."

"It's not the same. It's not the same at all."

He was silent and she saw that they were nearing the hotel. She wanted to add something more but she could not find the words to express what she wanted to say. She thought, He is angry with me. If I could let him know that only he matters, that nothing else in the whole world makes any difference to me and that I've wished I could die these weeks when I saw and heard nothing from him! That I did think that he was flirting with Toinette — I can't believe it now.

"Pierre," she faltered, "I tried to see you the night you took Toinette and her father somewhere in your carriage. I had Pascal take me to your hotel, for I needed to talk with you, but you were not there, and we passed the Planters'

House and I would not stop you." Surely he must realize what a daring thing she had done, risking her father's anger and any gossiping tongues.

"Why didn't you?"

"I hardly know. I saw you coming out of the lobby with them and I couldn't bring myself to speak with you."

He smiled down at her. She had been jealous then! That was more encouraging than her quick denial of jealousy a moment ago.

"You understood, of course, when you had my note the next day."

"Your note? You mean you wrote to me?"

"Yes, Charmian. I gave it to Pascal to deliver to you. Do you mean that you didn't receive it?"

"I had no note. I couldn't understand why you would ask me to marry you one night and the next time I saw you be taking another girl out." But what had happened to the note he had written her? Now that Pascal was back she would ask him. "What was in the note, Pierre?"

"I hardly remember, except that I was sorry that you weren't at the horse show

371

that day, and that I had expected you at the theater supper party. Mrs. Saucier planned it that afternoon at the horse show. You were to come in together from Ginger Blue and I was to pick up the colonel and Toinette and we were all to meet in the theater boxes."

Charmian had not heard anything at all about the theater party plans. But Pierre's protestations of love just a few moments ago had cleared up the doubt in her mind; his quick, tender kisses had swept away her jealousy of Toinette.

"Now, what was it you were going to see me about?" persisted Pierre.

"I came to warn you that my father had seen Negroes leaving the *Fresco* the night of our supper, when he went back to the offices. He said you were slave-running and he forbade me to see you again. That night you called for me, Pierre, he told you himself, though."

"And how do you feel about it, Charmian? Does that change your feeling toward me? Does my helping those poor devils get away into a free state — does that make you care any the less for me?"

"No. Never!" she said passionately. "No, Pierre, nothing could ever change my love — " She stopped aghast.

Her father's words came back to her, *Pierre Gregoire is not welcome at this house, and I forbid you to receive him here.* Tears filled Charmian's eyes and she started to move toward Pierre, but he was drawing up to the hitching rack. He jumped down from the seat and hurried around to help her out, polite as a stranger.

On the stairs inside he said, "Get your wrap and let me take you home, Charmian."

"But Blue is waiting."

"Let Blue wait! He can follow us, can't he?"

"But the dancing class — what about it? What will the others think?"

"Get your wraps, please, Charmian."

"Yes, Pierre," she said meekly. She slipped out of the borrowed cloak on her way and hastily found her own hanging on a hook on the wall of the narrow room. The 'St. Louis Polka' was again being scraped out by the fiddler in the next room and she could hear the clapping hands. She almost wished that Pierre had been willing to finish the evening here. The music stopped and she threw her own wrap about her, before someone should come out into the cloakroom. Pierre was standing in the stair well, buttoning his greatcoat.

"I think it's over," she said. "Let's hurry before the others come out." She glanced at him and he was smiling at her, and her heart beat quickly because her world was right once more.

The next morning Charmian remembered that Pascal had an undelivered note to account for. After breakfast she went out to get Whistlejackets, using him for an excuse to go to the stables.

"Tell Pascal to saddle him, and also to wait there for me," she directed Blue when he was filling the wood box for Sabetha.

Charmian did not bother to engage in pleasantries with Pascal. She pretended that he had never been away, although it was hard to disregard his downcast look and his hangdog expression.

She took up Whistlejackets' reins.

"Pascal, Mr. Gregoire tells me that he asked you to deliver a message to me some time ago.,"

"Oh, yes. Yes, he did, Miss Charmian. I brought it back one day at noon when I took your father to his office. I met Mr. Gregoire coming out of his own office there next to the silversmith's on Front and he asked me to wait while he wrote the letter. I do remember quite distinctly."

"Yes?"

Pascal frowned. "I was on my way up the stairs when your stepmother stopped me and asked me to build up the parlor fire. Before thinking, I said I would in a moment, that I was taking you a letter." He paused, brushing a hand over Whistlejackets' sleek back. "She took it, saying that she would see that you got it."

Charmian's face went white. "You're positive of this, Pascal?"

"By all that's holy, Miss Charmian."

Charmian raged inwardly. Her eyes stormy, she took a step toward the house. Then, turning back to Pascal, she said, "If you ever receive another message for me, bring it to me in secret, Pascal. I won't discuss this with my stepmother, but I know now what to expect."

"I'll do anything in the world for you, Miss Charmian," said Pascal. "I'll do anything for you." Bright tears flashed in his eyes. "And," he added, "so will Brigette."

# 23

THE next month was the happiest Charmian had ever known. She met Pierre after the dancing classes with the help of Blue, who faithfully followed them home so that Charmian could transfer to the Saucier carriage at the last bend in the road. Charmian held her breath for fear her father would learn that she was leaving the class early, in Pierre's company.

Sometimes she thought Llewellyn Saucier was so engrossed in his own troubles that he no longer kept his eye on her. Gabriella was openly sarcastic to him, and she seemed not to mind the servants hearing her. He was more withdrawn than ever, and grew thin as the month of December passed.

Pascal, who had seemed to age in the weeks he was gone, went about his work quietly and with marked contentment. Brigette refused to let him share her room for two weeks, but finally relented and, reacting just the opposite from what Charmian had expected, she had become less sharp of tongue, less demanding of Pascal. The servants fell into a routine almost as good as the old one of Florry's, and the house bustled with the activity of Christmas holidays, only slightly dampened by Gabriella's cheerlessness.

"Nothing seems to please her any more. She boxed Phoebe's ears over the dusting today," Brigette complained to Charmian one afternoon upon her return from a round of visits with Father Carmichael among the families in the waterfront district. "Phoebe sulked about it all day and that's not like her. It might do that fine lady some good to be poor again."

"Don't worry over it, Brigette. Has Papa come home yet?"

"No, and he's not likely to get here until supper's cold. It drives her wild to hold a meal."

"Yes, I know. Oh, well, let's forget it. It's almost Christmas, Brigette! I'm as excited as I used to be when I was a child. I bought Papa a present today at the leather goods store on Olive. It's here in my reticule." She fished out a package from Leonard's and opened it to disclose a finely carved wallet, highly polished. "Do you think he'll like it? The leather work was done in Spain."

"It's very handsome. I see some other packages."

"Don't be snooping, Brig," Charmian said, laughing, and the housekeeper drew back sharply. "Here, I didn't mean it. Here's a silk shawl for Gabriella."

"An' prettier than she deserves," sniffed Brigette.

"A French fan for Toinette. Some shoes and a dress for Peebee. Yours isn't here yet, Brig, so no use to go through my things tomorrow." She gave Brigette a quick squeeze. "Get down a fresh dress while I wash, won't you?"

"Better take off those shoes and put your feet in the tub of warm water a while. You look half frozen."

"It's not that cold out, Brig. It's glorious. The sun was out most of the afternoon. You should have been with us. Father Carmichael is lots of fun. He's not poky and solemn like you'd expect a priest to be."

"I don't like to think of your being out with him today. There could be talk."

"Oh, go on, Brigette! You and your fears. Won't the gossips leave a person alone, even when they're trying to do good?"

"As long as there's a man and as long as there's a woman in the world, there'll be talk." A tap on the door cut her words short. She opened it to Gabriella.

"I've been looking for you, Brigette. You'd better go down and help out with supper. Phoebe's worse than nothing in the kitchen. Keeps sniffling as if I'd half killed her this morning. Go on, Brigette. What are you standing there for?"

"I'll go as soon as I've finished helping Miss Charmian."

"And since when have you become Charmian's personal maid?"

"Since she was two years old," Brigette observed placidly.

Gabriella's hand went up and then fell, as though she thought better of striking her.

There was darkness in Brigette's face

and a frightening look in her eye as she muttered, "I'm telling you now, you hussy — don't ever lay your hand on me if you don't want to be taken apart." She marched to the mahogany wardrobe and took a bright red dress down and laid it out carefully on the bed for Charmian. She walked over to the washstand and picked up the pitcher of hot water and poured some of it out into the big white bowl and then laid a towel down beside it on the commode. Without another glance or a word to Gabriella, she turned and marched out. The only sound in the room was the snap of Charmian's hair underneath the brush as she wielded it.

"I won't stand for that woman to be kept around here any longer," screamed Gabriella.

Charmian did not raise her head as she continued brushing, her waist sharply bent, her head forward so that her long hair almost reached the floor.

"Out she goes this very day!" Gabriella said.

"I don't think I'd even suggest such a thing to Papa," said Charmian quietly. "Brigette's been the only mother I've ever had to remember. As long as my father lives in this house, Brigette stays."

Gabriella stared at her, her face bitter. There was nothing to say. Charmian's quiet tone precluded any argument. It held a warning which Gabriella was not too unintelligent to heed. She threw a look of hatred at Charmian and, stepping out, slammed the door until the things on the mantel shook.

Putting a pin in her hair, Charmian went over to the reticule and dug deeply under the top layers until her hand touched a small package, and she withdrew it from the net bag. She opened it and took it over to the lamplight on the piecrust table. It was a miniature of herself in colors, painted on ivory. The painter, Fitzgibbon, had been in St. Louis only a short time, but his miniatures were considered very fine, and Pierre had begged her to sit for one. Instead, she had had a daguerrotype taken one day, and asked the painter to make the miniature from it.

She was going to meet Pierre tonight and give it to him. There would be no chance to exchange presents on Christmas

Eve or Day — only the hope of seeing each other at Midnight Mass surrounded by other people.

She went on about getting ready for the evening meal and for the dancing class afterwards. It would be the final one before the holiday festivities started, and excitement was in the air. Her father was so late that she finally ate in the kitchen and had Blue take her into town before the carriage with Saucier and Pascal arrived.

They passed on the road, and Pascal slowed the horses and waited while Saucier talked for a moment to Charmian. "It's bitter cold out tonight, daughter. Are you wrapped warmly enough?"

"Yes, indeed. I have bricks from the fireplace at my feet, and this heavy buffalo robe. I'm all right, Papa, and it's just a short way."

"Don't stay out late, Charmian, please." He blew her a kiss from his gloved fingers and they passed.

Charmian's fingers were curled tightly about the miniature. She was glad that she had not had to dine tonight with her father and Gabriella.

Everyone was in high spirits at the dancing class. Toinette was radiant and Charmian thought she might have had a little too much wine at supper, for the colonel always served the best to be had, and Toinette loved it.

"Charmian! What do you think? We're all going to be serenaded on New Year's Eve! That is, all the belles of St. Louis. Come here," she called to Pierre across the room. "Do tell Charmian all about *La Guignolée*," she said as he came up to them, smiling at Charmian and bowing deeply.

"The young men deck out in masks and costumes and go about with baskets, buckets, or bags from house to house and sing '*La Guignolée*.' Contributions for a feast are given while they dance the rag dance, and then they go on to the next house. All collected, they meet with the girls and a party is held — "

"There's the professor! Don't tell her all of it now, Mr. Gregoire. Save some for later. You'll join in with the rest of us, won't you, Charmian?"

"It sounds like fun." I wonder what Papa would think if the young men came out to Ginger Blue. "Where is this *La Guignolée* a custom? I've never heard of it before."

"In the villages of France, it was always the custom," Pierre explained. "my brother thought it would be fun to revive it here. A few of us have been getting together and practicing the song."

He hummed lightly under his breath, '*Dansons la guenille, dansons la guenille, dansons la guenille.*" He bowed extravagantly and took a few crazy, capering steps of the rag dance, then finished, "*Bonsoir, le maître et la maîtresse, et tout le monde du logis!*"

Toinette clapped her hands and others joined in applause.

"Will the young man," shouted Professor Quenton, "who is demonstrating the rag dance come forward, please, and let us all observe? I'd like to know who is the teacher, sir! You, or myself? I come all the way from the East and waste my time with watching you perform that crazy step known as the rag dance!"

Charmian stood aghast. The professor was fiery, but she had seen Pierre angry himself. To her surprise, he walked calmly to the front of the room and bowed to the dancing teacher.

"It's not so crazy, *m'sieu*. Some of us like it. We'd be pleased if you'd teach it to us this evening. We're thinking of using it at our next party."

Professor Quenton threw up his hands. "But I thought it was the quickstep and the quadrille tonight! *Mon Dieu!* I cannot keep up with your thinking. But if you must have the rag dance, then rag dance you shall have!" He became as limber as the clothes flopping on a scarecrow on a windy day, and his arms and legs seemed disjointed. He straightened suddenly. "But it is no real dance, I warn you. This is merely clown capers, and does not take any brains."

Pierre led the applause when he finished, and the dour look on Quenton's face disappeared. "Let the young men come forward."

Such a half-hour! The young ladies were holding their sides from laughing and the two sitters who chaperoned the classes came out of exile to join the caperings.

*Dansons la guenille* —
*Let us dance the rag dance* —
*Let us dance the rag dance!*

sang Pierre, and the musicians took up the tune.

Quenton clapped his hands for silence. "We must go on with the lesson. All join hands!"

Pierre was beside her and Charmian felt her hand caught up quickly. "You're beautiful tonight, *Chérie*."

"And you are the handsomest rag dancer I've ever seen!"

She stood laughing up at him. "No, really, I cannot think which looked more like a scarecrow, you or professor Quenton."

"Do we dare come to Ginger Blue on New Year's Eve?"

"I don't know. Gabriella would like it, and if Papa didn't know you were there — the masks, of course."

"I'm going to risk it. We'll come. You'll join us after the serenade?"

Charmian nodded and then the music began for the quickstep. During intermission, Pierre had a moment to whisper that he had a gift for her, but she had not even a moment to say they would exchange, because Toinette was beside her.

Toinette was cross during the rest period. "I thought it was going to be such a beautiful evening. Captain Whitlake keeps trying to kiss me, and Dr. Sydney — well, he just plain has had too much to drink! I don't think Tom would like the things he has had to say to me. I think he might even challenge Dr. Sydney to a duel."

"Oh, Toinette, don't say such things!"

"Oh, lots of girls have had duels fought over them at Vicksburg. You do get shocked at the silliest things, Charmian."

"But duels aren't only silly. They're downright wicked. Don't pay any attention to Dr. Gregoire — he's just a little forward, I know. But you can turn your ear and you can cut him. Just refuse to dance with him."

"Pierre has danced with you almost the entire evening," Toinette pouted. "I've begun to think that you're in love with him."

Charmian did not answer. She could

not discuss Pierre with anyone, not even Toinette, although she had forgiven her for flirting with him.

"There's the music starting again. I think I shall go back to the hotel soon and retire," Toinette said as they joined the others. "It started out so jolly. I can't think what happened."

Charmian knew. Toinette had just begun to realize that Pierre was in love with Charmian. All these weeks Toinette had stayed on in St. Louis just because of him. Until tonight he had been more discreet, but tonight he had deliberately danced every dance but two with Charmian, cutting out Captain Whitlake and protesting his brother's request for one dance.

Charmian was glad when the lesson was over. She got into the carriage with Blue and drove to the customary place of transfer and found Pierre already there waiting for them. Blue went on ahead of them tonight. Pierre kissed her as soon as she was seated beside him.

"I have so much to say, *chérie*. I don't know how to tell you — I've bought a house! I've almost burst all evening with wanting to tell you. I closed the deal tonight at the Southern Hotel just before the class began."

A thrill shot through her. He had bought them a home!

"It's on the bluffs south of the city. It's quite an aristocratic place," he said proudly, lapsing into the adjective in vogue. "I hope you'll like it. It's the Barnett mansion."

"No!" she gasped. That was almost as grand as Ginger Blue, grander by far than the Manley place, Donneyleigh. She was ashamed even to have thought of the comparison.

"The old man doesn't want to have to keep it up now that his daughter's gone to live in Baltimore. Sydney told me about it, for I've been looking for one for some time. What do you think about it?" he asked anxiously. "It'll take some repairs, and paper and paint, and I want you to help decide on all of it."

"Pierre," she whispered, "It's so wonderful I'd not even thought about a house."

The reins lay slack in his hand and he put his arms about her and held her while her heart raced. She sat up.

"We'd better go. Blue will be waiting and wondering."

"My gift. It's a locket, Charmian. Please wear it the next time I see you."

She gave him her own gift, and they said a long farewell that would have to last them until they caught only a glimpse of each other at Midnight mass on Christmas Eve.

She found, when she was in her room at home, that the locket was exquisitely carved gold and that he had had an inscription engraved on the inside: *Charmian from Pierre. My love forever. Christmas, 1848.*

# 24

THE house glistened with its holiday polish. The rosewood furniture shone with a soft, rich glow under the candelabra and a great Yule log burned in the fireplace. Callers had been coming and going since soon after the supper hour. New Year's Eve brought out the old friends who had enjoyed the hospitality of Ginger Blue throughout the years, the Manleys, the Shaffners, the Lamonts.

Colonel Reaves and his daughter were lingering, and the talk was as festive as the day itself. Saucier, dressed in a fine dark blue broadcloth suit and a handsome silk stock, had cast aside his serious mood and urged more wine on his guests. Gabriella was pleasant once more under the excitement of the season, and was triumphantly wearing the beautiful necklace she had wheedled Saucier into giving her from the chest of jewels which had once belonged to Marie Louise.

Charmian, wearing a red satin dress, looked like the portrait of that other Charmian hanging in the gallery along with her great-uncle, Le Duc. To enter into the spirit of the events she was anticipating, she had dressed her hair like that other Charmian, and it gave her face a roguish, elfin appearance. The others in the room found themselves staring at her from time to time, and Toinette said, "I declare, Charmian, you look different tonight."

"She looks," said Saucier, "like her great-grandmother. I know you've seen the portrait in the hall upstairs."

Later, Toinette said again, "I'd hardly know you, Charmian, if I met you on the street!"

"I'm a little excited. I keep thinking of the party and I dressed to keep in the mood for it."

"Yes, I know," said Toinette, smoothing down the soft blue folds of her elaborate gown. "Every time Father takes out his watch and looks at me, I just shake my head. I want to be here when the serenaders come, and I told Dr. Sydney we'd be ready. Does Gabriella know?"

"No, I haven't breathed a word! I had Sabetha make some tarts, cakes, and other pastries. Two roast turkeys took a little scheming, but they're hidden in the pantry, locked away from even Gabriella." They were up in Charmian's room, smoothing their hair into place and adding a little rice powder to their petal complexions.

"Did you tell Blue they were coming?"

"Everything is all set. I don't know how Papa will take it!"

"Just like any other father. It would be almost an insult not to be serenaded," said Toinette. "I didn't know how we would manage it in the hotel, but when Gabriella invited us to call, I told Papa that it would be just perfect for me."

Charmian went to the window which looked out upon the white road, and pulled aside the heavy drapery. The moon was shining with a light almost as bright as day, and objects were clearly outlined below. "I think they're coming around the bend now," she said, her voice rising in expectation.

"Dr. Sydney said they'd come quietly and try not to make any noise until they started singing. Aren't you excited, Charmian?" Toinette joined her at the window and squealed, "Yes, it is! Here they come! Three carriages of them! The finest young men in the country will be piled in those carriages, and think of it — no chaperons!"

Charmian held her breath for fear the others downstairs would hear, for the quiet arrival of three carriages loaded with excited young men seemed unbelievable. Yet it was accomplished and the girls went downstairs innocently talking of their favorite subject, clothes, as though nothing important were about to happen. They settled themselves on one of the sofas near the door, Toinette, as though to distract the elders' attention, calling for another serving of wine, and both her father and Llewellyn Saucier leaped up to get it for her.

"What's that?" said Saucier, holding the bottle in mid-air.

"Someone singing. Yes, it is singing," cried Gabriella. "Listen!"

*"Bon soir, le maître et la maîtresse,*
*Et tout le monde du logis!*

*Pour le premier jour de l'année*
*La guignolée vous nous devez.*
*Si vous n'avez rien à nous donner,*
*Dîtes-le-nous;*
*Nous vous demandons pas grand'chose,*
*Une échinée — "*

"What fun!" Gabriella ran out into the hall before the second line was finished and threw open the great outside door. "Come in," she cried laughingly. "Come in and let us see you! Come in!"

They crowded in, and even Saucier laughed heartily at their crazy masks. You could not tell one from the other — tall men and short, swathed in mufflers and greatcoats, singing lustily, and masked so that not one particle of skin or even a shred of mustache was showing.

The open door made a draft in the room, and Saucier shouted, "Come in one and all; we'll hear you. Begin at the beginning again."

Charmian's eyes were bright with tears. Her father was as she remembered when she was small and the place had rung with his shouts and his laughter, when they had torn through the house, she riding high on his shoulders on a Christmas morning, to Brigette's pretended consternation. Now the male singers started once more:

"*Une échinée n'est pas bien longue —*
*De quatre-vingt-dix pieds de longue —*
*Encore nous demandons pas grand'- chose!*
*La fille âinée de la maison.*
*Nous lui ferons faire bonne chère,*
*Nous lui ferons chauffer les pieds.*
*Nous saluons la compagnie,*
*Et la prions nous excuser;*
*Si l'on a fait quelque folie,*
*C'était pour nous desennuyer;*
*Une autre fois nous prendrons garde,*
*Quand sera temps d'y revenir.*

"*Dansons la guenille —*
*Dansons la guenille —*
*Dansons la guenille!*

"*Bon soir, le maître et la maîtresse,*
*Et tout le monde du logis!*"

Everyone was shouting and laughing when they finished. "*Dansons la guenille*

— let us dance the rag dance, let us dance the rag dance!" had brought the serenaders to a comical closing and they cantered about in the big reception hall, eighteen young men, singing lustily.

"Good evening, master and mistress, and everybody in the house! For the first day of the year, you owe us the *guignolée*. If you have nothing to give us, say so. We do not ask you to give us much — a chine; a chine of pork is not very long, ninety feet long is all we ask. We do not ask much once more — *only the eldest daughter of the house!*" Three voices sang the translation, heartily and clear. "*Only the daughter of the house!*" they repeated. We will give her good cheer and have her feet kept warm. We salute the company, and beg them to excuse us if we have perpetrated any folly! It was only for fun and to make fun. Another time we will be more careful — *when it is time for us to come again.* Let us dance the rag dance," all joined in once more, "let us dance the rag dance. Good night, master and mistress, and people of the house!"

"A chine of pork indeed!" cried Saucier. "Such singing as that has earned wine and cakes and all of the best of the house. To the kitchen, what say you, Charmian, 'eldest daughter of the house,' and one or two young men to help you carry the victuals. Take off your masks, young men, and make this house your own."

"That we cannot do. But we will take your wine and cakes and anything else to make a feast! *Guignolée* is for our party, sir, for which we thank you." The young man who answered had disguised his voice so that even his companions laughed at him. "I will go with your daughter to the kitchen, and we shall hunt for food for our baskets."

"We'll ruin your carpets, sir. Our feet are snowy. We'll repair to the carriages outside," said someone more thoughtful than the others.

"Not until you've had a glass of wine! Gabriella, can you help me serve these gentlemen?"

"And be happy to do so! Such wonderful singing!" Gabriella cried, hurrying to get glasses from the sideboard in the dining room leaving Toinette with her father and the young men.

"Can you come with us, Miss Reaves? Can she, sir?"

"I wouldn't stop her if I might, lads. Yet, where are chaperons for the party?"

"All properly sitting in the ballroom at Montesano Place. We'll dance until morning, sir. Come along if you wish."

"What about Miss Saucier?" someone asked Toinette.

"I shall ask her to spend the night with me," promptly replied that young lady. "My father and I shall leave as soon as you have made your adieus, and we shall meet you at the hotel."

The Sauciers were back then with more wine and glasses. Masks were tipped up slightly to allow the gentlemen a few sips without disclosing identities.

There were a few more songs and the couple in the kitchen had not yet returned.

"It seems to take a devilish long time to round up food in the Saucier household," said Dennard Manley behind his mask. He was almost certain that the young man who had gone to the kitchen was

Pierre Gregoire. He had not been fooled by that clownish attempt at a disguised voice. "I shall go see if I can help them," he muttered, starting towards the kitchen hallway.

He hurried down the hall and cut through the second parlor. He stole softly across the dining room and paused outside the kitchen swing door. He could hear nothing, and he pushed the door open a tiny crack. The room was empty. It was a large square room with a high ceiling, and a huge walled-in fireplace in the east end, which was no longer in use since the advent of the cookstove, Sabetha's pride. Pots and pans clung snugly to the wall above it, and the shelves holding canisters of spices, tea, sugar, coffee, molasses, and other staples, were neatly in order. Dennard's eye caught the door of the pantry. He saw it open slightly, then close again.

Dennard strode quickly across the room and, holding the pantry door knob, jerked it open.

Charmian, deftly packing a basket with cakes and cold roast turkey, whirled in surprise. The young man, still masked, was packing things into another basket. Both were as silent as though they were servants working in front of a critical mistress. Charmian said, "Can I help, you Mr. Manley?"

"How could you know it is I?" Dennard said.

'But how could I help knowing?' She wanted to say, Only you would burst in that way. You were sneaking up on us, hoping to be able to tattle to my father.

"I'm all through now," she told the young man. "I hope, sir, that there is enough for a feast with the rest that you have gathered."

Silently the young man bowed. She washed her hands and asked him to turn out the gas light. Picking up the basket, she said, "Coming, Mr. Manley?"

Chagrined, Dennard followed her. He knew that she was aware that he was spying on her. "I don't think I'll go along with the rest of you," he said to the young man. "If you'll drop me off at my house, I've had enough."

In the same comical voice he had used before, Pierre said, "As you say, of course, but the night's only begun."

"It's begun to pall a little. I'm not much for this kind of an evening. Anyone can put on a mask and get into houses where he might never be invited without one."

"Anyone behind a mask in this house tonight," said Charmian hotly, "is as welcome as you, Dennard Manley."

"Little tinderbox! Hush!" said Pierre, no longer assuming the masked voice.

"So it *is* you, Gregoire! I thought as much!" Manley stood in front of him.

"And what if it is?"

"You wouldn't dare come to the door of Ginger Blue without a mask!"

"And you, Dennard, tattletale that you've always been, are going to run right to Papa and tell!"

"On the contrary, Miss Saucier, I do not care a tittle whom you entertain in your parlor — or behind the closed door of your pantry."

All the pent-up force of years of desire to slap Denny went into the kick Charmian planted furiously on his shin, catching him unexpectedly.

Dennard winced with pain and grabbed his shin in his two hands.

"The lady seems to be able to take care of herself, so I'll not need to give you the whipping you deserve," Pierre said before he followed her through the door to the hall which led to the parlor.

In another few moments the guests had gone with cries of appreciation for the heavy baskets of food and wine. Dennard did not even say good-bye to them, although he made no further pretense of keeping his identity a secret. The others chided him but he remained aloofly silent. Soon after they had gone, the colonel said they, too, must be going.

"Charmian, come and spend the night with me," said Toinette gaily, as if on sudden inspiration. "I won't sleep a wink and we might as well be together."

Charmian looked at her father and said, "I would rather like to, if you don't mind. Papa."

"Go along with you. But don't spend the whole night giggling and talking, you two young ladies. Try to get some beauty sleep."

"We'll try," said Toinette, turning her most charming smile upon him. "Come on. Let's get our wraps and get started. What a lark, sir! I thank you for letting her go."

# 25

THE air was crisp outside, and the snow crunched under their wheels. It was only a light skiff, the heavy snow of a week ago having thawed under the unexpected heat of a winter sun. Saucier had urged another heavy lap robe upon them, and they sat in the back seat, their feet on bricks kept conveniently near the fireplace to warm.

"I don't like to deceive Papa like this," Charmian said after they were well under way. Of course, she told herself, it wasn't any worse than meeting Pierre without her father's knowledge.

"Oh, pish! It's nothing wrong! There'll be others there whose parents may not approve."

"You may be sure that if I thought there was anything wrong about it," said the colonel, "I should lock this little harum-scarum in her room. But fiddlesticks, I was young once — and not so long ago but what I remember how sweet it was to dance until morning. Mind you both behave like genteel young ladies."

"Oh, we will, Papa."

The colonel grunted. He was not so sure that Toinette was always a genteel lady. It was hard to draw a line between coquetry and unladylike actions. Charmian was different, he told himself. Even now, she was afraid that she should not be carrying on this slight deception. A carriage was waiting for them at the hotel and the young men were seated before a blazing fire in the lobby still wearing the masks, to the amusement of the grinning clerk, who kept trying to discover their identities. The colonel objected to the girls' going with the men until he had the privilege of knowing them. They went into a private session in another room and he gave them a genial permit to start.

Then they were on their way to Montesano Place. Even in the carriage the young men would not disclose their names to the girls, and the drive was filled with outbursts as Toinette tried to guess. Charmian knew for certain that it was Pierre on the seat facing her, with Toinette at his side. She was almost as sure the other young man was Captain Whitlake, for she could detect his military bearing even under the strange coat he wore.

The regulations of the party were that they could not unmask until midnight. The big resort hotel was brightly lighted, and vehicles of every sort lined the hitching rails. The ballroom was filled with merrymakers and the music of the popular. 'Canderbeck's Quickstep' could be heard before they went inside.

Lights had been shaded, and laughter and music mingled, welding the excitement of the season with the mood of the celebrants.

Just before they went inside, one of the men handed the girls masks, gravely saying, "Everyone has to wear a mask, so that you are in the real spirit of *La Guignolée!*"

The four newcomers were out on the floor, sliding into the rhythm of the music as though they had not missed a step since it began.

"Charmian, you are a daring young lady," whispered the male voice into her ear which was partly covered by the mask. "Do you know that there's not a chaperon in the place? Do you know that this rousing New Year's party is straight from the simple folk who never considered chaperons necessary?"

"Whatever it's from, I like it. But I thought there'd be chaperons!"

He laughed. "They came, but they've gone — as good chaperons should! The French peasant dances the old year away with this custom, back in my small village. I can remember when I was a boy — but then you don't want to hear about that!"

"I do, though! Everything about you. Do you remember very much?"

"More now, it seems, than when I was smaller. But let's not waste time talking about that. I want to say I loved the miniature of you, although I cannot say how much."

"The locket is very beautiful, Pierre."

"Do you really like it, *chérie*? I'm glad that it pleased you. The music is stopping! Come, let's duck out of here and wait until the next dance starts."

They stepped out into the corridor

and like two conspirators stood for a moment listening for the next dance to be called. Then Pierre took Charmian's hand and led her toward a small iron-grilled balcony outside a narrow door. In the semidarkness he untied her mask and his own and kissed her. "It's not midnight yet!" she protested laughingly.

"I can wish you a happy New Year at ten o'clock if I want, can't I? At twelve, anyone can kiss you!"

"We must go back. Toinette is beginning to suspect that we are meeting secretly. I am almost sure of it!"

"It will not be a secret much longer." He held her tightly for a moment. "Promise me, Charmian. Make me happy tonight by telling me when you'll marry me. Remember, I have a house for you now."

The music eddied about them, and a deep voice sang, 'Thy Heart Is Like the Silent Lute.'

"In the spring, Pierre," she whispered. "Surely by spring. Listen! I hear someone coming!"

"Spring is a long time to wait," Pierre said, stepping away from her.

The door to the balcony opened. "Oh, here you are! Charmian! Your mask! And yours, too, Captain Gregoire!" said Toinette. "Ah! Now your identity is no longer a secret. Did you come out for a breath of fresh air? It's close inside the ballroom. Come on out, Captain Whitlake. Here they are. Let's drag them back with us and change partners for the waltz."

"May I have the pleasure of the waltz, Miss Saucier?"

"Certainly, Captain Whitlake."

Pierre fell into step beside the laughing Toinette and they went back to join the other revelers.

They were no more than halfway through the waltz when the young army captain swept Charmian through the same door that she had gone with Pierre. "Wait!" she cried.

"No, indeed, Miss Saucier. I never get the chance to see you alone. I've not been as lucky as some other people!"

She squirmed, but he held her firmly by the hand and pulled her toward the balcony.

"Don't try to get away. I won't bite

you! A little breath of fresh air won't hurt you. Let's look at the moonlight."

"Please. Please, let's go back," she said breathlessly.

"I couldn't think of it!"

"Then you're no gentleman."

"But it's New Year's. You don't have to be a gentleman on New Year's! Come now, Charmian. What a beautiful name! I've always wanted to call you by it instead of being so proper." Whitlake stripped the mask from his face, and before she could stop him, he had pulled the strings on hers.

He bent to kiss her and she drew her hand back and slapped his cheek. Laughing, he pulled her roughly to him. "I've waited a long time to have this chance! You've been kissed on this balcony before!" He pressed his lips to her and she could not move her imprisoned hands.

Her lips were cold beneath his and finally he released her and shrugged his wide shoulders. She stepped back quickly and ran through the door and down the hall. He remained on the balcony smoking.

Charmian stopped just as she reached the door. It was embarrassing to enter alone. She stood, hesitating to go in. Gathering her courage, she pushed open the door to look in. She recognized the mask that Dennard Manley had worn at her home, and wondered at his changing his decision. She didn't want to meet him just now, so she quickly closed the door again.

Whitlake was beside her then. "What's the matter?"

"You knew very well that I didn't want to leave. It's embarrassing to go back in," she said coldly.

"You appear to be a great observer of convention, Miss Saucier, and yet I've seen you under unconventional circumstances more than once. But to show you that my intentions are good, I want to apologize, I should not have kissed you, I grant."

"You are not a gentleman."

"I don't pretend to be. But I'm sorry. Let me escort you inside. That would be better than if you went in alone."

Charmian adjusted her mask, opened the door, and walked in casually, and

413

Whitlake took her hand to start dancing as though they had not been out of the room. The music changed to the 'St. Louis Polka' and the movement became swifter. She was flushed and her eyes glittered with anger beneath the slits in the mask. She was glad when the call to change partners sounded.

"Please think kindly about me," Captain Whitlake whispered into her ear before he relinquished her.

She was so upset that she was not aware that her new partner was Dennard until he said into her ear, "Here you are at last, Charmian. I'm glad I came. It's been a long time since I've danced with you."

She did not answer. Dennard was being charming, but it was too soon after the incident at Ginger Blue to make a good impression. She knew him too well. He could be pleasant one moment and hateful the next.

"You are looking most charming in that gown. May I be so bold as to say that there is not a gown so beautiful in the room."

"Thank you."

He was silent through several steps and then made another attempt at conversation. "I've been wanting to come and call on you, Charmian. It's been a long time since I have been out at Ginger Blue especially to see you."

"Yes, it has," she said, brightly casual.

His hand tightened upon hers. "I've been working very hard this winter with your father. We have great plans. My plans concern you, if you'll permit them." His voice had entreaty in it, a shade of subjection, and coming from Dennard Manley, who was always so sure of himself, it was a genuine compliment.

The thought flitted through her head, If only I could like Pinky. Nothing would please Papa more. But Denny would always be just a towheaded tattletale to her. He was overdressed, overbearing, and overegotistic.

"You have not answered me."

"Oh, I didn't know you'd asked me anything."

"I'm trying hard to say something to you of great importance. You make it difficult."

"I'm sorry. No one else has ever

accused me of being difficult to speak with. What are you trying to say, Dennard."

They were out of the door to the hall which led to the balcony before she knew it, and she stopped stock still. "Take me back to the ballroom."

"Oh, come, now, Charmian. You've known me all your life. It's perfectly safe for you to step outside with me on the balcony. It will give me a chance to tell you what I want to say."

"No!" She turned and he caught her hand.

"Don't make a scene. Please let me speak with you a moment."

"Very well," she submitted. "Just for a moment." She admired his withholding the accusation that she'd been out here before during this evening for she knew that he had seen her come in with Whitlake.

Dennard stood apart from her on the little balcony. Well, she thought, at least he won't try to kiss me! He seemed more assured now than a few moments before.

"I want to get your father's permission

to ask you to marry me," he said.

Charmian was stunned. Dennard asking her to marry him! They had always fought — she had kicked his shins this very evening. She could find no words to say.

"You can't be surprised, Charmian. You must always have known that I'd ask you to marry me. Our parents have always wanted it. Why, it's been discussed by outsiders since we were children. It's always more or less understood."

She took a step toward him. "You do me great honor, of course, but Dennard, I can't marry you." She tried to keep calm. The last thing in the world she wanted him to do was to go to her father about it. She knew how he would feel.

"You — can't — marry — me!" Disbelief was in his tone, as though the thought had never occurred to him that she would not jump at the chance. "But why?"

"Because I do not love you," she said honestly. She had taken the mask from her eyes and he saw that her face was quiet and serene in the moonlight. There was no trace of emotion, nothing but indifference.

She would never forget the look on his face. She knew that for once she had struck beneath his armor, but it gave her no pleasure. A trace of pity welled within her. She remembered then that she had seen him look almost like that once before, when they were very small, and Brigette had taken a jar of stolen cookies from him.

"If there is no one else, I refuse to give up hope."

"Dennard, please believe me, even if there were no one, I could never marry you."

"Then there is someone! Gregoire! You can't be in love with that oaf!"

"He is not an oaf. And you are mistaken — I *am* in love with Pierre Gregoire." She darted through the doorway, slamming the door after her. Tears spilled from her eyes. She had never intended confessing to anyone except Pierre that she loved him. Of all the impossible people to have told — Dennard Manley!

She could not go back into the

ballroom now. She hunted the ladies' parlor on the second floor. It was empty save for a fat Frenchwoman who, noticing her tears, fluttered around her, patting her shoulder and getting cool water and a fresh cloth to use for a pad.

"Men! Men! Men! Dogs, that's what I say. Come, come, come! No tears on the New Year's! *Mam'selle, je vous sou- haite une belle et heureuse année, et un gros mari à Paques!*"

"Thank you," said Charmian. Indeed! *Happy New year and a big husband at Easter!*

"And now I shall get you a glass of cordial and a plate of *croquignoles.*"

"No, no, please don't bother. This is so kind of you."

"Tears! Tears once before this evening. A beautiful young mam'selle. Such golden curls like the summer sun! Such blue eyes, like asters, and such a torrent of tears on the beautiful blue gown."

Toinette! What could she have been crying over? But then there was more than one girl in a blue gown at the ball. And more than one could have blue eyes

419

and golden curls. Nevertheless, the feeling that it might have been Toinette cleared up Charmian's tears quickly. They were more tears of rage than of hurt, and were much more quickly over.

"There, there, *mam'selle*. That's much better. A lady as beautiful as you need not weep over a man. Go back to the party! More than one dancing up there would stand on his head to marry you."

Charmian gave her a quick smile and the woman said, "That is much better; Be off with you. Men want no tears. They want only smiles and laughter!"

Dennard had gone, Charmian found when she returned to the ballroom. The hour was growing late. It was almost time to unmask. Dancing had stopped and the young people were standing around in small groups laughing and talking. Toinette and Captain Whitlake were standing alone, and Pierre Gregoire was cornered by two plump German blondes whom he managed to get away from when Charmian caught his eye.

"Good evening, *mam'selle*," he said in his disgiused voice of the earlier evening.

"*M'sieu.*" She dropped him a curtsy. For the benefit of the blondes, she pretended merely distant courtesy.

He took out his big gold watch and held it up so that she could see the hands. "Two minutes!" he said playfully, loud enough for the benefit of the nearest bystanders.

Then the whole place rang with cries, "It's midnight! Happy New Year! Out with the Old Year! Happy New Year!"

Masks were removed and kisses leaped from lip to lip. Merriment raged as the celebrants discovered each other's identities.

"Let us slip away," whispered Pierre to Charmian.

"But I promised to spend the night with Toinette! I must go back with her to Planters' House."

"Then one long kiss on the balcony, away from the rest of these people."

Toinette, on Captain Whitlake's arm, came up to them, and standing in front of Pierre, pouted her pretty lips.

"A happy New Year, Toinette," said Pierre casually, ignoring the offer of her lips, shaking hands with Whitlake and wishing him a happy holiday.

Whitlake, whose cheeks still burned with the sting of Charmian's hand, did not press his right to kiss her, and Pierre said, "We think it's time to go. What do you say?"

"*I'm* not ready yet," said Toinette, moving away, her hand on Whitlake's arm commandingly. She cast a swift look at Pierre. He was not the only man in the room! She was caught up abruptly and kissed by Dr. Sydney Gregoire. Charmian saw him look her way, and without a word she fled, with Pierre following, to the balcony. It was already occupied, and Pierre drew her into the hallway and kissed her lingeringly.

"I can't share you with the others, even though it is in fun!"

"Time to cut the Twelfth Night cake!" someone shouted.

They gathered around a large table upon which had been placed the refreshments collected by the young men who had organized *La Guignolée*. The Twelfth Night cake had four beans baked in it, and the girls who got beans were to become queens of the revels and each was to choose her king. This was the beginning of a series of balls which all present were expected to attend without further invitation. A night was to be chosen and the kings were to pay the expenses of the party.

The cake was cut and every girl was served a slice. Toinette cried, "I've found a bean!"

"Choose your king!"

"Captain Whitlake," she said promptly, although Charmian's heart skipped a beat, she was so certain that Toinette would call Pierre's name.

One of the plump German girls who had been talking with him when Charmian returned from the ladies' parlor discovered a bean in her cake and chose Pierre for her king.

The other two queens were not acquaintances of Charmian's, nor were their kings. Laughter and talk died down as plans were made. And so was inaugurated a series of parties which were to last until Shrove Tuesday and a final carnival.

"Isn't it wonderful?" Toinette said as they went to get their wraps. "All those balls one right after another!" She tied her bonnet ribbons securely. "I declare, Charmian, I hardly saw you at all! You were in and out of that hall door three times! You must have spent the whole evening on the balcony," she said laughingly, but there was an undertone of resentment in her voice.

Pierre caught Charmian's arm as they were leaving. He said in a low whisper, "I've just heard bad news. Some cholera cases came in on the *Amaranth* a few days ago from New Orleans, and the victims are scattered about all over the city. Sydney says it will spread. He was called away a few minutes ago."

# 26

THE *Amaranth*, docking on December twenty-eight with thirty cases of cholera, was followed by forty-six cases on the steamer *Aleck Scott*, and by the *St. Paul*, which brought in twenty-six more. Death notices in the papers brought but little comment from city authorities, and the immigrants were scattered over the city without any precaution to confine the disease in one area.

Dr. Sydney Gregoire, one of the few young and more advanced physicians, warned about chances of the disease's becoming epidemic in the city. By early February, the horror of cholera was well known in St. Louis. There was a new swing of advertising in the daily papers. Patent medicines which had formerly guaranteed cure of rheumatism, asthma, croup, spots before the eys, kidney disorders, and other organic troubles, suddenly became potent cholera remedies.

Llewellyn Saucier forbade Charmian to visit any of the homes which the disease had invaded. "I'll lock you in your room, Charmian, if necessary. I will not have you leaving Ginger Blue to care for cholera victims. You have no idea what it's like."

"If you ever obeyed your father, Charmian, do it now," urged Gabriella. "Remember, if you bring cholera here, although you do not die from it others in the family might. Don't consider yourself alone in this."

Gabriella was not looking very well. She was frightened over cholera and refused to leave the house. There had been no guests for a week, and she begged Saucier to discontinue his trips down to the docks.

"If you must go to your office, don't allow anyone to come and see you. Let your assistants do the work. You don't have to go every day." Her voice was on edge, and her eyes had lost their vivid green and were grayed with worry. "I've forbidden the Negroes to leave their quarters without permission."

"Battle Row and Shepherd's Graveyard

are full of cholera, Charmian," said her father. "The disease is spreading rapidly. New Orleans boats are bringing the victims in by the dozens. Although well when they leave, they're stricken on board. Six deaths occurred on the *General Jessup*. Something's got to be done. I don't want my boats carrying cholera victims. So far, we've been fairly lucky, but I've warned my captains not to take anyone on board but first-class passengers. Promise me, Charmian, that you won't continue your visits."

"Dr. Gregoire has forbidden me," answered Charmian, "so of course, I can't go. There's so little to be done by the time they know it's cholera — then it's too late to save them."

Charmian had seen Pierre only once since the New Year's party. He had made her promise then to give up her visits along the waterfront and in the poor sections of the city. Father Carmichael had called a meeting, and Charmian was determined to attend it, although she had decided not to ask her father's permission. There could be no harm in going to St. Mark's in the middle of the day, for she was not likely to meet anyone but members of the committee.

There was a sudden lull in the epidemic. People who had been frightened at first told themselves that it was over. Saucier resumed his daily trips to his offices. Charmian and Gabriella went to the stores to shop. The *Reveille* announced a new play opening at the theater and Gabriella excitedly insisted upon attending it. Saucier declined, saying that he had to meet a client at his office; and Charmian was not in the mood for a play.

"There were not many people at the theater last night," Gabriella said the following evening at the dinner table. She had slept late and had not seen her husband. "I was a little sorry I went. The Lamonts were not in their box and several other boxes were completely empty. The play was very good, much better than the last. Sydney said that it is the same cast as the one he saw in New York. Really, parts of it were quite funny."

"The theater should close," said Charmian.

"Really, Charmian! I guess it's not as bad as that now."

"Everything should be closed down until this epidemic is over — church as well."

"I wonder if the Reaves will stay on now," said Gabriella. "They talked last night about leaving."

"The colonel dropped into my office this afternoon. He was thinking of buying tickets for the next trip to Vicksburg. He doesn't want to go by way of New Orleans or to make any unnecessary changes."

"Tom is urging them to come home," said Gabriella. "I've always thought there might be something between her and Sydney's brother."

"What do you mean, *something*?" asked Charmian.

"One would almost have to be stupid not to see it. Last night I teased them a little, and Toinette almost confessed that she was in love with Pierre."

Charmian had not known that Pierre was going to attend the play, and she felt a sharp stab of jealousy to know that he had evidently occupied the same box as Toinette and Gabriella. It seemed altogether too much like a planned party. But he thought I'd be there, too, Charmian told herself.

"I think the colonel will have nothing to do with that abolitionist. Nor his daughter, either!" said her father.

"But you told me that they'd never been able to catch Mr. Gregoire!" exclaimed Gabriella. She bit her lip. She had not meant to let Charmian know they had discussed Pierre at all.

Charmian stared at them. Her father *had* reported Pierre! He was looking at her queerly, and she knew that her white face betrayed her. She was fiercely glad that they had not been able to catch Pierre. He had never discussed with her his helping escaped slaves. Perhaps, for all she knew, now that cholera was rampant, he was no longer hauling them from New Orleans. Of course, during the worst part of the winter season his boats had lain idle at the docks, like all of Saucier's boats.

She had to say something; Gabriella

and her father were looking at her expectantly.

"Toinette would not care if he believed differently from her. Friendship is based on much stronger ties than one's beliefs." She had to end her statement with a generality. Gabriella must not suspect that she and Pierre were planning marriage.

"I don't think Tom Benson was very bright going back home and leaving his fiancée here so long," Gabriella pursued the subject of Toinette. "Such a beautiful girl and such beautiful manners!"

"Humph!" said Saucier.

"Did you say something, Llewellyn?" Gabriella asked sweetly.

"Not yet, but I'm getting ready to. I've agreed with your ideas a great deal. I think a lot of Toinette and the colonel, but I won't agree that Toinette has beautiful manners. That, my dear, is really stretching the fabric a little. She is without doubt a little coquette."

"But — "

"Now, now, my dear. No use to argue. The colonel's an indulgent father, as he's told me himself. He admitted only this

431

afternoon he would like to turn Toinette over his knee and apply a vigorous hairbrush."

Gabriella laughed. "Oh, she's lively all right! She attracts men's attentions with her little tricks. And how they love it." She must write Tom. She had managed to get a letter from him last month by the sheer artifice of asking him to come to St. Louis and visit them at Ginger Blue. She had written:

> *Your little fiancée is having a wonderful time, Tom. You should surprise her with a visit. You might be able to get her to go back with you, but it seems as though Pierre Gregoire is quite interested.*

Tom had said, yes, he would surprise them all, probably in early April. He *must* come by April. Gabriella was bored with sitting at home. Since the holiday season, life had been very dull. One got tired of looking at expensive cloth, and yards and yards of laces, ribbons, and silks not yet made up.

Although Charmian was not going out every day as she had when Gabriella first came to live at Ginger Blue, the two women were not companionable. Gabriella took a long nap every day. Charmian liked to walk about in the snow and would tramp for hours in the woods behind the house. They seldom saw each other during the day except at the luncheon table occasionally, for usually Charmian preferred her noonday meal on a tray in her room, or in the kitchen, soaking up the warmth of the big kitchen stove and basking in the smell of Sabetha's freshly baked brown bread.

"I think we should have a party in March," Gabriella said as they rose from the table. "It's been so dull." She linked her hand through Saucier's arm and he absently patted it. "Come, come Llewellyn, we mustn't grow old and stodgy without making some effort to stay young. Charmian needs excitement and fun."

Charmian said, "Please don't worry about me." She kept thinking about Pierre and Toinette. She had not been able to see Pierre lately, but he would be certain to be at St. Mark's tomorrow.

"You look a little peaked, Charmian. Yes, Gabriella, I think a party is in order. A certain young man was asking about you, daughter." He took out a penknife and cut the end of the big black cigar he was getting ready to smoke.

She did not answer, she was so completely absorbed with thinking what she would say to Pierre the following day.

"Well, aren't you interested?" Saucier asked, reaching over and pinching Charmian's ear playfully.

"Oh, a little, Papa. I should ask who it was."

Gabriella suddenly seethed with anger. She disliked this friendly badgering between Saucier and Charmian. It was one thing which made her feel left out. She was sick and tired of Charmian, tired of having to be careful of everything she said and did in front of Llewellyn's daughter. She had seen her husband's expression at the table when she made the remark about Phoebe. Well, she had done it on purpose! She moved across the room and sat down a little apart from them, taking up a new Godey's Book, and although turning the pages, listening.

"Young Manley asked after your health. There's a fine young man."

"Yes, Papa, born to make his mark in the world!"

They laughed together. It was inane to say that Dennard would make his mark in the world. It had been made for him before he was born. He had inherited his astuteness from his father, along with a goodly estate from his mother. How could he help making his mark?

"Dennard is so dull, Papa."

"Yes, I know. I see him twelve months out of the year, every day except Sundays. It wears a little on me."

"I thought you liked Dennard Manley and hoped that he and Charmian would marry some day." Gabriella laid her magazine down. "I've always heard that, ever since — why, almost ever since they were babies. Let me think — the first time was at a ball here in your very house — the night Charmian ran away and was lost. You remember, Llewellyn, Denny came up and said that she was going to the slave quarters. You remember, don't you? I'll never forget how you looked when you brought her into the house. I thought then that nothing could ever come between you and her — that she was your life."

Fascinated, Charmian listened while Gabriella went on and on. It was so revealing that it should have been uncomfortable for Gabriella, but obviously was not, for she was completely unaware that she was thinking aloud.

Her voice stopped and the room was quiet. His cigar had gone out and Saucier sat, his shoulders hunched a little, his face stripped of its usual expression, and only memory engraved hard upon it.

A tear splashed on Charmian's hand; she had been too thoughtless all of her life. She wanted to throw her arms about him and cry on his breast. She moved slightly and her father's face resumed its familiar look.

A sob welled up within Charmian and she coughed to strangle it.

"I think I'll go up to my room and read a while," she said. Her father nodded, hardly turning his head.

Gabriella, frowning, had picked up her magazine again.

# 27

GABRIELLA'S proposed party was discussed for the next few days at all the elite gatherings of St. Louis — Sunday evening teas, the Home Circle, the theater at intermission, and even at church. It was to be a masked ball; they had grown in popularity and were in high favor.

Dr. Sydney Gregoire was not sympathetic with Gabriella's plans. "It's plain foolishness, as you ought to realize, Gabe. You're not just inviting guests. You're inviting cholera to come stalking into your door!"

"Fiddlesticks! You know very well that none but the elite will be invited."

"That's right. But cholera doesn't seem to be able to distinguish the elite from the common people these days. Three more cases at the Planters' House last night."

"But I thought you'd set up a quarantine station."

"We have, but that only takes care of

the cases coming in on boats. You must remember it had a head start before the mayor and aldermen got busy. The whole city is seething with cholera. Do you know how many funerals there were yesterday?"

"No, and I'd rather not hear about it."

"How would you like to have the cholera, Gabe? The first thing you know your belly starts swelling and hurting like blazes. You have a headache and you vomit while you're on the chamber. The same kind of thick whitish stuff. It's part of your intestines. How do you think that picture sounds?"

Gabriella's face was white. "You're just as nasty as ever, Syd. You said that just to shock me." Her eyes dilated. Sometimes she almost hated him.

"I'm sorry, Gabe, but that's the naked truth. It's pretty bad even to talk about it, but that's the cholera." His own face was thin. He had taken chances, but these poor devils — someone had to help them.

Gabriella backed a little way from him. "What about you, Syd?" she whispered.

439

"You don't go near it, do you?"

"You can't practice medicine in St. Louis today and keep your self-respect and not go near it. You don't have to go near it — *it comes to you*! Seven coffins were found this morning with cholera victims in them, floating on Chouteau's Pond. I wasn't going to mention it, but it'll be in the papers."

"Oh, I'm afraid, Sydney. What shall I do?" Gabriella's eyes were bleak. "Why did you ask to come today?"

"So I could pound some sense into that hard head of yours. I'm fighting this epidemic tooth and nail. My brother's helping me, and a few other people with a little common sense. Some of the city officials have fled. Parties have to stop; theaters have to close. People have to stay at home or leave the city."

"But where could one go?" Gabriella caught up his hand. "Oh, Syd, if you care for me, please tell me what to do."

"Stay at home where you belong," he said harshly. "Don't invite any people to come to Ginger Blue. Cancel your masked ball!"

"Oh, dear. I did so want the party."

"You fool! *You fool*, Gabriella!" He picked up his hat and strode toward the door.

"Oh, wait, wait, Syd! I'll call the whole thing off."

"All right. Now, perhaps we can talk quietly. Call your servants together. Better still, have your overseer take care of it. No one is to leave the place, and no one is to come on it. It's going to be hard, but it may be the only chance for Ginger Blue to come through the epidemic. The blacks are already scared stiff. Pierre and I have his place all lined up. I'm living with him in his new house for a while. I'll shoot any person at all I see coming to or leaving his premises without permission."

"You mean *anyone*?" Gabriella remembered that Tom was probably on his way to St. Louis by this time.

"I mean *anyone*!"

Ginger Blue became isolated from the rest of the world. Gabriella was terrified that cholera might be brought in with the groceries or clothing, so they went to their own storerooms for food, and no one either went into town or came out from town for three weeks.

The April fields were green with the early planting. The countryside was beautiful with spring. The late migrating birds and the flowers burst into song and bloom simultaneously. Life moved on, but it was different. Every time a Negro became even slightly ill, he was transferred into a cabin isolated from the rest, but miraculously they somehow escaped the disease.

As everyone appeared before her each day, Gabriella asked, "How are you feeling?"

Twice, for sheer devilment, Charmian said, "I'm not feeling very well." It was true; so long as she had to stay away from Pierre, she would probably never feel very well. But Gabriella sent a wide-eyed Blue for Dr. Sydney, who came on the double-quick, although Charmian had not meant it to go that far. She confessed to him behind the closed doors of her room.

"I'm sorry, Dr. Gregoire. I didn't mean for her to call you. I don't feel very well because I'm not sleeping properly. The situation is very bad, isn't it? I heard that the whole family of McGhintys was wiped out, and I keep seeing the baby. They named it for me, remember? The one we delivered together?"

"Yes, I remember," Sydney answered gruffly, noting her red-lidded eyes. "It's bad. There were three whole families wiped out in Shepherd's Graveyard last week." He sat down abruptly.

Charmian had grown to like and admire Sydney. Seeing him so haggard and worn, and knowing that he was fighting the epidemic almost single-handed, she felt a desperate urge to help him.

"We've got to do something! But what can we do? Father Carmichael is going right into the houses, administering the last rites, and trying to take care of the sick. He's gotten together a small group of those who have recovered to help with nursing." Charmian stopped abruptly. "I've got to help. Please don't forbid me any longer, Doctor."

"I must. I must for your sake and for Pierre's," he said quietly. "Your help would be so little. There must be other ways."

She was hardly aware that he had left, for he walked out so quietly. When she turned and saw that he was gone, she knew how hopeless it seemed. The dirty streets, the slop running along them in the poorer sections, and the dirty clabbered milk from the dairies, were a disgrace. Sanitation was what the city needed. Her father ought to help get up a petition. She would talk to him.

He was not in his room nor in the little study where he had spent many of the hours of their self-imposed quarantine. She rang for Brigette and asked his whereabouts.

"Pascal drove him into town this afternoon. A big shipment is due and the new boat is docking."

A little surprised at his leaving Ginger Blue, Charmian picked up some embroidery she had started since their isolation.

Gabriella, passing through the parlor later in the day, saw her and asked in mock surprise., "Are you all right? Is it safe for you to be down here?"

"Oh, yes, perfectly. I just had a headache. You really might have told me that you were going to call Dr. Gregoire."

"I'm sure that you looked all right." Gabriella smoothed down the wine-colored folds of her long house gown.

"I wasn't thinking of that, exactly. I could have saved him the trouble."

"He probably didn't mind," said Gabriella, stifling a yawn. "He visited with me awhile."

Charmian looked at her sharply. What did she mean by that? "To give you a report on my health?" she parried.

"Why, no. I can't remember asking." She was lying, of course, She would not let him touch her until she had made sure that Charmian had not been stricken with the cholera.

Charmian could not refrain from smiling. Gabriella's pretense at concern over her in Saucier's presence was sickening. "It's wonderful of you to be so considerate, Gabriella."

"There's no use for us to pretend, is there?"

"Certainly not." Charmian went on with her embroidering as though they were discussing a new book. She heard the wheels of the carriage and looked out the windows. Pascal was driving her father up to the side porch.

Gabriella had not noticed. She picked up the leatherbound book, *Omoo*, and turned to her place.

Charmian, glancing out the window again, gave a start. Someone was with her father. It was Tom Benson. A strange feeling went through her. It was mixed with dislike of the man, and elation that he had come. He would doubtless take Toinette back with him this time.

Gabriella heard them on the porch and assumed a wearied air for Llewellyn's eyes. Charmian smiled, because her stepmother was affecting the languor which might have come upon her after fatigue had taken toll of her energy. It was not what she would especially wish Tom to see. The chameleon change was amusing. Gabriella leaped to her feet, all smiles and friendly greetings when she heard Tom's voice in the hall. She went swiftly forward to meet the men. Her warm voice died down abruptly.

Charmian laid aside her handwork. She heard her father's tone and felt instinctively that something was wrong. She waited until they came in.

Tom was as white as death, and her father's expression was one of deepest pain.

"What is it, Papa?"

"You must prepare yourself for the gravest news. Toinette Reaves has been stricken."

A gulf of nausea struck Charmian. Toinette! She could not utter a sound. Toinette, pretty, lively, coquettish Toinette. Oh, she had been displeased with her, she had been jealous of her, but Toinette was the dearest friend she had ever known.

Gabriella said soothingly, "Oh, perhaps she'll be all right in a day or two. Perhaps it's not even the cholera."

Tom sank silently down on one of the sofas. "I need a drink, please."

Gabriella rang for Pascal, who had lately taken over the duties of Florry for guests and front service.

Charmian's hands were gripping the sides of her chair, and they were damp with perspiration. Toinette!

"How did you hear, Tom?" Gabriella pursued.

Saucier shook his head. "No, don't bother him, my dear. We talked to Dr. Gregoire. They called him in this afternoon."

Charmian moved toward them, her eyes blurring in the dusk. She said nothing, but passed them and went into the hall and up the stairs to her room.

Her father followed her. "Don't look like that, Charmian. Please, my darling. There's nothing that you or anyone can do. I feel so sorry for Tom. They wouldn't even let him see her."

"Where is she?"

"At the Planters' House. In her room. But there's nothing anyone can do, Charmian. She's very bad."

"Papa, I want to go to her."

"Yes, I know that. I knew that you would, child. But she is already dying. She wouldn't know you." he patted her arm. The hurt in her face was something he wished he could bear.

"I'll be all right, Papa. You'd better go back downstairs."

She would not go down for supper. Brigette sent a tray up to her by Pascal and he said, "Better eat a bite."

"Please take it back, Pascal. It would only choke me. Is Mr. Benson eating with the others?"

"No, he couldn't. I've not seen anyone suffer so much since your ma passed away and your pa took on just like that."

Charmian had no sense of the passing of time until a clock struck midnight. Poor Tom! She sat in the semidarkness of her room, with only the light from the low fireplace flickering about her. Toinette's sweet voice pealed out from every corner of the room. Charmian got up and went out into the hall.

The slow, body-tearing sobs of a man came from Tom Benson's room. Charmian's own tears started flowing. She crossed the hall and opened his door. The room was in darkness, but in the shaft of hall light, she could see him sitting in a chair, his head bent in his hands. She crossed the room and stood beside him.

"Tom."

He stiffened. He stopped crying but sat on silently. He finally said, "It's good of you to come in, Charmian. I'll be all right."

"If we can do anything for you, let us know."

"I intend to see her, Charmian. I'm going to see her!"

She could understand how he felt. Nothing could keep her from Pierre if he were dying.

"You mustn't go, Tom. Believe me, you would gain nothing. It would be suicide."

"I don't want to live without her. I was afraid I'd lost her. Gabriella wrote me — "

"What's this?" Gabriella stepped inside the room. "Well! I must say I'm a little surprised, Charmian!"

Charmian turned back to Tom and said, "If I can help you in any way, please let me know." Going out, she averted her face from her stepmother's and went into her own room and closed her door.

"If you don't want to make a scene, you'd better go now, Gabriella," Tom said dispassionately. "I'm leaving tonight. I'll go to one of the hotels."

"Oh, no, Tom, please don't go. I'm sorry. You mustn't go, Tom."

"It doesn't make any difference what I do any more." His voice harsh, he turned from her and started picking up his dresser appointments which Pascal had unpacked.

"Tom, please don't be foolish. I'm sorry about Toinette. Truly, I am. But you must know one thing: Toinette no longer loved you. She was in love with — "

Like a wild beast he turned upon her. He slapped at her, but Gabriella stepped back, avoiding him.

"You've done everything you could to keep us apart. You did everything you could to throw her and Gregoire together. Well, she was in love with him for a while. But I had a letter from her. I was going to take her back with me as my wife. I loved her better than anything in this world or the next."

Gabriella, staring at him, started backing out of the room.

"Don't, Tom. You'll waken everyone."

She turned and fled down the long hall.

He caught up with her and pinioned her hands to her sides.

Charmian opened her door and stood there helplessly. She moved forward and hesitated. Her father came around the corner of the hall, speechless with amazement.

"You can't keep us apart even in death," Tom shouted, "for I've gone to see her tonight! I've kissed her and held her in my arms, just as I'm going to kiss you — so you can have the cholera too, Gabriella. You'll like it!"

Gabriella broke loose from his grip, her face a white blur, her eyes distended with horror. She ran, ran past Saucier, past Charmian, and on to the balustrade of the great circular staircase. Tom caught her there, pressing her back against it and forcing his lips upon her mouth.

He released her. Her eyes pools of terror, Gabriella pressed hard upon the mahogany railing. With a great groan the balustrade cracked. Her body described a streaking white arc through the dim light. Her scream filled the stair well, echoing and re-echoing through the great house.

# 28

THE house stood in the quiet of death. Gabriella lay in the front parlor, her face in repose, the look of terror gone. She would have been pleased at her appearance for the few who would assemble early this afternoon. Brigette would not touch her, and it was Llewellyn Saucier who had dressed her in her most beautiful white satin gown.

"I will help you, Papa," Charmian had said.

"No. It is the last thing I can do for Gabriella. I will take care of her alone." Saucier had sat through the night in the study upstairs, and Charmian had not attempted to comfort him.

He had spoken only once that night and that was to Tom. "You'd better leave now, Benson." The restraint of his voice speaking the cold, quiet words cut sharply through the silence. Tom went like a sleepwalker into his room, packed his bag and stole out the back way into the moonless night.

No one slept. Pascal and Brigette tried to do a few things but at last went back to their room. Charmian could not help her father keep his vigil, but she sat by her window the rest of the night.

The servants went about their morning chores and at the field work as usual, but the same respectful quiet which shrouded the house hovered over them. At ten o'clock Father Carmichael came out from St. Mark's. Llewellyn Saucier would not see him, and Brigette begged Charmian to speak with him.

"A sad accident," said Father Carmichael. "I wish, Miss Saucier, that your father would see me. Perhaps there is something that I might say — some little word of comfort."

"Please, Father. Another time. But today, if you'll just say a few words at the grave — " Charmian's voice faltered over the word. The *grave*. That had always been the hallowed resting place of Marie Louise, her mother. "There will be just a few of her closest friends."

"Yes, it is better this way. Too much

danger from cholera to have a large funeral."

"Have you heard anything about Miss Reaves?" Charmian asked "How she is?"

The young priest shook his head sadly. "I was called there early this morning to administer last rites." Charmian looked through a blur of tears at the tears which rose in the priest's eyes.

The day would never end it seemed. Sometimes it looked as though the hands of the big clock in the hall did not move at all. Then it was almost two o'clock, and time for Llewellyn to come down from his study.

"He's not eaten a bite or touched a drop of coffee or anything else. He can't just sit there hour after hour," Brigette said.

"I'll go up for him," Charmian said resolutely. She climbed the stairs and knocked at his door. To her surprise, he opened it and smiled a little wanly.

"Daughter, come in."

Some of the grayness had left his face, and she thought, He will be all right now for the service. "Papa, it's time now for us to go down. Father

Carmichael is back." Dennard Manley and his father had sat in the second parlor over an hour.

"I'm ready." He had dressed in a dark suit and was wearing the proper mourning. "I want to say just one thing, and that is, we won't ever need to discuss the accident. I shall tell Brigette and Pascal. None of the Negroes know, and there was no one else in the house last night."

"Yes, Papa."

When the little cortege had wound back through the wood and up the terraces after the services, the Negroes were standing in a respectful, silent group. The new grave was not beside Marie Louise's. It was in a far corner of the lot where it would always stand alone.

The only things left to remind them of Gabriella were the new wing of the house which she had had built, the new grave, and a small pile of gray ashes behind the vegetable garden where Brigette had burned every vestige of Gabriella's clothes and other belongings.

Even that disappeared with the first gully-washer before Pascal could throw new soil over it.

Charmian spent most of the days with her father. They were remaining isolated, and it seemed now more than ever desirable. The lists of cholera victims reported by the daily papers had grown ominously. Ginger Blue had little contact with the city itself. Father Dennis Carmichael had driven out twice, the Manleys called once, and Dr. Sydney Gregoire sent a short letter of sympathy which Saucier burned without reading. A little pile of messages lay for a few days on a hall table before Charmian asked Brigette to destroy them.

April crawled by.

Blue brought a note from Pierre Gregoire to Charmian on the first day of May.

"Where did you get this, Blue?" she asked.

"Mist' Gregoire cut thu de woods back o' de co'n fiel's. He say let no one else see me gib it to Miss Ch'meen."

"Is he waiting?"

"No'm. He went on back."

"Thank you, Blue." Her hands trembled with eagerness to get it open. "Wait, Blue, take this to Phoebe." Charmian handed him a small pile of baby clothes she had been making and said, "Now, don't muss them. Here, I'll wrap them in a towel."

She read the letter avidly:

> *My own darling, I want so very much to see you. I've tried to observe a respectful amount of mourning time, but am afraid I cannot wait much longer. I don't like meeting you in secret, and this is not the time to cross your father. Please take every care of yourself. Sydney thinks the epidemic will soon be over. In the meantime, we must be patient. Until we meet once more, believe me, I am your obedient servant. With best love, I am, Yours, Pierre.*

She cried over the letter and carried it with her for two days before she could find a safe place for it. She was not above suspecting Brigette's ferreting.

On the morning of the seventeenth, Saucier went to his office at the wharves. He observed the wearing of mourning for the sake of propriety and curious acquaintances. Charmian, watching him at the table, thought that he looked better than he had at Christmas time. She preceded him through the breakfast room and took his tall beaver hat from the costumer and his cane from its holder and handed them to him.

"Thank you, rosebud," The name fell from his tongue from the long habit of yesterdays.

"You may kiss me, Papa."

"You little vixen! I may kiss you, indeed! Mind Brigette today."

"Yes, Papa."

Brigette, following them with a well packed lunch basket, sniffed. "She never minded a penny, as we all very well remember!"

"I'm going to do better, Papa," she said in a treble voice which sent a smile to his lips.

He cocked one eyebrow up at her, as of old. "Right, my little daughter.

I shall bring you a peppermint stick." he drew her to him and kissed her with tenderness and went out through the open door swinging his cane.

Brigette and Charmian looked at each other, their eyes swimming with tears. "That man!" said Brigette, staring out at him. Pascal was holding open the carriage door, and Saucier climbed in, hesitated, and blew a kiss toward the house. Charmian's hand flew up to wave at him until the carriage had gone.

"Now, we've got a lot to do today," said Brigette. "It's housecleaning time, and you can go up and take care of that rat's nest in your bureau drawers."

"Yes, Brig," Charmian said meekly.

Brigette stood at the foot of the stairway and stared after her. "An' don't go to planning about going to town or to go out making your calls."

"I wouldn't think of it!"

Charmian tidied up her bureau drawers until there was hardly a ribbon out of place. Starched petticoats and lace-trimmed corset covers lay in neat piles. I'd like to go, but I can't. I promised Papa and Pierre. And Dr. Sydney would turn me over to one of the Guards. He'd brook no disobedience.

The sanitation problems of the city were not solved yet. If only they could get rid of the cholera before extreme hot weather struck! The Eastern papers were critical of St. Louis, and stinging editorials were occasionally reprinted in the *Barnburner*.

"It's a sin to crockett what that paper prints! Such items will scare away trade and new settlers. The publisher ought to be tarred and feathered!" Papa had said.

"But, Papa, there's a lot of truth to that editorial. We do need a sewage system."

"We've got one."

"Even you must know it's not good enough to take care of such a large city. The gutters in Clabber Alley! Pfugh!"

The argument had died of its own accord, for they refused to get at crosspoints with each other.

Presently Charmian went downstairs, and through the kitchen hallway there was drifting a pleasant, but strong aroma of homemade soap. The windows throughout the whole first floor were flung wide, and the heavy lace curtains were pinned back to permit the cleansing breeze to sweep through. She paused a moment by the stair. The heavy hooked rug which for years had been at the foot of the steps had been removed and another had taken its place, the soft colors grayed through years of wear in the upper hallway.

She spent the day doing little things about the house and the lawns. She transplanted some rosebushes and ramblers, and talked with Pascal about new flower beds on the east terraces. She went for a ride on Gabriella's saddle horse because he needed more exercise than Ryan was able to give him. There was a new little Whistlejackets and she stopped at the old pasture gate and patted the colt and gave his mother an apple. She bathed and dressed for supper and sat out on the piazza waiting for Blue to bring her father from his office.

She heard the carriage coming and walked toward the mounting block at the side to greet her father. She saw when Blue turned into the lane that Saucier was not with him. That is so like Papa, she thought, working long hours on his first day back. She knew what Blue's message from him would be before he gave it to her.

"Couldn't Papa come home now?"

"No'm. He say tell you he havin' suppah at de Southe'n wif a gen'leman to talk bizness."

"All right, Blue. I'll go back with you for him."

"Yas'm, 'bout ten, he say, be at de Southe'n."

She ate a lonely supper and then went into the music room. It was the first time she had played since Gabriella's death. She went through the stack of music and selected some of her favorite songs. She played softly, and memories drifted in to haunt her. There were the nights she and Pierre had been alone. She clung to those memories the longest. It semed ages since then. So much had happened. In a few more days she would talk to her father about Pierre. She played for a long time, each song carrying her from one mood to another. Brigette came in and said good night at about nine, and Blue brought the carriage up a few minutes later.

It had been so long since she had driven into town that Charmian enjoyed every moment. Most of the lights were out in the houses as they neared the downtown section. It was still a little early, she noticed by the clock in the courthouse. They drew up before the Southern Hotel, and although it was a warm spring evening, there were not the usual loiterers about the steps.

"We'll wait out here a little while," she directed Blue.

Dr. Sydney Gregoire came out of the hotel. He hesitated for a moment, then came over to the carriage.

"Good evening. I thought I recognized Blue. I guess you're waiting for your father. He's talking business with someone from New Orleans. Are you taking good care of yourself?"

"Yes, thank you." Charmian studied Sydney's face and found it lean with fatigue and worry. The epidemic had been cruelly hard on the physicians. "How are you and your brother?" She got the words out, she was sure, without a quiver of an eyelash to indicate more than ordinary interest.

"Can't anything bother me much. Pierre is in good health. I've given him some special remedies and precautions and so far, he's getting along fine."

"And the new house?"

"It is foolish to undertake much work on it until this cholera epidemic is over. Can't have the workmen bringing it in." He straightened suddenly. "What's that?" he asked sharply. "Sounds like a fire engine!"

Then they saw the fire horses rearing and plunging down the street. A few men came running out of doorways and followed them.

"Well, I'll go along too. I can't afford to miss any excitement," said Dr. Gregoire.

Charmian said to Blue, "Go in and see if you can find Papa."

Blue hastened to tie the horses to the hitching rack, but Saucier appeared at that moment. "Where's the fire, Blue? Oh, you here, Charmian? You shouldn't have come."

"I wanted the ride, Papa. It's been so long."

"Well, you've not been exposed, I

guess." he stood by the carriage for a moment, his eyes seeking out the skyline. "There's a red glare over on the waterfront. Probably one of those shacks down near the river. Let's go see."

Charmian said, "It's getting brighter."

"There's a stiff wind from the northeast. Drive a little faster Blue."

Charmian caught the note of uneasiness in her father's voice. He leaned forward and urged Blue on again. As they neared Third Street, it seemed that one fire after another suddenly burst out in a long line.

"My God! It's at the wharves!" Saucier cried unbelievingly. "It's on the boats. Faster, Blue, faster!" he shouted. "My boats!" he moaned. "The *Charmian* the new one — "

The carriage tore along the street, Blue Whippet and Blue Bonnet lengthening their pace, their manes flying back in the wind. The street had suddenly become crowded, and once they narrowly missed a cart. All of the fire engines of St. Louis were turning out now, and the city was a bedlam of bells and whistles. Cholera was forgotten in the next few hours.

"You mustn't stay, Charmian, you must go home!" her father cried hoarsely.

"I'm going to stay, Papa. I'm going to look after you."

"Our new boat! It was almost loaded this evening, ready to depart tomorrow noon."

The vicinity of the Saucier boats was already sheathed in flames. Every boat along the waterfront seemed to be on fire. The St. Louis Grays were patrolling the mile-long landing. The carriage was stopped before they could get very close.

"Keep back!" shouted one of the men. "Keep back, you there! The whole levee is burning!"

Piles of incoming and outgoing freight which stood on the levee were already burning, with great volumes of smoke and leaping and crackling heat.

Saucier and Charmian got out of the carriage and stood as near as the soldiers would permit. Frenzied men kept running up to the scene, a few women appeared, and Saucier kept urging Charmian to leave him and go home.

"I'd like to have the money paid for firing the *White Cloud*," someone muttered in Saucier's ear.

"Who are you?" Saucier asked sharply.

"Watchman on the *Eudora*, sir. You're Llewellyn Saucier, owner of the *Charmian*. I've seen you many's the time."

"You say it started on the *White Cloud*?"

"Yes, sir, an old boat without a cargo, insured and valued at three thousand."

"That's pretty strong talk."

"Well, maybe it is. Maybe I shouldn't have spoke, sir. Forget what I said." In another moment he was gone, and Saucier saw him no more.

"It's pretty bad, sir," said Dennard Manley.

Saucier looked around. "Yes," he muttered thickly.

"I couldn't do anything, sir. The *White Cloud* broke loose and drifted down the river, setting fire to every one of the boats docked along the levee. "The *Edward Bates*' master is fit to commit suicide."

"The *Marmeluke*'s a better boat, though. Thirty thousand and insured for only twenty."

"Thank God, our insurance is in

good order and covers our cargo," said Dennard.

Llewellyn Saucier's face was white as he said, "But it wasn't. I canceled the insurance today and met with another broker tonight. But we couldn't agree,"

Manley stared at him. "You mean just on the *Charmian*? You do, don't you, Saucier? You couldn't have been such a *fool*!"

Charmian would never forget the sound of her father's voice. "I mean that we had no insurance as of today on either of our boats which are docked out there."

Dennard made no sound. He stood staring bleakly into Saucier's face, and then turned silently and walked away.

"The houses!" someone shouted.

"That building's on fire!" New terror struck. The wind had swept the flames onto the roofs of the nearest buildings and now the great conflagration was spreading into the city itself.

The small fire engines were hopelessly inadequate. Charmian's fears for her father's boats were transferred to fear for the people in the houses along the waterfront.

It was a night of terror. About one o'clock she saw Pierre Gregoire coming toward them out of a mass of people, his face blackened by smoke, his hair singed about his temples. Leaving her father, she plunged to him, crying, "Pierre, oh, Pierrre!"

He stood as if in a daze, then said, "Charmian, what are you doing here?"

"Pierre, you're hurt!"

"Only a little. I've been fighting this fire. We're going to use dynamite." he pushed her arms away. "I've got to hurry; there's no time! Stay away from danger. Go home, Charmian! Promise me you'll go home." He shook her arm.

"I promise," knowing that she would not go.

"What next, Gregoire?" Saucier asked, coming up to them.

"The water's giving out. The fire has its own way, sir. The only thing left is to blow up the buildings below Market Street."

"That's right." Saucier thrust Charmian toward Blue, who was still standing by, his wide eyes rolling, his hands hanging limply by his side. "Put her in the carriage, Blue, and take her home. I've got to help these men."

"Papa!"

"Hush, Charmian. Do as I tell you for once!"

"Yes, Papa."

She watched while he hurried after Pierre Gregoire. Tears dimmed her eyes. Pierre and her father were fighting — together, for the same cause.

# 29

ONLY one house remained standing between Olive and Market when the flames were subdued. Wholesale and retail dealers along the waterfront were burned out completely, the great piles of freight standing on the levee were lost, and the whole line of great boats themselves burned to the water's edge. Besides the boats of the Saucier Line, some of the others also lacked insurance; only a few of them were insured full value.

'The *Tagliona* out of Pittsburgh, valued at twenty thousand, cargo at twelve thousand,' reported the *Daily Union*, 'the *Marmeluke*, the *Prairie State*, the *Timore*, the *Edward Bates*, the *Charmian*, all beautiful Mississippi River boats, are great losses.'

The *Montauk*, the *Mandan*, the *Martha*, Pierre Gregoire's former boat, the *Redwing*, which he had sold in the early spring, the *Acadia*, the *Boreas*, the

472

*Belle Isle*, the *Eliza Stewart*, the *Frolic*, the *Kit Carson* the *White Cloud*, the guilty boat, were never to float again.

St. Louis lay in apathy. Only a few people were seen on the streets after the third and fourth days of digging into the ruins of the buildings.

Charmian begged her father to sell the stables and some of the land at Ginger Blue and use the money in his business.

"First, daughter, I shall pay off Dennard Manley every cent I owe him. Two of the Missouri River packets will take care of that. Thank goodness, there's a demand for them. We won't need to sell the stables. I still have two boats that will continue making us a good living and next winter I can build another."

She watched the papers for news of Pierre. Although she had taken food and hot coffee to the fire fighters and helped to find temporary quarters for the homeless, she had seen him no more the night of the fire. She had had the solace of praise for him from her father the next day.

"Young Gregoire worked like a mad-man. He's a brave young man, even if he is an abolitionist!"

"What about his boats?"

"Luckily he had all of them out on trips." There was grimness, but no envy in Saucier's voice. Charmian clung to his words gratefully.

The cholera was suddenly raging again. The mortality statistics for the first days of June rose sharply. The cholera victims in one week were given at five hundred and ninety-seven; total deaths, seven hundred and sixty-four. The *Daily Union* said:

> Shepherd's Graveyard is abounding in pestilence. There is a good accumulation of offensive matters, and the unwholesome practice of flowing the streets and alleys with slop waters should be stopped at once.

The steamer *St. Louis* was stationed at Arsenal Island in the southern part of the city as a quarantine hospital. The mortality lists became appalling, the daily papers giving details of reported interments for each day as listed by the cemeteries:

Total in one day, one hundred and thirty-one burials of cholera victims: German Protestant, twelve; Methodist, eight; New Catholic, four; City Cemetery, thirteen; Holy Ghost, twenty-three; Catholic, twenty-one . . .

Charmian read with sickening heart.

She could stand it no longer, She got into the carriage one day, disobeying her father, who was at the wharves; and driving straight to Dr. Sydney, who was living with Pierre in the new house, she asked for admittance when a frightened- looking woman finally answered her knock.

"Doctor said no one to come in," she said in a slow guttural voice.

"Tell him it's Charmian Saucier. I want to help. I've got to see him."

"Who is it, please?" The door was suddenly thrust wide. "Oh, it's you, Miss Saucier. Come in." Sydney Gregoire was haggard with sleeplessness. Gone was the careless, debonair spirit he had always displayed before in her presence.

"Come in," he said harshly. "So you want to help me. You must see me!" He laughed, and the sound was not pleasant. "I've not heard those words for a long time, I assure you."

Charmian walked into the room, her eyes roving over it and her mind straying from his coarse voice until she felt his fingers closing about her arm.

"If you're not just playing, perhaps you can be of help. Our brave officials are fleeing for their lives, and I can't say that I blame them. I'd counted on you, Charmian. But you took me at my word and stayed away. I couldn't do less than warn you, but you had broken bounds before."

"I wanted to come, but I couldn't leave my father. And, beside, what can two people do?"

"Pierre's helping. We've got to get some of public spirited people together. people who care or the whole blasted city's going to die of cholera! They're dying like flies, the people are. All the Sisters of Charity, all the doctors in this hellish hole won't do any good until we get some health regulations set up and send the people who disobey them to the guardhouse." Sydney was striding about the room in a frenzy of anger. "Seven hundred last week! One hundred and twenty-four last Tuesday!"

Fascinated, Charmian watched and listened to him. She did not hear the step in the hall until Pierre was entering the room. He came quickly up to her. "Charmian!"

He turned angrily to Sydney. "You talk as if it were her fault!"

"Pierre! It's partly my fault. Or at least the fault of people like me, so blind as not to help fight it! I think Dr. Gregoire is right. We've all got to help in this thing."

Pierre's own eyes were sunken in his head. "We've got to fight it. We're holding a meeting today."

"Holding a meeting's no good unless some regulations are set up, and we can shoot on sight anyone breaking the law," said Sydney grimly.

"That's drastic."

"So's cholera."

"Pierre, your brother's right. He's fine

to see this through."

Sydney sank into a chair. "I'm going to do my duty in this."

Pierre's hand touched his brother's shoulder for a moment. He glanced down and saw that Sydney was asleep.

"He's worn out. He hasn't been to bed for five nights." Pierre took Charmian's hand and led her into the next room.

He held her closely in his arms, and all the dreariness of the past weeks when she had not seen him changed into sharp happiness. "You are taking good care of yourself, Pierre?" she asked anxiously.

"Yes, of course. Charmian, darling, marry me now. Marry me, and we can fight this thing together."

"Give me a few days, Pierre. I want Papa to give his permission. He spoke highly of you the night of the fire."

"I'm sorry about his losses. I wish I could do something to help him. Manley wants to go in with me."

She could only stare at him, her eyes questioning him silently.

"Don't be a darling little goose! Of course I won't have him for a partner. Now, be a good girl and go on home and come back to Father Carmichael's manse later."

The meeting that afternoon cheered Dr. Sydney. Charmian marveled at his dignity in presenting sanitation problems and suggestions for the disposal of the cholera victims, the fumigation and the quarantine restrictions that were necessary to end the epidemic. Sixteen men and four women pledged themselves to see that the program was carried out. New city guards were appointed who would relax their vigilance only under pain of imprisonment.

"It will be a long vigil, and one that we cannot neglect. If we do not stop this disease, then you and you may also die," said Dr. Gregoire.

Pierre had risen before his brother sat down. Charmian would never forget the look on his face.

"We have just gone through another horrible ordeal. We have lost blocks and blocks of business houses, and our merchants have lost fortunes in boats in the fire. But we will build again. Nothing, neither fire nor pestilence, can stop our great city!"

It was late when Charmian returned to Ginger Blue. As she turned into the lane, she felt more cheerful than she had for many days. Suddenly she was rocked by a strange sensation. Lifeless silence wrapped the place. No one came running out to hold the horses; not even a leaf seemed to stir on the giant trees. Fear clutched at her heart.

She hurriedly hitched the horses and ran in at the side door. Hearing no sound in the kitchen, she called out, "Brigette! Phoebe!"

The swinging door was opened slowly.

"Brigette, what is it?"

Brigette tried valiantly, swallowing heavily, to say something. But Charmian already knew.

"Papa?" The querulous, stifled word escaping her lips sounded strange.

Brigette nodded. Charmian started slowly toward the stairs, but Brigette said, "You mustn't go in. The doctor won't let you. I'm taking care of him. Pascal and I are taking good care of him, Charmian."

Charmian did not answer. She climbed the stairs slowly. At the top she turned and called down, "I know what to do. I am going in."

Her father lay on the big walnut bed in his room. From the door she could see that his features were pinched, his eyes deeply sunken, and his skin dry and wrinkled. He was fully conscious. "Charmian, daughter! I beg of you not to come near. I'm feeling a little better."

His voice was a hoarse whisper, and she could see that her presence disturbed him. She had thought he might be unconscious. She wore a big cloth over her face, only two slits for the eyes revealing the terror within.

The agonizing cramps of his legs and feet and the abdominal muscles had spent themselves. Charmian knew something about the disease in its various phases — Gabriella had kept harping on its progressive stages. *Syd said that Mrs. Lamont seemed better all at once, that the pains were gone — but she was dead in half an hour!*

"Please stay out of my room, Charmian."

Her dry lips finally came to her aid. "I don't think I can possibly take it,

Papa. You've been drinking that water down at the office. Dr. Gregoire says it's contaminated. No one else at Ginger Blue is going to have the cholera."

"Charmian, my daughter — "

"Yes, Papa."

"You have always been very dear to my heart. My rosebud — " She saw the sudden movement of his body, the flash of agony across his face, and the cold sweat start out on his bluish forehead. The spasm lasted a moment. She reached for his hand, and it was icy. He tried to smile.

"I want you to be happy, above all, Charmian." His hand went limp.

Her lips moved, but no words came. She felt a touch on her arm, and Brigette said, "Come away, now."

Another spring came to Ginger Blue. New lambs frolicked in the meadows, a new litter of puppies tumbled about the green lawns, two new 'Blue' colts thrust wet noses over a rail fence down in the pasture lot. It was almost the Ginger Blue of two years earlier.

Gone were the dreadful days of the

cholera epidemic; gone Charmian's sharp anguish over her father's death; gone was the grief she and Pierre had known when Dr. Sydney Gregoire, fighting for others' lives had given his own.

Charmian and Pierre were married one sunny, quiet day in Father Carmichael's study at St. Mark's. Brigette and Pascal, uneasy in new clothes, were their witnesses. Cooing pigeons flew in and out of the eaves of the church next door, and their deep-throated accompaniment to Father Carmichaels' low voice was the only sound on the morning air.

Charmian heard the church bells as they began to ring, and her eyes caught a stray sunbeam which had found its way into the gray study as it danced and capered about on the wall for a moment. Father Carmichael's voice recalled her. She closed her eyes for an instant and it seemed that her father was with them, giving them his blessing.

Later, dismissing the carriage, Pierre and Charmian walked beside the Mississippi, high on the bluff where she had gone so many times with her father. They stood a long time at the edge of the cliff, watching the distant levee.

The wharf was swarming with activity. Piles of cargo, waiting to be loaded, stood high on the docks; teamsters, deck hands, roustabouts, and passengers thronged the waterfront. A ring of hammers, the buzz of saw, sounded loud in the clear air. That would be another new building on Olive.

Charmian smiled and said, "Listen!"

She was remembering his words after the fire last year when Pierre had spoken to the committee: 'We have lost blocks of business houses, and our merchants have lost fortunes in boats. But we will build again. Nothing, neither fire or pestilence, can stop St. Louis!'

They stood hand in hand as they heard the low, drawn-out whistle of a boat casting off from shore, and the confusion attendant upon its leaving. Black smoke ribboned out from its tall chimneys high above the river; steam hissed through the coroneted escape valves; a bell clanged sharply. The boat took a deep breath and nudged forward, slacking its headlines.

They heard the chant of the roustabouts, heard the people on shore and the passengers on deck picking up the words. The boat was out in the current now and the chant grew softer as the distance between decks and levee widened:

"*Juba in and juba out,*
*Juba, juba all about,*
*Dinah, stir de possum fat;*
*Can't you hear de juba pat?*
JUBA!"

*Other titles in the*
*Ulverscroft Large Print Series:*

## TO FIGHT THE WILD
### Rod Ansell and Rachel Percy

Lost in uncharted Australian bush, Rod Ansell survived by hunting and trapping wild animals, improvising shelter and using all the bushman's skills he knew.

## COROMANDEL
### Pat Barr

India in the 1830s is a hot, uncomfortable place, where the East India Company still rules. Amelia and her new husband find themselves caught up in the animosities which seethe between the old order and the new.

## THE SMALL PARTY
### Lillian Beckwith

A frightening journey to safety begins for Ruth and her small party as their island is caught up in the dangers of armed insurrection.

## THE WILDERNESS WALK
### Sheila Bishop

Stifling unpleasant memories of a misbegotten romance in Cleave with Lord Francis Aubrey, Lavinia goes on holiday there with her sister. The two women are thrust into a romantic intrigue involving none other than Lord Francis.


## THE RELUCTANT GUEST
### Rosalind Brett

Ann Calvert went to spend a month on a South African farm with Theo Borland and his sister. They both proved to be different from her first idea of them, and there was Storr Peterson — the most disturbing man she had ever met.


## ONE ENCHANTED SUMMER
### Anne Tedlock Brooks

A tale of mystery and romance and a girl who found both during one enchanted summer.

## CLOUD OVER MALVERTON
### Nancy Buckingham

Dulcie soon realises that something is seriously wrong at Malverton, and when violence strikes she is horrified to find herself under suspicion of murder.


## AFTER THOUGHTS
### Max Bygraves

The Cockney entertainer tells stories of his East End childhood, of his RAF days, and his post-war showbusiness successes and friendships with fellow comedians.


## MOONLIGHT
## AND MARCH ROSES
### D. Y. Cameron

Lynn's search to trace a missing girl takes her to Spain, where she meets Clive Hendon. While untangling the situation, she untangles her emotions and decides on her own future.